MW00935365

Spinstered the Novel

Sharyn Kopf

Jackie ~
Thank you for your
help and encouragement
as a writer and a friend.
Enjoy the journey!
Sharyn Kopf

LoJo Publishing
2014

First Printing: 2014

ISBN: 978-1-312-44725-7

LoJo Publishing
803 E. Sandusky Ave.
Bellefontaine, OH 43311
www.sharynkopf.wordpress.com
www.girlsnightin40.com

Special discounts are available on quantity purchases by corporations, associations, educators, and others. For details, contact the publisher at the above listed address.

U.S. trade bookstores and wholesalers: Please contact LoJo Publishing, tel: (937) 407-7943 or email sharynkopf@gmail.com.

To my mother, Lois Joanne Kopf, who told me to chase love until it caught me. If only it hadn't taken me so long to figure out what she meant.

Though she's been gone for over three decades, she still impacts and inspires my life.

Acknowledgements

All my thanks to:

My Colorado Springs and Ohio friends—who inspired so many of these characters and situations. (But if you recognize yourself, it's just a coincidence.)
Treshia Kuiper—for being the first person to point out the fact that I was grieving my singleness.
Zena Dell Lowe—for pushing me to stop getting distracted by other things and write this novel.
Asheritah Ciuciu—for being the perfectly insightful editor I was looking for.
Alycia Morales—for cleaning up the manuscript and making it shine.
Kathy Carlton Willis—for showing up as a mentor, encourager, and friend right when I needed her most.
Susie Jarvis, my beautiful and talented sister—for sharing her skills by creating a gorgeous cover and taking great headshots, and for making me an aunt to the three best kids around.
Dr. Paul Kopf, my dad—for providing the support I needed to get through the lean years … and for consistently encouraging me—through words and deeds—to not give up.
And to my Lord and Savior—for putting this calling on my life then lovingly forcing me to see it through.

I am forever grateful to you all!

Prologue
Catie

I fell in love with Lawrence Poole at the coy and clueless age of seven. He gave me a pink wildflower and a whisper-wet peck on the cheek after he caught me under the monkey bars during a lunchtime game of tag. In that moment, I was smitten. Not so much with Lawrence. Oh, he was nice enough and cute as corn. But the girl in me liked the boy in him and that was enough. I followed him around the playground like a homeless puppy, hoping for more. I didn't know what I wanted more of. I just couldn't forget how that kiss made me feel.

Three years later, Lawrence stopped coming to school. "Leukemia," I heard Mom say to Dad one night. The next day, she took me to visit the first boyfriend I never had. He didn't talk much as he floated in a pool of fluffy, white pillows, his skin blending in with the hospital sheets. I wanted to ask him why he only kissed me once, but the room was full of soft-talking parents with sad eyes. So, I sat in a folding chair by the bed and chattered on about all the homework I had to do and how I wished Mrs. Effelbaum would stop blowing her coffee breath in my face when she helped me with math. Mom didn't tell me I was there to say good-bye. When he died a few weeks later the whole class cried. And, somehow, I felt more alone than ever.

After Lawrence, no other boy tried to kiss me under the monkey bars. Or behind the bleachers. Or in the stairwell. Or anywhere else, for that matter. I went on a few dates in high school, but boys made me nervous, and

I didn't let them do anything more than hold my hand. These polite and good church-going young men agreed to my terms. And never asked me out again.

I wandered around in my twenties and thirties without even a hint of a proposal, always believing the right man was out there, just around the corner. He would be charming. I would be clever. He would love my dry sense of humor and restless red hair. I would be surprised by his wit and love the way he smelled like cold wind and leather. It all played out so perfectly in my mind.

Still, forty came and went and nothing. I immersed myself in my work. If I didn't need a man, maybe I'd stop wanting one. Where my lonely barrenness was concerned, I let a thin, hard shell form around my heart. Tears couldn't get out; pain couldn't get in. I focused on anything else and tried to forget the fact—

I was spinstered.

Chapter 1

Catie

I am more single today than I have ever been. I see this truth reflected in the eyes of just about every man I meet. Including the blue-eyed barista at the local coffee shop who takes my order, gives me a brief once-over, then turns away to pump foam and an extra squirt of espresso into my cappuccino.

Maybe he doesn't like redheads.

As I wait, I pull out my phone, check my e-mail, and remember Gary Reynolds from Indiana. He's the last guy I dated, and that was almost eight years ago. Gary went out with my friend Uli first, but it didn't last. Probably because every time she was around him, she would sing that song about Gary, Indiana, from *The Music Man*.

Not long after they broke up, he asked me out. We drank coffee at Panera Bread and talked about work. We clung to the possibility of a relationship for about a month. During that time, our dates included more coffee, more shop talk, and less chemistry each week. Then he left Colorado Springs to be closer to his family in the Midwest. He said he would write, and he did. Well, his fiancée did, sort of, when they sent me a wedding invitation.

Since then, nothing. I can't remember the last time I flirted with someone or had a reason to buy a new pair of shoes, other than practicality. The absolute worst reason to buy shoes.

Barista boy hollers my name, and I grab my cup

before heading to my car. The restaurant where I'm meeting my friends is just a few blocks away. I'm the first one to arrive. No surprise. Certainly not to our regular waiter, George, who leads me to a table and asks if I want him to bring our drink order while I wait. Sure. Why not? We always get the same thing: one iced tea and three diet Cokes, two with lemon, one without ice. I sip on my capp while I wait. And thank God for caffeine. And wonder why I'm thinking about past relationships today.

One past relationship.

Where is everybody?

Every other week, I join my three best friends at Applebee's for what we call Accountability Monday. In truth, it's a three-hour discourse on work, men, hopes, dreams, faith, and whatever's annoyed us recently. We laugh. We cry. Sometimes we get into an argument, and we work through it. Then we pray about whatever issues came up. It's just a good way to start the week.

Jolene Woods arrives first and slides into the booth across from me just as George drops off our drinks. Her eyes sparkle at the tall, blond waiter, and she thanks him in a voice as smooth as the black suede jacket she's wearing.

My flirtatious friend's brown skin glows with the warm sheen of coffee after you stir a bit of cream into it. She's pulled her mass of thick, black hair away from her face with a zebra-patterned headband but she didn't even try to tame it, so the sheer volume of hair triples the size of her head.

Jolene grins at me as she draws the glass of sweet tea toward her. "You look great, Catie. New highlights?"

"Just a bit on top. You like it?"

"Yeah, I love it. It's more of a strawberry blonde now. But still red." Jolene glances toward the door. "Any signs of my roommate yet?"

"Are you kidding? Since when is Uli on time?"

"Maybe she'll surprise us."

I grunt. "And maybe George will ask me out."

Jolene's eyes twinkle at me. "Stranger things have been known to happen." She grabs a menu. "I would think you'd be used to her tardiness by now."

"You'd think." But I'm not. So I guzzle down the rest of my coffee to keep from saying something snarky, even if it would be appropriate.

A grimace of disapproval mars Jolene's face, though it's hard to say whether it's directed at me, Uli, or the entrée options. I look behind me, see Tess Erickson gliding in our direction, smile, and wave her over.

Tess plops down next to Jolene, grinning as if she just talked a policeman out of a speeding ticket. "I have news," she announces, her voice sing-songing "news" like a soprano.

And then she doesn't say anything but picks up and peruses the menu so intently I consider tossing my spoon at her.

We wait. I tap out a rhythm on the table. *Seriously.* Finally, I clear my throat. "Well, are you going to tell us or are we supposed to guess?"

"Of course I'll tell you," Tess says. "As soon as Uli gets here."

"But it's good?"

"It's *so* good."

Jolene asks if anyone wants to go in on some potato

skins with her. That discussion leads to the decision to share several appetizers instead of entrees. We're trying to choose between chicken quesadillas or buffalo wings when Uli rushes in, out of breath and complaining about Colorado Springs traffic as she slips into the seat next to me. Since her permed, shoulder-length blonde hair is still a little damp and she smells like coconut body wash, I suspect she decided last minute to take a shower. Uli Odell has never been good at gauging how much time something will take her. Which explains why she's usually late.

"You're just in time," Jolene says. "We're about to order half the appetizers on the menu."

"Sounds good." Uli thanks me for the diet Coke, picks up her straw, rips the top off the paper wrapper, and blows it at Jolene. After taking a long drink, she relaxes against the seat with a sigh. "So, what's up?"

"Tess has big news," I tell her. We all look at Tess, whose gleaming hazel eyes and room-lighting smile promise something life-changing.

"We have a new GWP."

GWP is our code for a Guy With Potential. Lately, though, sighting one has become rarer than catching a glimpse of Bigfoot, as evidenced by the deep breaths taken by Uli and Jolene. They seem incapable of talking, so I say,

"Where, at church?"

"Of course at church. He's going to check out our class this Sunday."

As the pastor's executive assistant, Tess often knows when someone new is about to visit our group. This comes in handy if the person is a single, available, age-appropriate male. With Tess around to give us a heads-up, we have a chance to make sure we look our best. And freak out. And blast our expectations so high not even Johnny Depp could compete. Yet this is what we do to ourselves, every stinking time.

"So," Jolene says, "what's his story?"

Tess opens her mouth to spill the details, but she's interrupted by George, who takes our order for a three-appetizer platter and a large, oriental chicken salad to share.

Once he's gone, Tess leans across the table and whispers, "He's forty-four." That's the most important detail, and my friends take another delighted breath. He's about the right age for either Uli or Jolene. He's too old for Tess, however, and a bit too young for me. Then again, five years doesn't seem as much of a barrier now as it was when I was, well, younger.

"What else do you know?" Uli tries to act casual. But the older she gets, the less casual she feels where men and marriage are concerned. I know because she told me. And because I've had similar feelings. It doesn't help that she's about to hit the big four-oh. You can almost feel the desperation radiating off of her like heat waves. I can't blame her. Though none of us wants to come across as anxious or, even worse, desperate, the thought of a new GWP makes hope bubble to the surface for three of us.

Not for Tess, though, who's never been interested in a long-term relationship. She pictures herself as a modern-day Amy Carmichael, preferring to follow her heart to the mission field rather than down the aisle. But that doesn't stop her from keeping her eyes open for the rest of us. I've only dated one guy in the last eight years—yes, Gary from Indiana—and Tess introduced him to me.

Anyway, Tess tells us his name is Brian and he's an anesthesiologist, which makes Uli's green eyes widen. She and Jolene throw smiles at each other. I can practically see them ticking off must-haves from their checklist. Usually they would hide their enthusiasm, but this is a safe place where we're free to express our deepest dream: that God has just the right spouse out there, somewhere, for each of us.

This latest prospect is one of many California transplants who escaped to the Springs for a better career opportunity. One thing Tess can't tell us is what Brian looks like. Everything she knows about him she gleaned from a short phone conversation when he called the church to find out more about services and the denomination's core values. Tess guided him to the website, then dove into a carefully conducted interview.

"So, yes, I asked him a few questions, but I didn't want to seem too nosey," she says. "You will all just have to wait to find out more on Sunday."

"Mm-hmm." I pull out my iPhone. "Do you know his last name?"

"Kemper. Why?"

"Maybe he's on Facebook." I wink at Tess as I type in the name. A dozen results pop up, no surprise, but one works for the Colorado Springs Medical Center.

Uli looks over my shoulder. "Whoa. Is that him?"

"I think so." I click on his page, put the phone in the middle of the table, and everyone leans in.

"He's cute," Jolene says. "Nice eyes; a full head of

hair. Most guys our age have already started working on their comb-over."

"He's short." Uli heaves a sigh and sits back.

"Ooh, he has a post about going to Panama with Christian Medical Mission. That's a good sign," Tess says. "What do you think, Catie?"

She looks at me. They all do. We have an understanding that I have dibs on any incoming GWPs since I'm the oldest. Still, we can't force chemistry, so we prefer to leave any actual love-matching in God's hands. As much as I appreciate their generosity, the problem is—

"He's too young."

Uli scrunches up her nose. "For you? No, he's not."

"I prefer older men."

"You prefer to be high maintenance." Jolene says this in a whisper, as George is in the process of setting down four empty plates and several platters of food. It takes about five minutes to split up spinach-artichoke dip and chips, potato skins, quesadillas, and salad between the four of us. I take advantage of the distraction and say,

"So, I saw that *Wicked* is coming to Denver. Should I get tickets?"

Jolene scowls across the table at me. "Nice try, Miss Delaney. But we *are* going to talk about how you push guys away." She takes a small bite of quesadilla. "And yes, you should definitely get *Wicked* tickets."

"I don't push men away. I'm cautious."

"You do kind of put up walls," Uli says. "When's the last time you let someone kiss you?"

"Kissing is overrated."

"Spoken by someone who's never really been kissed."

Jolene nods in agreement. "Uli's right. One drunken kiss in the backseat of a car ruined you."

"It wasn't that bad."

Uli smirks at me. "You said he tasted like dirty socks."

"Ew. Hang on a minute." Tess holds up a hand. "I haven't heard this story. What happened?"

"Nothing." I glare a warning at Uli and Jolene. They chuckle. I'll find no mercy here. "It was a mistake. I'd like to think I've put it behind me. Can't we forget about it?"

"One of Catie's few indiscretions," Jolene says. "We all have our moments."

Tess looks at me. "And …?"

"And …" I glance at Jolene, who smiles almost apologetically. "First of all, I was only twenty-three. I went out with friends one night and felt a little daring, so I had a few rum and Cokes … and ended up making out with the bouncer in the backseat of a station wagon."

"You didn't."

"I did, and it was terrible. But," and I have to laugh, "I fell asleep. I woke up and thought, 'He's still kissing me. Why is he still kissing me?'"

"Oh dear. Catie." Tess shakes her head. She's relatively new to our group and hasn't heard much about any of our backgrounds. It's possible she has even less experience with the opposite sex than I do. Crazy, but possible. "So what happened?"

"I finally came to my senses and realized I was in danger of doing something I would regret. So, I crawled over him, pushed open the door, and ran to my car, which was, fortunately, parked close by. And I haven't had even a sip of alcohol since."

Uli adds, "She also hasn't kissed anyone since."

Tess turns to Uli. "She hasn't?"

"Nope. It's been over twenty years."

She says "twenty years" like she's reading an obituary.

I'm suddenly aware of the hum of voices around us, the smell of sizzling fajitas and burgers fresh off the grill, and the sound of a Sugar Ray song tripping from the speakers. If I focus my attention on anything else, maybe I'll finally forget that stupid mistake and the two decades I've gone since without being touched—in an intimate way, that is—by a man. I take a deep breath. "Can we talk about something else?"

Jolene reaches across the table and covers my hand. "Sure."

Because I know if we don't change the subject, I might end up spilling all my secrets. And I'm just not ready for that yet.

Chapter 2
Jolene

She sits across from me, her back straighter than my mama's moral fiber and her mouth full of teeth. I can see every one of 'em. I get it.

This girl is happy.

My clients bring me all kinds of emotions: anger, remorse, sadness, even a thirst for vengeance. But pure joy? That's as rare as bacon in a synagogue.

I followed the call to start Cocoon House five years ago, hoping to give women shifting from prison life to the rest of their life a better chance. Lord knows I've met all kinds since—recovering addicts, heartbroken mothers, frightened girls, and a lot of angry women who think the world is out to get them. But not this girl. Her shiny, brown hair curls softly around her face, and her eyes, the same gentle russet color as her hair, brim with hope. It's something I'm not used to seeing at Cocoon House. Certainly not on someone's first day.

Yep, Benita Jensen is definitely different.

I shuffle through her application papers. The dome-topped grandmother clock I inherited from my mama's side of the family ticks away the silence, adding a steady rhythm to the sounds of traffic from the busy, nearby intersection. We sit in my small office right off the front hall. Sparsely furnished with a pair of mismatched leather chairs, a desk, and a bookshelf, the office—like most of the rooms in the house—is lovingly decorated with items donated by ministry supporters.

From the kitchen, the smell of garlic and bread and

tomato sauce wafts down the hall, and my stomach grumbles. SueAnn, my right hand, lives to cook, and the whole house can't wait for her Italian feasts every Wednesday night. I check the clock. If I finish this interview early enough, I'll have enough time to whip up a batch of Ghirardelli brownies to go with the meal. Mmm.

But first I have a job to do.

Benita shifts in her seat, stuffing her hands into the opposite sleeves of her pale-blue, zip-up hoodie. Underneath, a plain, white T-shirt peeks out. A pair of beat-up jeans and cheap, white sneakers complete the look. Pretty standard for my girls. So often, in their attempt to put the past behind them, they try to disappear into plainness. The exceptions go to the opposite extreme: gaudy jewelry and clothing accompany faces coated in layers of makeup.

Still, it doesn't matter how they dress or what they've done, everyone has a shot at a place in Cocoon House. But since we only have room for six women at a time, our referral and acceptance process is, well, tedious but thorough. I smile at Benita. She's made it this far. Might as well just dive right in.

"So, you were at La Vista on a ten-year sentence for armed robbery. Is that right?"

"Yes, ten years, but I only served seven." I catch a smidge of an accent and see on her application that she lived in Tampico, Mexico, until she was eight, when her family moved to Pueblo, Colorado. Her English last name came from her stepfather. She shrugs and sends me a shy grin. "Good behavior."

"What did you do before prison?"

"I was a schoolteacher."

My pen slips from my hand and falls with a clunk onto the desk. I pick it up before looking back at Benita. "A schoolteacher?"

"Yes. Fifth grade for three years."

Dang. She's braver than me. The application indicates she's thirty-five. Single, no kids. "Would you like to teach again?"

"Si, I think so."

Putting the application aside, I lean forward. "I have to know. How on earth did you end up involved in a bank robbery?"

She sighs. Apparently, I'm not the first person to ask her that. "Have you ever fallen for a guy who was completely wrong for you, Miss Woods?"

Ooh. There's a question. I glance at her application. "I take it you're referring to Diego Chavez."

"He made me feel ... exotic and exciting and ... not afraid." Her faraway smile says he still makes her feel that way. Not good.

"And you're not over him."

That breaks the spell. Benita takes a deep breath. "I could never forget him, even if I wanted to, but I've put that relationship behind me, Miss Woods. I'm ready to move on."

"How do you know?"

"How do I ... what do you mean?"

"If Diego Chavez were to walk through that door"—I nod toward the one leading from the office to the hall—"what would you do?"

"Honestly?"

I nod.

"I'd run. Fast. Just like Joseph."

"Joseph?"

"From the Bible. He didn't stick around and try to work things out when his boss's wife came onto him. He just got out of there. Seems like a good idea."

Bless her heart. She tells the story like a child explaining what she learned in a Sunday school lesson. Though they probably didn't use the phrase "came onto him" in the telling. I hold back a smile. "How do you know about Joseph?"

"Church, of course." She tilts her head. "Who doesn't know that story?"

Once again I wonder how on earth she got involved in a bank heist. Then I realize Diego found her innocence appealing. It made her weak, pliable. Easy to manipulate. *Honey, I need to run an errand. Can you drive me? You are such a doll. What's one felony when I love you, baby?* Yeah. I know the type. I spend 75 percent of my time schooling my girls on how to blast these losers out of their lives. But getting them out of their hearts? I'd have an easier time churning butter. I ask,

"How long have you been going to church?"

"All my life." She pauses a moment as she plays with the zipper on her hoodie. "But it didn't really mean anything until a few years ago. The prison chaplain, she taught me things."

"What kind of things?"

"What real love looks like. God's love. How it's … sacrificial. Diego didn't love. He amused himself. He played with my heart like it was Silly Putty."

Yep, I definitely know the type. "When's the last

time you saw him?"

"Not since the trial."

"His or yours?"

"I testified against him. He wasn't at mine."

"That must have been hard."

She smiles. "Which part?"

"Either. Both." Naïve, yes, but quick. "So, tell me, Benita. Why do you want to live here? What brought you to Cocoon House?"

"Well, the prison chaplain told me about it."

"Mm-hmm." She knows I already know that.

"I just … want a fresh start. And I think maybe I can help other women." She holds up a hand, but I wasn't about to interrupt. The best way to learn is to listen. "Yes, I have a long way to go. I'll work hard, though, and listen ·and do whatever I need to do. I feel … I believe, with the support of this ministry, I can get to a place where I can make a difference." Benita stands and walks over to a window that looks out at the house next door. Her gaze focuses on something outside as her fingers continue to fiddle with the zipper, sliding it up and down.

"Miss Woods, about four years ago I realized God had a purpose in all this. Nothing was an accident. And I could see it that way and figure out why, or I could feel sorry for myself and settle for whatever life throws at me. I've watched a lot of women just give up." She rubs a hand across her forehead, and I wonder what she's remembering. Finally, she looks at me. "I don't want to settle for anything but God's plan for me, Miss Woods. Does that make sense?"

I nod. Everyone deserves a second chance, even if

not everyone wants one.

"Benita, I have just one more question." With a smile, I close her file and set it aside. "Do you like lasagna?"

◊◊◊

Later that night, back home in the cookie-cutter two-bedroom apartment I share with Uli, I browse potential date profiles on comegetyourrib.com. As I do, Benita's comments about God's purpose, even in the bad stuff, won't leave me alone. Do I see God's purpose in the events of my life? Can a person make horrible, wicked choices yet still trust His plan will be accomplished? Or is it all a series of ups and downs and sideways beyond my control, without making sense or having a reason, other than to smother me in regret and guilt? Is my singleness holy retribution? It is, after all, what I deserve. Uli sees herself as *being* spinstered whether she wants it or not, which she considers ridiculously unfair. She can't find anything good in her unmarried status, and she's made some, from what I can tell, desperate decisions as a result. Catie, on the other hand, seems to have just given up.

Well, it's not like I'd be more content married than I am single. It doesn't matter if God intended it all along or not. This is where I am and who I am. Yes, I'm still haunted by the mistakes of my youth, but God has forgiven me. Besides, I love the freedom of being on my own, making my own plans, following whatever vision God gives me. Most of the time, I'm very happy with my friends, my home, my career. It's highly unlikely I would have started Cocoon House if I'd had a family to care for. And I can throw all my kid-love on my nieces and nephews. I adore them.

I click on a profile with the screen name "Boaz." Ruth is one of my favorite Bible stories, so he's certainly worth a look. Two comments catch my attention: He says he can cook, which includes "putting together a mean Toaster Strudel," and, under *hobbies*, he wrote "frog jumping and sunset watching, not necessarily in that order." At least he's trying, so I send off a quick hello. Next I respond to Tim, a man I've been communicating with for about a month. We've finally scheduled a date and will meet for miniature golf on Saturday afternoon. He looks cute and just past the cuddly stage of fat and seems a little needy but still worth a try. This is no time to be picky.

The variety of profiles I scroll through range from too cool to be believed to just plain sad. Some have thumbnail photos that look worse than a mugshot; others clearly took the picture with their cell phone. If his hair is trimmed and he's wearing something nicer than a T-shirt, I take notice. But that's all surface stuff. I have a list of must-haves I need to get through first. Then I'll worry about appearances.

First of all, his faith has to be strong and church must be a vital part of his life. He also needs to be open to the idea of having children. I'm always disappointed by how many men state they have kids and don't want more. If he won't even consider the possibility, he's not for me. He'd better want to adopt children as much as I do. Then there's his work, his relationship with his family, and his political viewpoint. And he absolutely cannot be a smoker.

Yes, it's exhausting, but I only need one to work out. He's got to be out there somewhere.

By the time I shut my laptop for the night, I've connected with three more Guys With Potential. I then pick through my closet for twenty minutes, finally deciding on a flirty, lilac-colored blouse and my favorite jeans for my date with Tim. Lucky man. What he won't know is I'm saving my best and brightest yellow skirt and top for church ... and Brian Kemper.

If it doesn't work out with Tim, I'll pick myself up and dust myself off with an orange creamsicle float on the way home. I might even buy a bouquet of sunflowers and daisies to cheer up the dining room table. And, of course, there's always the new guy on Sunday.

It's good to have options.

Chapter 3
Oli

I stub my toe on a wrought-iron chair as I try to find my way across the room in the dark. I'm not sure what bothers me most: that I know someone who decorates his bedroom with patio furniture or that I'm stumbling around his house in the middle of the night. I'm not worried I'll wake up Cole. If I could wake him up, actually, I would. Why should he be snoring peacefully while I'm once again abusing myself, physically and mentally? But the man sleeps like he's been nailed into a coffin. Besides, I would hate to have to talk to him now.

I don't want to talk to anyone.

Finally dressed, I grab my bag and slip out the door, shutting it behind me. I don't close it fast enough, though, because shame and regret follow me all the way to my car and all the way home. The legs of shame wrap around my neck while regret pounds on my temples with sharp, little fists. I can't escape the guilt. Tears drip down my face, and I let them.

When I get to my apartment, the entryway light is still on, meaning Jolene expected me to slink in late. On the coffee table, a coupon flyer from the Magic Mountain miniature-golf park reminds me she had a blind date this afternoon. Well, if nothing else, we'll save money on our next putt-putt outing. And Jolene always gets at least one good story out of her online dating adventures.

I tiptoe to my room, even though Jolene's is on the opposite side of the main area from mine. No need to risk waking her. She probably knows by now why I stay out so late, but we've never talked about it even though we've been roommates for almost three years. The one time she met Cole—when he came over to fix our dishwasher—only let her know I was seeing someone. I made it seem like a casual, brand-new thing. And though she laughed at his jokes, she raised an eyebrow at me more than once and, after he left, she said, "A guy who wears wife-beater shirts? Really, Uli?"

At least she's not standing in the hallway, waiting for me, arms crossed and toes tapping while she wonders why I can't be more like her. I doubt she's ever had an impure thought in her life.

As I get ready for bed, I push aside thoughts of my latest failure. Or how disappointed God must be with me. Instead, I scroll through my story. It's become something of a nightly ritual; a pre-fortieth birthday pep talk: *Cole loves me. He's there for me. If I just hang in there, someday he'll marry me. We've been close to an engagement before. He even bought a ring. I just have to be patient. These things take time.*

Cole loves me. He's there for me. If I just hang in there ...

These things take time. But, really, how much time do I have? I do *not* want to start over with someone new. What a terrifying thought. And would it even be possible at my age? Besides, I feel bound to Cole and not just physically. I'm trapped in our relationship by time and opportunity and because I'm older than dirt.

Maybe this new guy, Brian, has potential. Maybe starting over wouldn't be so bad. Maybe there's reason to hope. All I know is something has to happen soon, or it will be too late. And I can't bear the thought of being that spinster-girl no one ever wanted to marry.

That can't be God's will for me. It just can't. Clearly, He expects me to put more effort into the pursuit. I wish He'd help out a bit but, until then, it's all on me. My mother always told me to chase the guy until he catches me. Maybe I need to try harder. Run faster.

Yeah, I won't get much sleep tonight.

◊◊◊

Sunday morning dawns crisp and clear. It's late September, and the aspens outside my bedroom window twinkle gold in the early sunlight. Hope filters through me. It's like what *Anne of Green Gables* said: "Isn't it nice to think that tomorrow is a new day with no mistakes in it yet?" I'm ready for something wonderful to happen.

I'm so ready.

Squeezing into my black jeans, I choose not to stress about the thirty pounds I need to lose. Maybe today I'll take a walk instead of opening a bag of Hershey's Kisses. The dark chocolate ones. *Stop it, Uli.* It's a new day, and anything is possible. I pull eight sweaters and five shirts out of the closet and try them all on before finally knocking on Jolene's bedroom door and getting her opinion on my final three options.

"This one, definitely," she says, pointing to a white cardigan covered in big black and gray flowers. It's lightweight, which is good because fall afternoons in Colorado can still simmer on the warm side. I wear a simple, white tank underneath and wrap a red scarf around my neck for color.

After spending thirty minutes trying to get my hair to do something even remotely cute, I finally pull it back with some black clips, leaving a few curly tendrils free to frame my face. Dangling, silver earrings; strappy, black sandals; a hint of Charlie Red, and I'm ready to go. Since Jolene has been yelling at me to hurry up for the last ten minutes, I grab my purse and chase her out to the car. She streaks ahead of me like a ray of sunshine in her bright, happy outfit. Or like a big, yellow chicken. Brian will definitely notice her. And I'll make a nice, neutral backdrop.

I have a tough time paying attention to the service. It's hard to listen to a sermon about the power of grace when you're craning your neck for a glimpse of the new guy. Especially when you're trying to look without looking like you're looking.

Jolene elbows me and whispers, "Can't you wait another thirty minutes?"

"No." I grin at her and glance behind me ... right into the clear, silver-fox eyes of Brian Kemper. Wow, he actually has an up-to-date Facebook photo, except his dark hair is shorter and there's some gray at the temples. His eyes are a little close together, and he has a rather large, hooked nose, but it works for him. Especially when he smiles, which he does, and I realize I'm staring. Then he nods at me. One of those polite, "what's up" nods. Like we work in the same building and, every once in a while, have to wait for the elevator together. What a disappointingly unromantic meeting! I can't tell our kids *that*. "Our eyes met across a crowded room ... and he nodded at me." Blah.

I want a do-over.

Though it's too late now, I look away, feeling the heat crawl up my face. Well, that's that. Then I make the mistake of glancing at Jolene. She has a serene, perfect, speak-to-me-Lord expression on her face. Good grief, the woman knows exactly where Brian Kemper is sitting. She's probably known since we walked into the sanctuary.

Jolene: one; Uli: zero.

Catie, however, seems completely oblivious. She's sitting on the other side of Jolene, scribbling notes faster than Pastor Owens can get the words out. I shouldn't say "scribbling" because her writing is neat, bulleted, and laid out in columns. It looks like an Excel spreadsheet. But her short, cropped, red-gold hair frames her perky but somewhat plain face just right and, though I'm not fond of business suits personally, her striking blue one makes her seem taller and, somehow, adds a few curves.

"What did he just say?" Tess, to my right, leans closer. Well, he didn't *say* anything, he's— Oh, wait. The sermon. She means the pastor, not Brian. Right. I shrug my shoulders. "Sorry. I missed it too." She gives me a crooked, behave-yourself smile. Boy, do I wish my friends couldn't read me like a book. Not all the time, anyway.

So, I turn my attention completely to the pastor until the last amen is uttered. We stand for the closing song, and as the final strains of "Your Grace Is Enough" echo through the sanctuary, the music morphs into the chatter of several hundred voices.

I do not fight my way through the crowd or hurry to our class meeting room but wander around, greeting acquaintances and chatting with whomever I happen to run into. On occasion, I catch a glimpse of Brian. He's surrounded by people. What could he have done to be such a favorite already? He's definitely an extrovert. And he's cute in an older-guy-with-laugh-lines-and-no-sense-of-style kind of way. The group around him seems completely captivated. They laugh at almost anything he says. Hope simmers through me like that first sip of hot chocolate.

Please, God. Please let something happen.

Eventually, I make my way to the classroom where our group leader, Scott, greets everyone with a Squiggy-like "hello" and hands out his weekly list of discussion questions. Thirty-one-year-old Scott Jones works at Home Depot and treats every girl like a sister. Which would be fine if he didn't see himself as the annoying little brother who pulls your hair and drops ice cubes down the back of your shirt. Okay, he's not that bad, but I'm pretty sure the thought has crossed his mind. To his credit, though, he does an adequate job keeping our small group on track.

I set my Bible and notebook on a chair before turning to dash back through the door, heading to the restroom for one last, quick check in the mirror. But I take the corner too fast and run smack-dab into Mr. GWP himself. I don't just run into him; I practically bowl him over, stumbling like a drunken sailor, knocking a cup of coffee out of his hands and to the floor, where it splatters all over our shoes. Strong fingers grab my arms, helping me get my balance. With a deep breath, I look up into gray eyes that flicker startled, then amused.

"Steady there," he says.

I laugh. What else can I do? This meet-cute might be more interesting than a nod but only if it leads to something. If he never asks me out, it will forever be merely an embarrassing memory. So, of course, my imagination jumps to a happier outcome. One where I tell our kids about how I ran into their father ... literally.

Once I'm no longer tilting, he drops his hands away. "Are you all right?"

"Yes, I'm fine." I pick up the now empty Styrofoam cup and hand it to him. "How about you?"

He smiles. "I've survived worse. So," he says, looking around, "are you running to something or away from it?"

To something. Definitely. But I say, "The restroom," like a ditz. I'm always so much more clever in my mind.

We gaze into each other's eyes for a suspended-in-air moment. Then he says, "Where can I get something to clean this up?"

"What?"

"The coffee."

Shake it off. "Right. Of course. I'll take care of it. You go on. I'll be there in a minute."

"Where's that?"

"Oh, um ..." *Good grief, Uli. You sound like a stalker. "Hello, stranger. I know we only met a minute ago, but I know exactly where you're going."* Out loud I say,

"I meant ... aren't you ..." I point pathetically toward the door I just lurched through.

He looks past me. "Is that where the single

professional class meets?"

I nod and am, I'm sure, about to say something completely *not* brilliant, when Jolene sashays out into the hall.

"Well, hello there!" She flicks her head my direction and flashes a smile that actually outshines her dress. "Uli, are you gonna introduce me to your friend?"

Jolene: two.

Once again I stammer out something nonsensical as Brian steps forward, hand outstretched.

"Hi, I'm Brian. Your friend—Uli?—and I just … ran into each other." He grins back at me and suddenly hope springs up again like a jack-in-the-box, shocking me with its sudden reappearance. Two minutes after meeting and the new guy and I already have a past, a history, an inside joke.

Uli: one.

My friend and roommate takes his hand. "Jolene. Nice to meet you." Then, instead of letting go, she practically pulls him into the classroom. "Let me introduce you to the rest of the crew."

I look down at the puddle of coffee soaking into the carpet, tempted to just leave it. It's old carpet, anyway. That would be wrong, though, so I hurry to get some paper towels from the kitchen.

It would be unwise to leave Brian in Jolene's grasp too long. If all's fair in love and war, then I need to prepare for battle. My roommate, after all, is a seasoned campaigner.

Chapter 4
Catie

During the forty-five minutes allotted to our Sunday school class, I watch Uli and Jolene scuffle over Brian with all the finesse of a slickly choreographed dance. Or the tangled mess of a car accident. Call it what you will, you can't look away. If I suspected he had a clue, I might be embarrassed, but he doesn't, so I enjoy the show. Besides, he's too busy discussing sanctification with Scott. Brian has some interesting thoughts on the subject and expresses them without reservation. You don't often meet a man who can jump right in so comfortably. It's an attractive quality.

My friends, apparently, feel the same way.

I suppose I should throw my own log on the fire if I want a shot. Not that I have a log. Or even a stick. What do I have to offer, other than the wrinkles, sags, and salty attitude of a forty-eight-year-old spinster? Do I even want a shot? Is Brian someone I could be interested in or just the only new thing on the horizon? Sure, he seems like a nice enough guy. Not bad looking. Maybe a little opinionated.

Perhaps I'm done with the whole idea of marriage. What a relief that would be! No more stressing about how I look or freaking out about the latest GWP who happens to show up at work or church or across the tomato bin at King Sooper's. I could just be me. Lonely, grumpy, cynical me.

On the other side of the room, Uli tucks a loose curl behind her ear and smiles at Brian. He just made some comment about the Apostle Paul coming across as somewhat arrogant in his letters to the churches. I can practically see her wheels turning.

"Was he arrogant," she says, "or just confident? Sometimes the two can seem similar."

"Yes, I suppose it's a little bit of both," he responds. "But he even admitted in Corinthians that God gave him a thorn in his flesh to keep him from becoming conceited. He evidently recognized it was a problem for him."

"Even if it was, that doesn't make what he wrote any less valid." Tess holds up her Bible. "He was still writing the inspired Word of God."

Brian nods. "Exactly. All I'm saying is, you don't have to look too closely to see the personality of some of the biblical authors coming through. Moses was self-deprecating. Peter was passionate and quick to express an opinion. John was modest and humble."

"Well, that was a good discussion," Scott says, reeling things in. "Does anyone have any prayer requests?"

Of course people do, so we spend a good twenty minutes sharing needs and praise, followed by prayer. We also take some time to discuss the upcoming fall retreat, scheduled for mid-October. For as long as I've been a part of the group, caravanning up to a gorgeous, A-frame lodge in the mountains near Buena Vista has been an annual adventure for us. It's a highlight of the year. But when Brian tells Scott he wants to sign up, I suddenly have more to look forward to than long hikes and shopping in cute souvenir shops. Which means I'll spend the next few weeks mired in anticipation. Great.

With class officially ended, we get into a fifteen-minute discussion on where we want to go to lunch—a weekly ritual. It always takes us forever to decide whether we prefer burritos at Margaritas or burgers at Wendy's. I am usually out-voted, and we end up at some fast-food place, which is fine. I make more money than a lot of people in the group. It's not something we talk about, but it creates a bit of a wall.

So, after a great debate over what everyone's in the mood for— interrupted by Jolene telling us about the time a meatball sub and a skateboard ruined her favorite pale-pink blouse, a story that makes Brian laugh so hard he chokes—we finally decide everyone will get whatever they want and bring it to Palmer Park in one hour. We'll picnic then head out for a long afternoon hike. Perfect.

Uli and Jolene each ask Brian at least once if he'll be there, and Jolene stomps all over Uli's artistic toes when she draws him a map of directions. It's never good when Uli's insecurity slams up against Jolene's clueless enthusiasm. All of which means Uli will push harder while Jolene will be more teeth and temptation than any one man can handle.

Poor Brian doesn't stand a chance.

And neither do I.

◊◊◊

An hour is more than enough time to run home, change into jean capris and a T-shirt, grab a flannel jacket for warmth, and whistle for my golden retriever, Luna, to follow me out to the car. After a quick stop at

Subway for a BLT, I'm on my way to Palmer Park. Why we can't make something like this happen in thirty minutes or less I will never understand, but that's the way it is. I'm so used to waiting, I always keep something to work on or read in my SUV.

Once I reach our agreed-upon meeting place, I unload my lunch and a copy of John Maxwell's *The 21 Irrefutable Laws of Leadership* from the car. Luna follows after me. I pour some water for her into a bowl I keep in my trunk.

Since no one ever shows up on time, I should have a good fifteen, twenty minutes to eat and read. But five minutes after I've set up shop at one of the picnic tables, a car pulls into the parking lot. I can't think of anyone in our group who gets anywhere early, so it's most likely a random hiker or another group of picnickers. At least, that's what I think until Brian Kemper steps out of the tan Volvo. He sees me and waves. I'm stunned. There he is, not only on time but early. *What do you know about that?* He leans back into the car and pulls out a plastic grocery bag and a huge water bottle. Then he walks toward me.

There's something almost skippy about his gait, like he's trying not to break into a run. He lopes right up to me and drops his bag on the table. Luna watches him closely, barks once, then takes up a post beside me. She growls occasionally, her eyes never leaving the newcomer. Brian points at her and says,

"Your dog?"

"Luna."

She growls again.

Brian smiles at her. He seems hesitant. "I don't

think she likes me."

"It might take her a while to warm up to you, but she won't hurt you." I shrug. "Unless you come after me, of course."

"Of course." He finally sits across from me and looks around. "This is great!"

"It is?"

"Sure. Beautiful place. Great company. I was worried I'd be the first one here or no one else would show up." He tugs a large store-made salad, a packet of balsamic vinaigrette, a container of grilled chicken strips, a fork, and some napkins out of the bag. "Isn't it great to have someone to eat lunch with?"

I nod and take a bite of my BLT.

Brian points his chin toward my book. "What are you reading?"

"It's about leadership." I wipe my mouth with a napkin. *Oh please, don't let there be any mayo on my face.* "There's a VP position opening up at my company, and I want to apply. So, I'm trying to improve my chances."

"Oh yeah? That's great! What do you do?" Brian adds the chicken and dressing to his salad, stirs it around a bit, and digs in.

"I'm a project manager at an IT company."

"Nice." At least, I think that's what he says, since his mouth is full. Turns out, eating and talking at the same time is a bad habit of his. Not an appealing one but also not a deal-breaker. I guess.

We spend the next five minutes chatting about work, completely wasting the opportunity. I should be getting to know the new GWP on a somewhat more personal level now, when there isn't a gaggle of girls around fighting for his attention. I try to maneuver my mind into WWJS mode: What Would Jolene Say? I've never met someone as natural or flirtatious with men as Jolene. She would *not* talk about work at a time like this. Well, maybe she would. Her job is certainly more fascinating than mine.

Say something, Catie. Anything more interesting than blubbering on about work (boring) or the weather (yawn). So I ask,

"How long have you been in the Springs?" Not the best start, but it could lead to something. And it's a good way to get a feel for his views on long-term commitment. Does he like moving from place to place or is he ready to settle down? Over the years I've developed a knack for catching the subtext in male-female conversations … among the single population, anyway.

"I just moved here a few months ago," he says, giving me a glimpse of mashed lettuce and carrots.

"Oh really? Where did you live before?"

"California, near Oakland."

"And you moved *here*? I hope you're not a Raiders fan."

He pauses in his chewing. Raises an eyebrow. "Raiders fan?"

"Yeah, the football team."

The eyebrow doesn't move.

"They're one of the Broncos biggest rivals."

Still nothing.

"You know … football." Yeah, because that's gonna help.

With a shrug, he says, "You lost me," and dives

back into his lunch. He's right. Brian lost interest in this conversation faster than it took Elway to throw a touchdown pass in Super Bowl XXXII. And that man could release the pigskin quicker than anyone.

I say, "I take it you don't like sports."

"Well, I like to play sports, like volleyball or racquetball. But sitting down and watching a game on TV isn't really my thing. I don't even own a TV, actually."

"That's too bad. About football, I mean. I love it. In fact, I have season tickets to the Broncos' games." The words dangle out there like an invitation. *And just what do you expect him to do about it, Catie? He already said he doesn't like to watch sports.* Still, maybe he'd enjoy actually going to a pro football game. Or, my heart whispers, maybe he'll find the idea of attending a game with me appealing.

But Brian simply says, "That's nice," and checks his watch. I might be more boring than the weather.

I swallow the last bite of my BLT then gather up my trash. A heavy weight sits on my head, and a voice tells me I've failed. Again. The voice whispers, *Why would anyone want you?*

To my relief, another car pulls up. I see Jolene—or, rather, her hair—silhouetted through the front windshield. Might as well concede the loss and pass the torch to my friend. She heads our direction, and I wave.

Once she joins us at the picnic table, Jolene whips a peanut butter and jelly sandwich, a Ziploc baggie of tortilla chips, and a Fuji apple out of a brown paper bag. Leave it to Jolene to pack a lunch like the one my mom used to send with me to day camp and still come across as chic as if she were eating foie gras and caviar on the French Riviera.

I say, "Where's Uli?"

"She wanted to drive separately."

"Really?" As a freelance graphic designer and photographer, Uli rarely has money and tries to save whenever possible. Since her car is typically overflowing with everything from old magazines and fast-food wrappers to prints of finished work she needs to get to clients, she usually catches a ride with her roommate.

In response, Jolene looks at me pointedly, jerks her head surreptitiously toward Brian, and winks. Oh. Uli might be a skinflint, but she sure knows how to make the most of an opportunity. And she's not one to let carpooling get in the way of spending as much time as possible with Mr. Potential.

Brian puts his now-empty salad container back in the plastic grocery-store bag. He asks Jolene, "Do you usually drive together?" as he reaches across the table, grabs my Subway trash, and tosses it in the bag with his own.

After explaining her and Uli's roommate status, Jolene embarks on a funny, of course, story about their apartment search and how one particularly lecherous landlord tried to talk them into a skanky—her word— studio apartment near Chapel Hills Mall. She's just getting to the good part as more people from our group arrive, including Uli in her beat-up red Toyota.

Must be time for lunch.

◊◊◊

Another forty-five minutes of munching and chit-chat eats away at daylight before we're finally ready to get moving. Besides Brian, Jolene, Uli, Tess, and me, we're joined by Scott, a girl named Ellen with gray-streaked hair who never seems to fully understand what's going on, and our token married couple. Doug and Lindsay met and courted as part of the group and, ever since they got married over a year ago, they've had a hard time pulling away. Truthfully, we like having them around. They don't shove their wedded bliss in our faces, and they give us a sense of stability. Maybe even a little hope we all still have a chance.

While Brian and I wait, the rest of the group packs up or throws away their stuff, tightens the laces on their hiking boots, and grabs their water bottles. I know Palmer Park like my own backyard and suggest we take the Edna Mae Bennet nature trail, which curves around and past the horse stables—another option for exploring the area. It's a tough climb that takes a lot of work, but it also has one of my favorite views of my favorite city. Everyone agrees, and we head off, starting in the northwest direction.

The familiar Colorado sun comes close enough to provide a layer of warmth. The air feels as crisp as a Granny Smith apple and carries the faint scent of burning leaves. Thin patches of clouds speckle the sky. I end up walking with Tess as Luna scampers ahead, ready to protect us from man or beast. Tess skips along beside me, more upbeat and talkative than usual. And that's saying a lot. It's like someone lit her from within. We quickly take the lead as we make our climb along the switchbacks crossing the side of the hill. Tess bubbles on about how much she enjoyed the morning service, and how she's looking forward to the upcoming sermon series on Nehemiah.

"I love Nehemiah." She hops around a boulder and glances over her shoulder at the group coming up behind us. "He was so … gutsy."

"What has gotten into you?"

Tess takes a sip from her gray REI water bottle as we make another sharp turn. "What do you mean?"

"You just seem really enthusiastic today."

"Why shouldn't I be?" She throws her arms wide, like she's a nun exploring the Alps and singing about the hills being alive. "Isn't it a perfect day?"

"This is Colorado. It's almost always a perfect day."

"I suppose. But this one seems so much more …" Tess pauses. Then she sighs. Not from exertion or because she's enjoying the view but from something else. Something she doesn't explain.

Maybe I can help. "So much more … blue?"

"Catie." She stops and places a hand on my shoulder. "You're just gonna have to accept the fact that I'm in a good mood."

"You're delightful."

"And your sarcasm has no power here. In fact," she quirks an eyebrow at me, "maybe I can rub some of my enthusiasm off on you."

To test her theory, she massages my arm then laughs and pulls me into a bear hug. She's actually strong enough to lift me off the ground and shake me like a rag doll. Luna barks and circles us, wanting to be included. This gives the rest of the hikers a chance to catch up.

Great. We lost our lead.

Near the back of the pack, Uli huffs right along and somehow manages to stay close to Brian and keep a conversation going at the same time. I can't help but admire her tenacity. She certainly seems relieved when there's a pause in our forward movement, giving her a chance to rest a moment and get her breathing somewhat back to normal.

Jolene, meanwhile, lags behind and doesn't quite catch us before we start moving again. She's never been fond of hiking. She once told me, "Only crazy white people would climb a mountain for no reason." Jolene's idea of exercise is flipping on a light switch. If, however, a hike means an afternoon with a GWP, she'll make the best of it.

Her typical strategy is to take her time on the uphill portion of the trail then make her move on the downside. Since one of her mottos is "Never let them see you sweat," she has to take it slow. I guarantee her designer backpack not only has a bottle of ice water and a fresh blouse, if needed, but also contains a washcloth and a small, battery-powered fan. As soon as we reach the top, I predict she'll spend more time cooling off than admiring the view, because that's what she always does. She doesn't really need to go to so much trouble, though. Jolene always comes across as calm and collected.

Once I shake myself free of Happy Tess, she drops back to walk with Uli. The other groups also morph into different dynamics and, before I know it, I'm striding side-by-side with Brian. Well, not technically, since Luna places herself decidedly between us. She doesn't trust Brian yet, but I'm sure she will in time. I stare at the rocky path ahead of us, wishing I wasn't such a failure when it comes to casual conversation. I don't have anything new to say. Didn't we cover it all at lunch? I am this close to making some lame comment about the weather when Brian saves me by saying,

"Have you climbed Pikes Peak yet?"

"Yes," I say. "Have you?"

"I'm training. I hope to make the climb before summer. Maybe in May."

"Wow. I'm impressed."

"Really?" He rubs the back of his neck. "I thought climbing the Peak was something everyone did around here."

I laugh. "Well, it's certainly something most Coloradans talk about doing. Tess and I have made it to the top twice, but you couldn't pay Uli or Jolene to go."

He glances over his shoulder. "I guess it's not for everyone."

"No, it's not."

We march on in silence for a moment. Or two. Long enough for me to wonder if he thinks I'm the most tedious person he's ever met. Then he says,

"Have you ever taken that train to the top?"

"The cog railway? Um, no. I've always wanted to, but—"

"I've been hoping to check it out since I moved here. Would you want to give it a go, maybe next weekend? I wouldn't mind getting a better feel for the mountain. And what I'm getting myself into."

By some miracle, I manage to keep up a regular hiking pace. Only my heart stumbles. Did Brian just ask me out? If he did, he has the most casual approach I've ever heard. I glance over. He's chewing on a drinking straw, which throws me as I don't remember him having one earlier. His eyes are focused straight ahead, and he seems completely relaxed. What am I supposed to think about this?

Somehow I manage to say, "Sure. Sounds like fun. What time?"

"Let's go later in the day. Then we can get something to eat after. Does that work?"

"Yes." Next thing I know, he's asking for my phone number.

Maybe he likes me after all.

I just hope Uli and Jolene didn't hear our latest GWP ask me to climb a mountain with him. One freaked-out, single woman at a time seems like more than enough.

Chapter 5
Jolene

This is my day off, for heaven's sake. The Lord's Day. A day of rest. So why I'm spending it trudging up the side of a cliff is beyond me.

First, Tess and Catie sprinted ahead like gazelles toward a mountain stream. Brian was in a deep conversation with Doug and Lindsay, with Uli tagging along, followed by Scott and Ellen. And I trailed in the back like a caboose.

There's a joke about the size of my booty in there somewhere.

Now, Brian seems completely entranced by Catie, and I'm still bringing up the rear. I see my red-haired friend glance over at our GWP, a look of complete shock on her face. What on earth are they talking about? I'd love to chat with Uli, who's huffing along next to me, about what's going on ahead of us. But, Lord have mercy, I'd rather breathe at the moment.

I really can't stand hiking. We're human beings not mountain goats. A drop of sweat slides down the back of my neck. The climbing shoes forced on me by life in Colorado are beyond ugly. There's grit in my teeth from the dust we're kicking up, and I'm wheezing like an asthma patient without an inhaler. Not to disparage asthma patients. My younger brother has asthma. Still, this is no way to make an impression, good or otherwise.

But I hang in there because I refuse to let a pile of rocks come between me and Mr. Possibility. Too bad he's still such a mystery. I haven't had a chance to interview him yet. Not that I want to do a full-blown, "Who's-your-mama?" interrogation, but I do have a few must-know questions. Who doesn't? At my age, I know what I want. And what I don't want.

We finally gasp our way to the apex of the trail. While everyone else oohs and ahhs over the view, I find an as-good-as-you're-gonna-get boulder to sit on. At last a chance to freshen up. I gulp down some water, letting the icy coolness work its way through my insides. Then I pull a few musk-scented hand sanitizer wipes from my bag. Each swipe takes away a little more grime, a bit more grit, and I start to feel like myself again.

Ooh. Ahh.

Now that I'm refreshed, I take a moment to observe the dynamics of our little group as they mill around. Brian stands on a rock near the edge of the cliff, shooting pictures with his smartphone. Uli patiently listens to Scott drone on about who knows what. I doubt she has a clue either since she keeps glancing toward Brian. She has her bottom lip clamped between her teeth, which means she's planning something crazy and trying to talk herself out of it. Or into it.

I'm about to go over and stop her when my cell whistles at me. Caller ID says it's my friend Trevor, so I answer.

"Hey, stud."

"Hi, gorgeous. You busy?"

"Not at the moment. I'm just sitting on a rock in Palmer Park."

"You are not."

"Oh yes, I am. And don't mock. I worked hard to get to this rock."

"Uh-huh."

"Seriously. I have the sweat to prove it."

"Okay, now I know you're joking. So, sweating aside, are we still on for tonight?"

Trevor and I get together on Sunday nights to watch *The Amazing Race* and eat homemade pizza. We also swap online dating stories. Whoever has the best tale gets to stay behind while the other goes to pick up ice cream for dessert. I rarely have to leave.

But tonight I'm reluctant to commit. I glance toward Brian, who's gesturing wildly. I hear the words "third-world mission trip" and notice how Tess perks up.

I say, "I'm not sure. Can I call you later?"

"If you can make it just come over. Otherwise, yeah, call me."

"Well, don't wait for me. If you want to make other plans—"

"Jolene."

"Yeah?"

"Just do what you have to do. There's always next Sunday."

I hear the smile in his voice and realize I would probably regret it if I missed our weekly non-date. Trevor and I have been friends since we met at a Bible conference in our late-twenties. No one gets me like he does. It would be perfect if we were attracted to each other, but we're just not—even though Trevor Jakandé is one of the best-looking men I know, with skin as black as night, a smile no woman could resist, and the most perfect bald head I have ever seen. He moves with the strength and grace of a panther. Twenty years ago, he made the Olympic track team just out of college, winning a silver medal and two bronze. Now he works for the U.S. training center in Colorado Springs as a therapeutic recreation specialist. I'm as proud as I could be of his success. Kind of like how a sister feels about her big brother.

And that's the problem. Great guy. Godly man. Hot as pavement on the Fourth of July. And he's just like a brother from another mother, as they say. Have I mentioned I already have three brothers? And three sisters. Siblings I have. It's a husband I want. I look up, and my eyes meet Brian's. He grins, waving me toward the group.

"Trevor, I'll call you later, either way. I have to at least tell you about my date with Tom."

"I thought his name was Tim."

"Tim, Tom. It didn't work out."

"Big surprise. He's the dog walker, right?"

"Dog *groomer*. It's a job that has given him some particular skills."

"I'm sure."

"Talk to you later?"

"You bet."

We say our good-byes, and I click the phone shut.

Time to show the new guy what I'm all about. I won't have any trouble breathing on the way down. And I mean to spend every moment of the trek finding out all I can about Brian Kemper.

◊◊◊

It's like interviewing a goldfish. His answers tell me practically nothing.

"If you could live anywhere, where would you choose?"

"I *can* live anywhere."

Cheeky.

"But if you could move to anywhere in the world. An-y-where."

"I'm happy enough here. Moving is such a pain."

Well, I suppose stability is a good thing.

"So, do you plan to settle in Colorado Springs?"

"For now."

For the love of pickles.

I don't give up, though I do ease off a bit after Catie sends me a "give-the-poor-man-a-break" eye roll. By the time we reach the parking lot, I know three new things: Brian is interested in short-term missions, he doesn't like to move, and he's allergic to feathers.

Actually, I made up the third thing. If he's allergic to anything it's a good conversation.

We all stand around our cars for a few minutes, making plans to get together for a movie and dinner on Friday night. Once that's settled, everyone takes off except for Catie and me. I can tell she wants to talk. And I really want to hear what happened between her and Brian. We stroll over to the picnic table while Luna finds a shady spot under a tree and promptly falls asleep.

"So," Catie begins, "Brian asked for my number."

Not what I was expecting to hear. "Wow, he did?"

"Yeah. What do you think it means?"

"I think it means he wants to call you."

She takes a seat on the bench, facing out, and leans back against the table. "That's what scares me."

I park myself next to her. "What? Why would that

scare you?"

"I don't know if I'm even interested in Brian. We just met."

"Okay. But that's why you go on dates. To find out if there's something there."

"I suppose."

Turning slightly, I wrap an arm around her shoulders. "Catie, I know men make you nervous."

She shrugs and tries to pull away. "It's not that."

"Are you sure?"

Catie stands, takes a few steps, and turns back to me. "You think I'm really immature where men are concerned, don't you." It wasn't a question.

"When did I say that?"

"You don't have to say it, Jolene. We both know it's true. I don't have as much … experience as you do."

"Wait a minute. There's no need to—"

She holds up a hand. "I know. I'm not comparing your choices to mine. I'm just saying that sometimes being around people who have actually had sex makes me feel like a child, whether they mean to or not."

"Now back up. We're talking about dating here. How did sex come into it?"

"Sex always comes into it."

"Well, eventually. After marriage. But can't we take things one step at a time?"

"No. We can't." Catie brushes a strand of hair off her forehead. She doesn't look at me. "The thing is, you're right. My lack of experience—even with something as everyday as kissing—makes me nervous around men. And I don't know what to do about it."

I somehow get to my feet, which isn't easy since my

calves and thighs are stiff and achy and on fire after the march to the apex of hell and back. But once I manage to stand, I take one of Catie's hands in my own. "I know you think it is, but that's not necessarily a bad thing. I would give anything to have your innocence." I really would.

"It's not that simple."

"What isn't?"

She takes a deep breath then smiles at me. "Nothing. I just have a lot to work through. I wouldn't wish me on any man right now."

"Oh, don't say that. All you have to remember is that the right guy will see you for the great catch you are. And he won't care if you're nervous."

"I hope you're right."

"Of course I'm right. And Catie? I can't wait for the day you find out there's nothing 'everyday' about kissing."

She grimaces, though it might have been a half-hearted attempt at a grin. Poor thing.

I'm not much help, so I backpedal a bit. "Well, never mind all that, what exactly did you and Brian talk about?"

Once she's finished recapping the details of her surprising conversation with Brian, I tell her to be open to whatever happens. Her wide, uncertain eyes suggest she's not quite ready for that. How anyone could be almost fifty and still not be able to handle a potential relationship is beyond ...

Seriously, Jolene? Are you sure you're that much better at this than she is? Give her a break.

So I say, "Anything could happen, Catie. You just

need to relax and have fun and not worry so much."

"Really?"

"Absolutely. It's way too early to freak out."

She grins at me, and this time it's genuine. "It's never too early for me to freak out, Jolene. You should know that."

When I ask if I can pray for her, she nods. Afterward, we hug and say our good-byes. As soon as I'm in my car, I call Trevor. He answers right before it goes to voicemail.

"Hi, gorgeous."

"You still in the mood for company tonight?"

"Sure. I'll make the pizza dough if you bring the toppings."

"See you at six."

Maybe he's not my soul mate. But he sure makes Sunday nights easier to get through.

Chapter 6

Uli

"So, what did you think?"

Loaded down with groceries, I barely get through the door and Jolene waylays me, ready for an in-depth breakdown of the new guy. The one who had so much potential not too long ago. I say,

"Well, I have to admit, I wasn't that impressed. Sure, he has a lot going for him but … I don't know. He's cute enough. Just not my type."

Jolene follows me to the kitchen, where I drop my bags on the counter. That's when I remember I didn't get more diet Mountain Dew. Great. Now I have to go back to the store. I hate shopping. Well, I suppose I should drink more water anyway. As I put my stuff away, my roommate rummages through the fridge, looking for who knows what. She finally emerges with a bottle of flavored water, a block of mozzarella cheese, and a bag of Canadian bacon.

"Sometimes you have to give attraction time to grow," she says, opening the water and taking a long swig. She then puts the cheese and bacon in one of my now-empty grocery bags, along with cans of tomato sauce and mushrooms she pulled from the cupboard. Oh, right. It's her night to hang out with Trevor. Now there's a good-looking man. Why she doesn't sling him over her shoulder and carry him to the altar, I can't begin to understand. She says she's not attracted to him. Mm-hmm. Maybe she should take her own advice. If your best friend looks like Taye Diggs and you're not attracted to him, there's something wrong with you.

"First, I have to decide if he's worth investing that much time in." Time I don't have.

Jolene sips at her drink as she studies my face. "To be honest, I wasn't feeling it either. He's nice, but I think he might be a better fit for Catie."

"Really?" I fill a tall glass with ice then add some water. "You think she can get past the age difference?"

"I think she only brought that up as a defense mechanism. Then, if he's not interested, she can say she wasn't either."

"That makes sense." I take my glass over to the dining room table—my office, for lack of a better space—and fire up my Mac. "The last thing Catie wants to do is make herself vulnerable around a man."

"Which is exactly what she needs to do." Jo's chocolate-brown eyes meet mine, and we both giggle. "Now if she'd only listen to us, she'd have a man like that," and she snaps her fingers.

"It's almost like she doesn't think we know what we're talking about."

"Impossible." And we laugh again.

"Well, I have to run some errands," she says, grabbing her things. "Then I'm going to Trevor's. See you later?"

"Where else would I be?" Because I'm not going to Cole's.

After Jolene leaves, I briefly consider calling him anyway. I'm sure he's home, and I know he won't call me. I blow a heavy sigh into my bangs. I can't even play hard-to-get with him anymore.

Hmm. Admitting that feels like something of a

breakthrough.

So, instead, I get to work. Several families asked me to take their Christmas photos for them, which need to be edited, and I have a holiday flyer to put together for a local strip mall. 'Tis the season. I turn on my computer, set the channel to the classic movie station, where I discover Barbara Stanwyck turning Henry Fonda into malleable clay in *The Lady Eve*, and dive into work.

I'm definitely not going to Cole's.

Two hours later, most of the photos are done, Henry and Barbara are finally honeymooning on a train, and hunger pains force me out of my chair. That's when I realize I haven't checked my phone all day. I left it in my glove compartment during the lunch-hike, and, sure enough, I find it still hanging out in my car. Clicking the phone on, I see three missed calls from my mother. Oh blast.

I think about calling her back. I might as well since I'm not going to Cole's. I think about calling her back while I make a pot of chili. I think about calling her back while I eat the chili with crackers and a little cheese as I watch a DVR'd episode of *House Hunters*. I think about it during another useless hour of jumping around our cable channels, watching three different shows while not really settling on anything. By now, it's almost seven. And that's when Mom calls again. So I stop thinking about it and answer the phone.

"Hi, Mom."

"Honey, are you okay?"

"Yeah, I'm good. I just forgot to check my phone."

"All day?"

"Well, I was gone most of the afternoon."

"Oh, right. Your church group. How did that go?"

"We had lunch then went for a hike. It was fine." Now, what my mom really wants to know is if I met Mr. Right. That concern is always at the top of her agenda. I'm sure I'll give up all hope long before she does. I don't know if it's sweet or optimistic or just annoying. Maybe a little of all three.

"Did you meet anyone new?"

This probably isn't the best time to tell her about Brian. If I haven't told her about Cole, why on earth would I mention a new, potentially datable man in my life? No reason to get her hopes up. Okay, there's no reason to give her one more thing to pester me about. I can hear her now: *Were you friendly? Did you smile a lot? Why aren't you attracted to him? But if he asks you out, you need to say yes!* Because I clearly don't have a clue about men.

Clearly.

"It was, pretty much, the same group."

"Oh. Well, you hang in there, honey. I know you'll find someone. You just need to put yourself out there more."

Here we go. If she only knew. I almost say, "Like you?" but hold my tongue.

"Mr. Right isn't going to just knock on your door. If you could be more vulnerable—"

"Mom."

"—flirt a little more—"

"I know."

"—and not be so picky!"

"Okay. I need to go. I have work to do."

"Work? Did you get a job?"

Oh, that's just perfect. I just threw her onto her other favorite topic: my unemployed/underemployed/self-employed status.

"It's a freelance job."

"Of course."

"Mom, can we talk more another time?"

"Yes, that's fine. I just want to see you stable and settled, Uli. You know that, right? At this rate, you'll never be able to even retire. Do you really plan to work until you die?"

"Actually, I do. I love being an artist."

"Uli—"

"Good night, Mom."

She heaves a sigh that's so loud and expressive, I swear I could have heard it all the way from her condo in Iowa without the phone.

"Good night, sweetie."

I hang up. And call Cole.

◊◊◊

Twenty minutes later, I'm sitting on Cole's couch, and he's kissing my neck whenever the Sunday night football recap goes to commercial. It's devastatingly romantic. Well, maybe not romantic.

I ask, "Who's playing?"

He looks at me like I just signed up his firstborn son for ballet lessons.

"The Broncos. Don't you live here?"

"I thought their colors were blue and orange."

"Yes, but sometimes they wear their old uniforms, and those were brown and yellow. They said it's *refro*."

"Retro. That means it's something from the past."

"Oh, of course. Excuse me, Miss Smarty Pants."

"There's no reason to get testy."

"Shhhh." Because the game is starting. I don't mind that Cole likes football. My dad and, later, my stepdad watched it all the time, so it reminds me of my childhood. I don't understand the appeal. But it doesn't bother me.

He leans over and kisses me in an absent-minded apology and somehow manages to keep watching the game while doing it. The indirect approach causes his stubble to scratch against my chin. Each fall, Cole grows his "winter face," which means he gets Santa-ized with a bushy, gray-streaked beard. He knows I hate it. It would be one thing if it was just unattractive, but he looks ridiculous. My boyfriend—the man I've chosen to love and to whom I would promise my life forever if he just asked me—wears wife-beater T-shirts and shorts, year-round. That's his style. But in the winter that's his style, with a beard. He looks like an ice-road trucker at the beach.

I get it. Really. Cole dresses the way he does because he's never hot and he's never cold. And he doesn't care how he looks. When we go out, though, he will put on a T-shirt with actual sleeves and, if I beg, a pair of jeans instead of cargo shorts. It's a shame, really. With his black hair and intense black eyes, Cole Moretti would look amazing in sharper clothes. The streaks of gray through his hair only make him look more distinguished. From the neck up, anyway. I fantasize about seeing him in a deep-blue dress shirt and black blazer. He can even keep the jeans. I mentioned the idea once.

Once.

So I learned the hard way that this is a battle I can't win. Better to concentrate on the ones I might still have a chance at.

I say, "Can we talk?"

"Can it wait until the next commercial?"

"You want to hold a conversation in three-minute intervals every ten or fifteen minutes?"

"That'd be great."

"Cole."

"Uli." Ah, sarcasm. My favorite.

I say, "This is important."

"So is this."

"But I think we should—"

He grunts like a linebacker and looks at me, anger slanting through his eyes. "I just missed what they said about the lineup."

"So rewind it."

"If you'd quit nagging I wouldn't have to rewind it."

"Right, 'cause that's such a hardship."

He swears. His hands clench into fists. "Seriously, Uli, could you shut up for two minutes?"

Yes. Yes, I can. Even longer in fact. The chili rolls through my stomach like rocks tumbling down the side of a mountain. Too much spice, too many beans. I glance at Cole, who snorts and leans back against the couch cushion. Maybe I shouldn't blame the chili.

Maybe I should leave.

I should definitely leave.

If I can just make the move from sitting to standing to walking out the door. I'm about to do just that when

Cole puts his hand on mine. It would be nice if he was sorry for being such a jerk and would say so. But he just doesn't want me to leave. Not yet anyway. I'm so frustrated with myself I can't breathe.

Then my stomach rumbles again.

Cole looks at me. "What was that?"

"Chili."

"Well, don't let it out here."

Now I can stand. I get my purse and say good night.

Maybe I should always eat chili before I go over to Cole's.

◊◊◊

Once again, I end up crying all the way home. But I clean myself up enough for drive-thru Dairy Queen and get the biggest chocolate ice cream cone they have. Because it will help settle my stomach.

I'm crunching away the last bit of the cone as I walk through the apartment door. Jolene sits at our kitchen table, checking e-mail or surfing dating websites or posting goofy cat videos on Facebook. Or all three.

Jolene looks up. "You're home early."

"So are you."

She tilts her head. "Are you all right?"

"Yes." I slant my head the other way. "Why wouldn't I be?"

"You have chocolate on your chin and a little on your shirt."

I glance down. Blast. My loose, three-tiered, pink blouse looks like an ice-cream-coated child got his hands on it. *Well, it's not the end of the world.* A few squirts of

Shout should take care of it. But as I stare at the drizzles of chocolate staining my shirt, my barely controlled emotions spill out, and the next thing I know I'm sobbing as if everything has been ruined. And, I suppose, that's about right. The wreck I've made of my life can't be Shout-ed out.

"Mercy, Uli, calm down." Jolene walks over and puts a hand on my shoulder. "Seriously, sweetie, it's not that bad."

I pluck a tissue from a box on the end table and dab the tears and, hopefully, some of the chocolate off my face. Okay. Good. I'm weeping because of my shirt. If Jolene believes that, it's far better than what she'd do and say if I admitted the truth. So I sniffle a few times and whimper, "I know. I know. It's just ... it must be that time of the month."

Well, not exactly, but she knows that. Two women living as roommates for three years will eventually become aware of each other's cycles. Another harsh reminder of how single I am, even though I'm in a stupid relationship with a man who doesn't love me and I will never get married or pregnant so my cycle is nothing more than a monthly nuisance. These thoughts don't help, and the tears start dripping all over again.

"Oh, honey, I know how you feel. But if the stain doesn't come out, why not see it as an excuse to go shopping?" Now Jolene has her arm around me, and her eyes are sympathetically sad. You'd think I just told her I have a terminal disease. Then she chuckles. "I'd suggest we go get ice cream to make you feel better, but—"

"I don't know if there's anything that will make me

feel better."

Fatalism. Gotta love it.

"Well, I can think of one thing."

"Oh yeah?"

She goes to the window and flips up the blinds. There, just peeking over the apartment building on the other side of the parking lot, is a glorious autumn moon.

"Now," Jolene says, "how about you grab your camera and we drive to the top of Palmer Park? It's a perfect night for you to get some great stock photos."

She's right. Nothing relaxes me like setting up my camera, getting the right angle, composing a dream shot. Besides, stock photos are my bread and butter most of the time. And my client would find a set of full-moon pics particularly appealing.

"I'll change my shirt."

"And I'll grab a few napkins. Or maybe some wet wipes would be better."

I pick up a copy of *People* magazine from the end table and fling it at her. "You're a funny girl."

Jolene skitters out of harm's way. "Hurry up or you'll miss all the good photo ops."

Once in my room, I change into a heather-gray Help-Portrait T-shirt, which represents my annual attempt to give a little back by taking family Christmas photos for those who can't afford them. If I made enough money, I'd do something like it all the time. The people are wonderful, and the whole event makes me feel so … useful. I like that feeling.

Last December my day included photographing the Lennox family—mom Audrey and her kids, Jason and Kara. Audrey lost her husband in a car accident the spring before and was, like all of the Help-Portrait families, struggling to get by.

"All my dreams died with him," she once told me, as tears brightened her dark blue eyes.

I can only imagine.

Over the months since I first took their pictures we've become friends, and I help her out by watching the kids every Wednesday afternoon so she can run errands. We also do fun stuff, like going to the Denver amusement park or spending a summer afternoon at the apartment complex pool, watching the kids swim while Audrey and I guzzle frosty Dews and talk about the latest episode of *The Bachelorette*. It's a different kind of relationship than the one I have with my church friends.

And she's the only one who knows everything about Cole and me. I'm not sure why I find it easy to tell her so much but still can't say a word about it to Catie or Tess. Or even Jolene.

"Come on, Uli," my impatient roommate hollers from the other room. "Moon's a-wastin'!"

I grab my camera bag and a black hoodie and stuff all my secrets down as far as I can. If Jolene suspects something, she can be relentless. I've avoided a discussion with her about my sinful indiscretions for over a year. I don't want her to tell me what I already know.

If I can hang in there until Cole's ready to do what's right and marry me, everything will be fine.

Chapter 7
Catie

Get out of the car, Catie.

I drove into the garage almost ten minutes ago, yet here I sit. It's not my fault the particular radio station I tuned in keeps playing one good song after another. Each one seems perfectly suited for the day I had. The kind of workday that would make most girls cry for their mommy. I deflected so many potential disasters they should give me an honorary flak jacket. At least the new system updates I was put in charge of implementing will be done in a week, and I can, hopefully, move on to a more appealing project.

At least turn off the engine.

A twist of the key and quiet fills the space. I power down the garage door, shutting out the blinding sunlight as it drops over Pikes Peak. At times, I like to sit somewhere quiet and dark with only the sound of my breathing. It's so peaceful. Especially when everything around me seems so frantic.

But I can't stay here forever—not with my dog whimpering inside the house and my stomach reminding me I forgot to eat lunch, and all I had for breakfast was blueberry yogurt and a banana. That means I poured a lot of coffee into a mostly empty stomach.

Once inside the house, I don't even go upstairs to change but deposit my keys and purse on the hall table and shuffle to the living room where I collapse onto the leather couch. Luna follows me from the moment I walk in the door, of course. As soon as I sit, she drops her soft-blonde head on my lap and stares at me with empathetic brown eyes.

"Did you have a tough day too, girl?" I scritch behind her ears. Her tail wags. "You're such a good dog."

Too bad I'm too hungry to relax. I should have bought take-out on the way home. It requires every ounce of energy, but I push myself to my feet and head to the kitchen. My beautiful, granite-coated, stainless-steel-applianced, open-to-the-main-room kitchen. The center of my home, if you can call a woman, a dog, and a great kitchen a home. As I pass my laptop, I click to a soft jazz Pandora station and turn up the sound.

Dinner consists of a simple turkey-and-cheese sandwich, some leftover cucumber salad, and water instead of coffee. I read the paper while I eat, dropping occasional bites of meat and cheese for Luna. Once I finish and the kitchen is clean, I consider watching a movie. But going to bed early and reading the Michael Connelly novel I'm halfway through sounds far too tempting. I'm on my way upstairs when my cell phone rings. I know it's work. I should ignore it.

Turns out it's not work. I don't recognize the number. I let it ring three times before finally deciding to answer.

"Hello?"

"Hi. Is this Catie?"

A male voice. A nice male voice. I don't recognize it.

"Yes?"

"Oh, hi! This is Brian."

"Brian?" Brian Kemper?

"Yeah, from church. We met on Sunday?"

"Oh right." That sounded casual. Good start. "How can I help you?" And now I sound like a flight attendant. Or a customer service rep.

"Well, I'm calling about that Pikes Peak idea. I've changed my mind."

No, please don't say that.

But he continues, "I think I might hike up the Peak on Saturday instead of starting with the train, like we talked about. Might as well get right to it. At least part of it. So ... would you still be interested?"

"Pikes Peak? Saturday?" *Catie. You're not a parrot.* "What time would you want to get started?"

"Let's go early. Maybe seven-ish? I thought we could climb for about three hours then head back down. And maybe grab some lunch afterward?"

"Oh, so, make a day of it." How long should I pretend I don't know if I want to go or not? *Who are you kidding?* "That actually sounds great, Brian. Where should I meet you?"

I hear a sigh through the phone. Maybe he's as nervous as I am. That would be nice. Though it makes far more sense that he's thinking it through.

He asks, "What part of town are you in?"

"Do you know the Springs Ranch subdivision, at Powers and Constitution?"

"I know Powers. Is that near Woodmen?"

"South of there. Where are you?"

"I live in a duplex on See-Saw."

"Ah. The playground." I used to live in that neighborhood near the north-center of town, only I was on Teeter-Totter. "Well, it probably makes more sense for me to either come to your place or meet you somewhere."

"My place is fine." He gives me the address and says good-bye with a friendly, "See you Saturday!"

After I hang up, I mentally punch myself. *You really couldn't think of anything else to talk about?* Not that we won't have hours to talk on Saturday. And, just like that, I'm overwhelmed by the realization I have to be interesting for six hours straight. Probably more.

He's going to be bored out of his mind. I can't do this. I start to dial him back to cancel. But I call Jolene instead. She answers with a "Hey, Cate, what's up?"

"Brian just called. He wants to go hiking on Saturday. This Saturday. That's in two days! Not even two days. Two nights. One day. Thirty-six hours!"

"Whoa, wait. Stop throwing numbers at me and calm down, honey. We can do this."

"No. I can't. Maybe you could, but I don't have a good track record for appealing to men. We'll be an hour up the mountain, and he'll suddenly realize he left the oven on."

She laughs. "Okay, let's not freak out. Not yet, anyway. Can you meet me at Pikes Perk in twenty minutes?"

And so, half an hour later, I'm sitting in the little coffee shop with Jolene—and Uli, who tagged along—gripping my cappuccino between cold, tense fingers. I told them what happened and now we're just staring at each other. I say,

"He wants to hike for five or six hours, then get some lunch. But it's not a date. Right?"

Jolene shrugs. "It's hard to say. Did he call it a

date?"

"No."

"But," Uli says, "you're the only one he asked to go."

"As far as I know."

Uli blows on her hot chocolate. She's been blowing on it for almost ten minutes. "Well, then, you should treat it like a date until you have a reason not to."

Jolene rolls her eyes. "What kind of advice is that?"

"The optimistic kind."

"She doesn't need optimism; she needs honesty."

"Exactly. And she honestly might be going on a first date on Saturday."

"Oh, and what's the chance of that?"

"Wow," Uli says, "could you be a bigger Debbie Downer?"

"Debbie Downer? Really?"

"If she doesn't treat it like a potential date, then she's doomed to fail."

"But if she does and it's not, she's setting herself up for disappointment."

It's like watching a tennis match. One I'm not playing but that I'm still, somehow, losing. "Thanks, guys. So I'm either going to fail or be disappointed? Those are my options? This is not helping."

Jolene glowers at Uli. "Sorry, Catie. You're right. But, seriously, you don't have anything to worry about."

Uli nods. "You'll be fine. He's going to think you're great."

"Yeah," Jolene says. "You're smart, funny, successful. Just be yourself."

She doesn't say pretty. No one describes me as

pretty but I'm used to that. Some people are average, and that's OK.

They both look at me like "be yourself" is the only advice I need. Like it's that simple. All these years of constant singleness, and my only problem is I haven't been myself. That's so funny I want to cry.

"So," I say, "just be myself? As opposed to being … who? I don't even know how to be anyone else. *Myself* is the problem."

Jolene puts down her mug of chai tea. "If you really think that, Catie, then I don't know what to say. Other than maybe you need to stop seeing yourself as the enemy and learn to like yourself the way you are."

"Thanks, Jolene, but why don't you save the psychoanalysis for your ex-cons."

Uli leans back and sips at her hot chocolate, which, it would seem, has finally cooled off enough. She's let us know, several times, how much she hates confrontation—something to do with her mother—so I'm not surprised to see her remove herself from the conversation. Jolene, on the other hand—

"There's no need to get snippy. Or to take your issues out on me."

"You're right. I'm sorry, Jo. I'm just so frustrated."

"You over-think things too much."

"I over-think. I don't like myself for who I am. I push men away. Yes, I get all that. But what's frustrating is these are new problems. Ones I didn't have fifteen, twenty years ago. You know, when I was young and hopeful and still believed someone could love me just the way I am."

My friends don't respond to that. They feel the same

way. We've lost something to age we can't ever get back. And at the top of that list is the freedom to be ourselves. Now we're trapped in the pressure to be what we think—no, hope—men want. Except what men our age really want is younger women. Preferably fertile blondes with sparkly teeth and plenty of their own money. Even Jolene, for all her confidence, knows we're at a disadvantage. It shows up on her face when she thinks no one will notice—a flash of fear she can't cover up. And poor Uli, who tells us about this guy she's dating but never brings him around, no longer tries to hide her disappointment. Even with a boyfriend, she doesn't have a lot of confidence she's in a relationship that's actually going somewhere. It doesn't matter how much we want to believe there's a reason to hope, we can't ignore the truth.

"Sorry to be so blunt," I say, "but you know I'm right."

Uli stares into her mug. She takes a deep breath. "I need another hot chocolate."

Jolene looks back and forth between the two of us before grunting with all the attitude of a retired professor chewing on cigars and ripping through his chess opponents without mercy. "Look at you two, wallowing in your cups over what you don't have. Has it occurred to you that a man isn't the answer? That marriage won't solve your problems?"

"Really, Jolene?" I throw up my hands, and let them fall onto the table with a slap. "That's the kind of cliché we hear from married people. I don't expect it from you."

Uli sighs again. "I think I'm ready to call it a night."

Her voice catches, and when I glance her way, her eyes shimmer with a hint of tears. She looks at Jolene. "Can we just go?"

Unbelievable. They're actually trying to find a reason to get away. "Wait a second. You came here to give me a pep talk and help me feel better about Saturday. Well, here's a news flash: Now I feel worse. And you're just going to leave me?"

Jolene raises an eyebrow. She's the most compassionate person I know and yet, at times, she's as cold as a car door handle on an icy morning. She calls it tough love. "I'm just not sure what else we can do," she says. "But I do hope you'll be able to relax and have a good time."

"And be myself."

She stands and gives me one of the most you-poor-thing smiles I've ever seen. "Whenever possible, yes. Be yourself. Any guy would be lucky to have you."

They say good night, leaving me there with a cold cappuccino and a dozen more reasons to call Brian and cancel the hike.

But I don't, which means there's still a part of me, small though it may be, that thinks love may be a possibility. Even if it's a long shot.

Even if it won't solve any of my problems.

◊◊◊

Saturday dawns overcast and cold, which is admittedly unusual for Colorado. At least it's not snowing on the Peak, and there's always a strong chance the sun will come out eventually. It usually does.

The weather calls for layers; the climb requires jeans and hiking boots, lots of water, and a few snacks. I throw the latter items into a small backpack, along with gloves, a scarf, my little red Nikon camera in its case, and an extra sweater. I'm ready by six-thirty, which gives me plenty of time to get to Brian's by seven. I whistle for Luna, who trots out ahead of me and leaps into her spot on the front seat, tail wagging and tongue panting. She loves an adventure.

I arrive at Brian's and he meets me at the door wearing jeans, a gray, long-sleeved Henley, and a ragged, blue-plaid flannel shirt. Locking the door behind him, he says, "Do you want to drive?"

"Um, sure. That's fine."

As we walk toward my SUV, he whistles a nondescript tune. I glance over, and he grins at me. "You ready for this?"

"I think so." I hope so.

It takes me a minute to drag Luna from the front seat to the back. Brian laughs, pats her head and says, "Maybe next time, old girl." Like the first time they met, she growls at him. There's no threat in the growl, but it still throws me. She usually takes to new people in my life faster than this.

The first half of the hike is as I feared: a series of long silences punctuated by Brian's whistling and several awkward snippets of conversation—a good majority of it about work and my dog. Worst of all, I discover we don't have much in common. Is it too much to hope this will be a case of opposites attract? I regret my decision to not invite Tess. She's so upbeat and easygoing, I could have relaxed and, well, been myself.

Instead, I'm the brace-face girl who ends up standing too close to the star quarterback in the cafeteria line.

And this is what I'm thinking when I twist my ankle.

After a good three hours on the trail, we've turned around and are on our way back down the mountain. Clouds still cover the sky, only now we're closer to them. So close it feels, at times, like we're in them. I'm sure we are. Luna bounds around us from one side of the trail to another. Her tongue lolls out of her mouth, she's so happy. Partly because she believes she's protecting me and partly because she's already seen several squirrels and hopes to spy more.

A chill cuts through my jacket as the wind picks up a bit. We still haven't seen an inch of sun. I'm glad I brought an extra layer. The path is rough and rocky and much harder to navigate as we're descending. We move faster than we should, which throws me off-balance. So when I step on a rock just right, my foot twists beneath me and down I go.

Brian tries to squat beside me, but he's hampered by a rather large and decidedly fretful mass of a dog. Luna licks my face, and I say, "It's okay, girl." The fall knocked the wind out of me and, when I can breathe, all I gulp in is dog hair. "Luna, calm down."

Somehow, Brian finally manages to maneuver past the canine and is rewarded with a growl. He puts a hand on my shoulder. "Ouch. That looked painful." His eyebrows scrunch together. "Are you all right?"

"Um. I'm not sure. My ankle." Could I sound any more wimpier? "Maybe if I can stand on it ..."

He helps me to my feet. When I put my right foot down, though, pain slices like a knife all the way up the side of my leg. I try to hide the shock, but a gasp escapes. I grit my teeth and mutter, "It's fine."

"Yeah, right. Here, put your arm around me."

I try, but our height difference makes it awkward. Before I know what's happening, he sweeps me into his arms. My heart slams up into my throat. I'm suddenly very glad I'm a girl. I relax and discover my face fits perfectly in the curve of his neck. I can smell his shaving cream and the coffee he drank on the drive to the trailhead. For the first time in my life I have an almost-irresistible urge to murmur, "Oh my." But I don't. I force myself to think about something else. Luna weaves around Brian's legs so closely it's a miracle we don't all tumble to the ground.

"Are you sure I'm not too heavy?" I don't know what's happening to me. When did I start talking like the damsel in distress in some cheesy romantic movie? I'm horrified and fascinated at the same time.

A part of me has always wondered if the right man—the one for me—would feel so natural, all of my doubts and insecurities would vanish in his arms. Many of my married friends and acquaintances have told me, "When you meet the one for you, you'll just know."

Is this what they meant? It's not that I feel comfortable with Brian. But something's different. Like maybe I could be at ease if he gave me just a hint of interest. All he has to do is look at me and tell me he likes me just the way I am.

Instead, what he says is, "It's not that far." Which makes me wonder what he would have done with me if it had been "that far."

We're probably at least half a mile from the parking lot. But Brian takes it in stride, moving slowly and keeping his eyes on the path ahead. A sense of something unfamiliar washes over me, and I can't figure out what it is. After a few moments of trying to name it, I give up. I close my eyes and enjoy the moment as my arm tightens around his neck. I no longer care what he thinks.

We reach my SUV far too soon. He opens the back door first and Luna jumps in. She's asleep in seconds. With no pomp and very little circumstance, Brian deposits me in the passenger seat. He makes sure I'm comfortable then rubs my ankle. His hands are strong and gentle and his touch sends tingles up and down my leg. It's all I can do not to groan out loud.

"It's not broken," he says, "but I wouldn't be surprised if it's sprained. You'd better stay off of it as much as possible, until you can get it checked out."

I don't trust myself to speak, so I nod instead.

He looks up at me, his face only inches away, and we stare into each other's eyes for a lifetime. Something races through me. Is he holding his breath too? Then the moment ends. He gives my leg one final pat and smiles. "If I get you home could one of your friends take you to Urgent Care?"

Well, sure. Though I wish he would have offered, I guess we have only known each other for a week. It's better if I call Jolene. But before I do that—

"Could we ..." I gulp down the last bit of nerves and say, "get something to eat first?"

"Oh, yeah. If you're sure you're up for it. What are

you in the mood for?"

"How about Beau Jo's?"

He walks around to the other side of the car and hops in. "Beau Jo's? What's that?"

"It's a pizza place. Really good."

"Sounds perfect." As we head down the road, I prop my foot on the dashboard, give Brian basic directions, and down a couple of Advil with a whole bottle of water. My leg won't stop tingling, but I don't know if it's because of the sprain or because of the man.

◊◊◊

"So, why are you still single?"

That's the question he asks when my mouth is full of sausage-and-mushroom calzone and his is, for once, only full of words. Thankfully, this gives me time to formulate the right response. Not that I haven't been asked that question before. So many times. But how you answer when talking to the man you're attracted to is different, and it requires some finesse.

I need to avoid the typical responses. For years, I answered with, "I guess I haven't met the right guy yet." Except that usually led to the "Maybe you're too picky" response, to which I had to reply, "Or maybe God wants me to be single—for now—for a reason." Eventually, I decided it worked best to jump right to blaming God. Since He alone can do something about my singleness but chooses not to, I presume His shoulders are wide enough to take the responsibility.

Still, I feel like a traitor to God for even thinking such things. I glance around the crowded restaurant. *No one can hear your thoughts, Catie. No one knows what a turncoat you are.*

In a room filled mostly with families, the couple to our right stands out. They notice nothing, they're so completely absorbed in each other. He holds her left hand in his right, gently rubbing her ring finger and the giant rock blinking off of it. They can't be more than twenty-five. No wrinkles. No worries. Just youth and love and plenty of time. I turn back to Brian. Even if he could be the one, how much of a life could we actually have together? It's unlikely I could have children at this age. Grief burns the back of my eyes, and I push it down.

Don't go there, Catie. Not now.

So I chew, swallow, and say, "I suppose God hasn't brought the right guy into my life yet. What about you?"

"I thought I met the right girl once. But I was wrong."

"What happened?"

He takes a long gulp of Pepsi. "I'm not sure. One day we were together The next we weren't."

"But until then, you thought it was pretty serious?"

"To be honest, I had been checking out the prices of engagement rings when she told me she didn't think it would work out."

"Ow." Again, I look at the young couple. They don't know how good they have it. And if their pure-joy gazes are any indication, they may never know how bad loneliness can feel. My eyes meet Brian's. "Is that the real reason you moved to Colorado?"

He laughs without a touch of humor. "I had many reasons. None of which are as interesting as they might seem."

I have nothing to say to that, so I let the conversation lapse into a much-needed silence while I chew on a bread stick. It's a comfortable quiet. I feel closer to Brian than I've felt to a man in a long time. Maybe ever. He shared something personal with me. He didn't have to. It's so wonderful to be here, at this table, sitting across from this man, and I wish he'd take my hand. Slide his fingers through mine. Pull me into the warmth of a possibility I hope we're both longing for.

We finish eating and, as I hobble out of the restaurant, Brian puts his arm around me.

It feels right. And that's when I realize what the unfamiliar feeling was as he carried me down the mountain.

Security. Like I'm finally home. And safe. And that I could, some day, be loved.

I am in so much trouble.

Chapter 8
Jolene

I should have stayed in my hiding place. Lord help me, the bounty hunters are hard on my heels, and I can't escape them now. I zip around the corner into the living room—where the three lying in wait hit me full force just as the four pursuers jump me from behind.

It's no use.

They pull me to the floor, and I'm engulfed under a pile of squirming, giggling kids.

"Okay, okay, I surrender!" I say, laughing so hard I can barely breathe. But there is a way to get out of this. I start tickling the ribs closest to me.

"No, Aunt Joey! Don't tickle me!" Three-year-old Milo squirms away, which puts Toolah, who's a year older, within reach. She tries to wiggle out of range. And that's when I go completely still. The twisting mass of children freeze too.

"Uh-oh," says Klinka, who's the oldest at thirteen. They know what this means. To them, I'm a lion ready to pounce, a geyser about to blow. Klinka jumps up and the beads on her tightly braided hair *tip-tap-click* with the movement. She yells, "Run!" and takes off.

Within seconds I'm free. The patter of little feet lets me know the kids have shot off in two directions, though they are certainly all headed toward the second floor.

"You can run but you can't hide!" I hop up, throwing out my most evil "muah-ha-ha" laugh. When I reach the bottom of the stairs, I'm just in time to see the tushies of a handful of nieces and nephews disappear around the upper banister. But a voice stops me as I'm about to put a foot on the first step.

"Are you kidding me, Jolene?" My younger sister's raised eyebrows and crossed arms echo the inherited attitude of decades of black soul mothers who don't mess around. I'm lucky she doesn't throw a shoe at me. Mama would be so proud. "I'm trying to get the kids to calm down before bed, and I don't need you to get 'em all riled up."

"Relax, Freddie. We're just having fun."

She scowls.

I hold back a grin. My sister's never been fond of the nickname Freddie, but no one will call her Fredericka. Though she prefers Rickie, her husband, Sam, is the only one who uses that name on a regular basis.

"Besides," I say, "they'll be so wiped out, they'll fall asleep in no time."

"Oh, really?" Now she smiles. I've been afraid of that smile since the first time she asked me to babysit, when she only had three kids. It's a miracle I didn't have to shave my head after Oscar, her second oldest, put gum in it.

"Well then," she says, "why don't *you* put them to bed?"

I love my sister.

For the next hour, I slip from room to room, tucking in fidgety little bodies, reading *Goodnight, Moon* and *Where the Wild Things Are* until I know them by memory, and exchanging enough melt-into-you hugs and sweet kisses to last me a week. I treasure my seven nieces and nephews as much as I would my own offspring. My heart drops at the thought, and I push the ache away. *Focus on what you do have, Jolene. You have children in your life to love.* Children who bless my single heart like butter on a biscuit.

When I finally make my way downstairs, I find Sam and Freddie snuggling on the couch watching a Hallmark movie. Well, now I know who won the arm wrestle for the remote.

"All tucked in," I say, falling onto a leather arm chair. "They went down easy, except Toolah. She said she can't sleep until Papa kisses her good night."

Sam pushes himself to his feet. "I'm on it."

He's barely out of the room when Freddie says, "That's the last we'll see of him tonight."

"I know. He'll fall asleep in the girls' room. Poor thing. He'll miss the end of the movie."

Freddie giggles. "I don't know how he can sleep not knowing if the shy doctor and the brave firefighter end up together or not."

"I thought it was a brave doctor and a shy firefighter."

"Either way, if it's not a happy ending I'll be so disappointed."

"No kidding." I grin at her, then say, "So, I put your kids to bed. The least you can do is give me ice cream."

"We might have some Cherry Garcia, as long as the munchkins didn't find it."

"What are the chances of that?"

My sister looks at me like she can't believe I'm that dumb. "You have met my children, haven't you?"

"Oh, right."

We chuckle as we make our way into the kitchen,

where she pulls a paper bag hiding a quart of Cherry Garcia from the back of the freezer. You can never underestimate Freddie when it comes to ice cream. Two spoons later, we're digging in. I say something about the calories I freed up chasing her kids and Freddie laughs.

And I'm reminded how glad and blessed I am to have her in my life.

You couldn't find a braver woman than my sister. The quarter-inch of wispy hair covering her scalp testifies to her recent battle with ovarian cancer. Her bright eyes and rosy cheeks tell the world she won the fight. After a terrifying year that started with such severe bleeding we almost lost her before we even knew she was sick, I still can't believe she's here. And she's going to make it. I don't know what I would have done if I'd lost her. Not for the first time, I draw in and breathe out a deep prayer of gratitude.

Freddie chews silently on frozen cherries and chocolate pieces for a moment, then says, "So, what about your happy ending?"

"What do you mean?"

"Shy firefighter, brave doctor, online stalker, Olympic contender. Just wondering if you're any closer to choosing your man."

"Wow, that's beautiful. I'm so glad romance lives on in our family."

She puts her spoon down. Which, in Freddie's world, means business. Woods women don't mess around when it comes to dessert. "Come on, Jolene. You move from one guy to another like you're trying on shoes. You know what that makes you."

"Content? Happy? A smart shopper?"

"A serial dater."

"And that's ... bad?"

"Joke all you want, but it won't get you a man."

Freddie snaps the lid on Cherry Garcia and sticks him back in his hiding spot in the freezer.

Well. I wasn't done. I purse my lips at her and say, "I'm just being cautious."

"Hmm." She grabs the spoons and drops them into the dishwasher, then turns back to me and crosses her arms. "Can I be straight with you?"

I flip up my hands in surrender. "Aren't you always?"

"Just because I love you doesn't mean I'll ignore what's really going on here. As long as you keep jumping from one man to another, you never have to make a commitment. And I think that word terrifies you."

Oh, that's just ridiculous. "Now why would you say that? It's not like I'm some slouch, living in my parents' basement, making sandwiches for the King Sooper deli part-time. I run my own ministry, for heaven's sake. That's a big commitment."

"A business commitment is very different from a heart one."

She turns and walks away like that's the end of the discussion. I follow her back into the living room, where we both collapse on the roomy leather sectional like we just darted up a flight of stairs. She picks up the remote, but I snatch it out of her hands. This conversation is far from over.

"Seriously, Freddie, you don't think my heart is in my ministry?"

"Of course it is. But that's not the same kind of risk."

"I don't see a difference. Besides, I'm not afraid of a relationship. It's just better to be single than to be in a bad marriage."

Freddie tries not to grin but fails. "Did you really just say that?"

Yeah, I'm a little surprised myself. I abhor married people clichés almost as much as I loathe hiking. "It's okay if I say it."

"It would be okay if I thought for one minute you believe it."

"I know."

"Actually, it's a stupid saying."

"I know."

"It assumes facts not in evidence." Freddie briefly studied law before choosing Sam and motherhood. Every once in a while her inner defense attorney comes out. "It would be like saying … you shouldn't eat ice cream because you're allergic to coconut. Because it's better to avoid ice cream than to get sick from it."

Huh. I never thought of it that way. "Wow, I like that. It doesn't mean you should avoid or stop wanting ice cream. You just need to stay away from any ice cream with coconut in it."

"Exactly. I would suggest you find yourself a good, godly, coconut-free man."

From my purse on the hall table, my phone beeps, announcing a new text message. It's probably Trevor. I'm sitting next to the only other person who texts me regularly. I glance toward the hall, curious. Why is he writing me so late?

Freddie says, "Do you know anyone who fits that description?"

I look her square in the eyes. "I'm not allergic to coconut."

"Jolene."

"Besides, you know I love being single."

"I know that's what you say."

"You don't think I'm happy?"

She leans back and studies me for a minute. "I think you've done a great job of convincing yourself you're happy." She's a straight shooter, my sister.

"Oh, I see. What you're saying is I can't really be happy without a man." I can shoot pretty straight myself.

"Can you?"

"Well, you tell me. You're married. You've been married since you were, what, twenty?"

"Twenty-one."

"Right. So more than fifteen years." I cross my arms and raise my eyebrows. "Are you happy?"

"Deliriously." She leans back a bit. "Oh, come on. That can't surprise you."

"No. But you *should* be happy. So should I. Kind of goes along with that whole 'be content' command."

"I'm not saying you're not content or that you shouldn't enjoy your singleness, Joey. I just want you to be honest with yourself about what you really want. And if you want to get married, you have to be intentional about going after it."

"You don't think meeting and dating is intentional enough?"

She tilts her head and harrumphs with all the charm of our grumpy Uncle Stan. "Online dating doesn't count."

"What? Of course it does. I meet at least one new guy a week."

"And?"

"And what?"

"And … nothing happens. You go on one date, decide you don't like how his nose whistles or the way he chews gum, and that's the end of it."

"I don't see why I should waste time on a guy I'm not interested in. If there isn't any long-term potential, what's the point?"

"The point is relationships take time to develop. When's the last time you went on a second date?"

"Two weeks ago." Ha.

"Uh-huh."

How does she do that? Sees right through me. "All right, I ran into this guy I went out with while standing in line at the bank, and we chatted for a few minutes."

"Like I said."

"Yeah, yeah, you're so clever." I can't not laugh. "Anyway, it was awkward, and he kept staring at my chest so it felt like a date."

We both giggle until Freddie leans forward, right up in my face. "Serial. Dater."

I breathe in slow then let it out. I did not come over here to have her persecute me on my dating habits. As I chew on a thumbnail, I wonder if I should ask the question she brought up.

Why not?

"So … Freddie. When you were listing potential men, you said 'Olympic contender.' Why is that?"

"I was talking about Trevor."

"Yeah, I figured out that much. But why? You know we're just friends."

She laughs, reclaims the remote, and turns the TV back on. Seriously? As she flips through a couple dozen channels, I wait for an answer. No one can use silence to make someone suffer quite like my sister.

Freddie surfs her way to an antique auction show. We're both auction junkies—we call ourselves auctionistas—and dream of the day we snag a big enough deal to retire on. Well, actually, I don't want to retire. But it would be fabulous to drop a nice chunk of cash on Cocoon House.

So, I sit back and store away mental notes on how to recognize a real Margaret Mitchell autograph, should a vintage copy of *Gone with the Wind* ever fall into my lap, while I wait for my sister to lay me out flat with today's lesson. The women in my family simply don't know how to keep quiet, which means the only reason Freddie hasn't said anything yet is because she's trying to unnerve me. Or because she wants to make sure whatever she says is as effective as she can make it. Or both.

All right, so Trevor and I do make some sense, in a let's-make-a-sandwich-out-of-the-last-two-slices-of-bread kind of way. Two fine-looking and fun-loving people who enjoy spending time together probably should be a couple. We certainly turn heads. He makes me laugh, and we're on the same page on a lot of things, like religion and politics. What's not to like?

Well, the biggest problem is, he's too gorgeous. I like what I like and the athletic pretty boy just isn't it. I want someone scruffy, a little nerdy, and desperate for me. Which is exactly what I tell Freddie. Who rolls her eyes at me—not the first time—and tells me I need to stop making lists.

Actually, what she says is, "You're an idiot," but I prefer my own interpretation. It's one of those things only family can throw at you, yet you still know they love you and think everything about you rocks the fabulous train.

But she brought it up and now it's out there. Circling above me like a vulture, ready to totally unnerve me the next time I hang out with Trevor. I'll take one look at him and the word, "Boyfriend!" will leap into my brain. And I'll have to swallow my tongue to keep from shrieking like I did when I was twelve years old and my signed Shawn Cassidy poster finally came in the mail. I don't want to see Trevor that way. Everything is fine the way it is.

So I glare at my sister for the rest of the auction show and completely miss crucial information on how to tell the difference between an antique credenza and a well-built knock-off.

Chapter 9
Catie

It's a regular Thursday, and I'm sitting at my work desk on trying not to get distracted by last night's heat-inspired dream about a dark-haired, gray-templed, whistling anesthesiologist, and failing miserably. I've gone over the same spreadsheets so many times the numbers are starting to blur. Should I just call Brian and give up all pretense of being coy and waiting-to-be-pursued? And that's when my phone dings the news I have a text message. From Brian.

NEED COFFEE. WANNA MEET TONIGHT?

My heart jumps as I quickly respond: SURE. PIKES PERK @ 8?

Seconds later: C U THERE!

My much-improved sprained ankle throbs along with my heartbeat. When was the last time a guy made my whole body react? *Dear God, please don't let me mess this up.*

The rest of the afternoon is a torment, but I throw myself into the tasks at hand and am, at the end of the day, satisfied with the amount of work I've accomplished. I'm far enough ahead, in fact, that Friday will be a breeze. Now I can enjoy my date with Brian without anything hanging over my head.

But is it a date? I probably shouldn't use that word if he didn't. I do like the way it sounds, though. As I file away papers, clean off my desk, and gather my things for the night, I decide I can call it a date for one hour only. Then I have to go back to saying it's "just coffee with a friend."

Three hours later I'm still trying to convince myself it's "just coffee" as I trot into Pikes Perk. I look around, but Brian isn't here yet. So I stare at the menu board, waiting, wondering what I want. Maybe I'll try something new.

A shiver runs up my spine as soon as the door jingles open. Then I hear whistling. I turn around and Brian strolls in, grinning. His silver eyes twinkle with the promise of everything I've ever wanted. I don't know whether to laugh or cry. Years of hope tug around my heart and pull me toward this man. *I want him, God. This is the one I want.*

Gulping down my nerves, I smile back and say, "You made it."

"Yep. You been waiting long?"

So long. I shake my head. "Haven't even decided what I want yet."

"Well, go crazy. It's on me." His eyes flash again as if looking at me strikes a match inside of him.

I laugh. "Okay. If that's the case I'll take a Belgian coffee."

He raises his eyebrows. "Mmm. Sounds rich."

"Pure decadence. But I'm in the mood."

"Is that all?"

Feeling reckless, I say, "Make it a large."

So maybe *reckless* isn't the best word for it.

Still, for some reason that's enough to make us both chuckle. When the barista offers to take our order, Brian says, "Two large Belgian coffees." Then he winks at me and adds, "With extra whipped cream."

Nice.

Once seated, coffees in hand, he asks me about the upcoming retreat. I'm not sure what I say exactly because he chose to sit on the couch next to me, not on the adjacent club chair. Actually, it's more of a loveseat, which means we're close enough for his arm to brush against mine every time he takes a sip. And I realize if I shift just this much, our knees touch. What is wrong with me that the slightest tap of contact makes my mouth dry up like land without rain?

He finally breaks through my daydreams when he says, "You're riding up with me, right?"

"Where?" *Get a grip, Catie.*

"To the retreat. We might as well carpool."

"We might as well."

He flashes his teeth. He has a slight gap between the two top front ones. No wonder he likes to whistle. "Great. You do know where we're going?"

"Oh, sure. I've been there a dozen times at least."

"Really? On retreats?"

"Retreats or long weekend getaways with the girls. But the fall retreat is an annual thing. And my favorite event of the year."

Brian scratches the stubble on his chin. "What do you like so much?"

"Spending time with friends, mostly. Buena Vista is gorgeous too, which doesn't hurt. Have you been there?"

"Not yet. Guess I need more adventurous friends." He elbows me. Then, as if worried he might have hurt me, strokes the same spot on my arm with his hand. *Wow.*

I nudge him back. "You think I'm adventurous?"

"Sure." He shrugs. "Of course, I don't know you

that well yet."

Yet. I love that word.

All right then. Time to do something adventurous. "You know, you could get to know me better this weekend." *Where did this girl come from?* "If you don't have any plans ..."

"That would be fun but, unfortunately, I'm busy Friday and Saturday. I'll definitely see you at church on Sunday though."

He doesn't explain his busy weekend, and I don't suppose I should ask. It's frustrating. I want to see him on Friday, Saturday, Sunday and every day next week. And have decades-long phone calls on the nights we can't get together. I just want us to be a couple already. But I'll wait until he decides to take things to the next level.

In the meantime, what can I do to get my mind off of him until Sunday? Maybe the girls want to go to a movie. Or have a game night. Anything would be better than sitting at home alone, wondering, wishing. At least I wouldn't ...

I look at the man sitting next to me and realize he's staring. At me. He looks at my eyes, my nose, my mouth, pausing there for a moment. What is he thinking? I feel heat crawl up my chest, claw its way across my neck, and settle over my face, suffocating me. *God, if You love me even a little, You've blinded him temporarily so he doesn't notice I'm blushing.* For a moment, it's as if we're both holding our breath, sensing the start of something and willing to wait long enough to let God make it beautiful, perfect, and worth every second. I somehow manage to keep from licking my lips.

Then he clears his throat and looks away. Just like that, the moment passes, and I can't help but feel I blew it. I should have done something to draw him toward me. But always in the back of my head is the key question: Does he want to kiss me or not?

We chat a little longer about stuff he'll need on the retreat and how much various activities might cost. And then, it's time to go.

As our evening ends, Brian walks me to my car. The Colorado wind has kicked up and as we head across the small parking lot, a breeze lifts my floaty, navy, knee-length skirt just enough to border on inappropriate. I make a sound that, thankfully, is not too squeal-like and push my skirt down, but not before I catch a glance from Brian. The glint in his eyes tells me he noticed and didn't mind one bit. I slide into my car, brave and blushing and bold. He whistles all the way to his.

Without him saying a word, I feel feminine and attractive, even a little sensual. Maybe I shouldn't, but I do. And I cannot wait to spend a whole weekend with him at the upcoming retreat.

Something's going to happen. I'll make sure of it.

◊◊◊

Three days. Three days until I shake off all the stresses of work and an unknown relationship and escape into the mountains. And then I'll enjoy three days of possibility. *Watch out, Brian.*

In the meantime, after a month of overtime and underpay, the system conversion is done. I'm proud of the work I've accomplished as overseer of the project.

My boss said she never even considered asking someone else to take care of it. If this doesn't get me a raise—maybe even a promotion—I don't know what will.

Good timing too because now I can sit back and look forward to the weekend. Not just the weekend, but a future full of opportunity. Especially if it includes Brian. Other than church and lunch on Sunday, I haven't seen him since our coffee-date. But he did call last night and we talked for two hours. The chance that he and I are moving toward something real and incredible fills me with electricity.

Is this how Hannah felt after God finally gave her a child in First Samuel? Year after year she begged Him for a son and, at long last, He answered her prayer. He saw her heartbreak and knew her pain and remembered her. Is it too soon to hope He's remembered me? I'm not walking down the aisle yet. I grit my teeth to keep my hope in check. What if I'm imagining the whole thing? Maybe I am.

I don't care. It's better to feel something—even if it hurts—than nothing at all.

My computer alerts me to a new e-mail message from my department vice president, June Sorenson. She wants me to come to her office right away. My boss's boss. She never meets with me except to talk about a change in my employment status. This could be bad news, but after the month I've had, I feel comfortable thinking positively. I snag my iPhone and head her way. Even if I don't get a promotion, she might still hand out a bonus check for all the extra work I put in over the last few weeks. Either way, a one-on-one with June has always resulted in good news for me. A little more cash would come in handy this weekend.

Arriving at her office, I rap twice on the door and open it when I hear her invite me in. She doesn't return my smile, no surprise. June is notoriously serious.

This meeting is no exception as she gets right to business. "Catie, have a seat."

I take the chair closest to her desk. June pats her hair, which doesn't move. It's as stiff as meringue. I swear it was molded into a bouffant in 1975 and she hasn't done a thing with it since. Whatever happens, June is always ready to pose for a Glamour Shots photo.

"First of all," she says, "I want to commend you on the work you did on the system transfer."

"Thank you."

"You have been an exemplary and committed employee, and it's been great having you on our team."

Was that past tense? Am I getting the promotion just like that, without an interview?

June continues, "That's what makes this so hard."

And that's when I notice she won't look at me.

"As you know," she says, "we've been making efforts to cut costs. Our main goal with the technology transition was to save money. Unfortunately, it isn't enough." She folds her hands in front of her like a child dutifully taking the prayer position. "We have no choice but to start downsizing."

Now I know why I'm here. The realization buries me like the blizzard that shut down Colorado Springs for two days last May. I've never let myself think about what would happen if I lost my job because it was too horrifying. Work grounds me and gives me something to focus on besides loneliness. Without it, I ...

My mind freezes there. Her voice sounds muffled as if we're actually in that storm. June expounds on what an asset I've been to the company and how they'll miss having me around. Then she presents the details of the generous severance package I'll receive—enough to last me at least a year, as long as I stay frugal. All I want to do now is get through this nightmare without breaking down. But the possibility of making it from here to my office long enough to grab my things and still have to stumble through the building and to my car, all while managing to remain dry-eyed, seems unlikely. As if to prove the point, a single tear pools in my eye and threatens to drip down my cheek.

"You're still an employee until the end of the month," June says, "but you don't have to stay. In fact, you can leave now, if you prefer. Or you can continue in your job until your official last day. It's entirely up to you. Your exit interview will be"—she double-checks her calendar—"on October 30th at 10:00 a.m. Okay?"

She finally looks at me, not a trace of emotion for the woman who has given more than two decades of her life to this company. As far as June Sorenson is concerned, I'm already gone. My heart seizes in the ache of realizing just how much she doesn't care.

Though I don't trust myself to speak, I mutter, "Yes, that's fine."

June stands and holds out her hand. I shake it out of habit. She doesn't even try to hide her relief to have this meeting over. "Of course, I'll write you a strong recommendation, Catie. You won't have any trouble finding another position."

I nod, staring down at the suddenly useless iPhone

clutched in my left hand. In a mere ten minutes, my life has drastically changed.

Tears have turned to quiet sobs by the time I'm mere steps out of June's office. Somehow I manage to make it to my car without running into anyone. It's as if they all know what happened and purposely avoided me. And I'm okay with that.

I don't call anyone because it's still too raw. When I get home, though, I send a mass e-mail to my closest friends, letting them know what happened. I don't pray about it. I won't give God the satisfaction. I do want to talk to Brian, though. Should I call him? Has our relationship reached that place yet? If only it had. Then he'd be here, holding my hand and telling me everything will be all right.

Instead, I turn off my phone and my laptop, curl up on the couch with my dog, and cry myself to sleep.

I haven't felt this alone since my mom died.

Chapter 10

Oli

If I close my eyes long enough, maybe I can trick my mind into falling asleep. I open one eye and blink several times, trying to focus on the cat-shaped digital clock propped on the armoire across the room. Things clear up in time for me to see it tick over from 4:03 to 4:04. In the morning.

Insomnia, you are my Kryptonite.

I try to do the math—which is about as much fun as plucking coarse, little hairs off of my chin—to figure out if I can still get enough sleep. I have a photo shoot for a church family's Christmas card at ten. It will take half an hour to get to their home and another half hour to set up. Add the hour I need to shower and get ready, and I have to throw myself out of bed by eight, at the latest. So if I fall asleep right now … I'll get less than four hours.

But I'm not going to fall asleep right now, am I. No, I am not. I'd be more upset about this if I wasn't used to it, yet insomnia has been my dear companion for decades. The most important thing I've learned is to not let it get to me. Though this probably means I'll yawn my way through the photo session in the morning, I should be able to take a nice, long nap in the afternoon.

Oh, the joys of being self-employed.

I flip my pillow over to the cool side and punch it a couple of times. My brain won't stop working. Mostly because I'm worried about Catie, who hasn't answered her phone in the two days since she sent her cryptic "I-just-lost-my-job" e-mail. Jolene and I have taken turns trying to check in on her, but she isn't responding. If we don't hear from her today, we intend to go over to her place after Jolene gets off work. She can't avoid us forever. Besides, we're leaving for the retreat tomorrow. Surely a weekend in the mountains will do her a world of good. She's not the first person to lose her job.

The other reason my mind keeps racing would be this little fact-tidbit: Cole mentioned the "e" word at dinner last night. "E" as in *engaged*. "Dinner" as in we were eating cold pizza while he watched baseball. During a Doritos commercial, he turned to me and said, "If you ever expect to get engaged to me, maybe you should learn how to chew without making so much noise. It's disgusting."

I didn't say it was a romantic use of the word, but it did come up.

Flip the pillow. Punch it. Wonder why I'm still dating Cole. More importantly, why am I still sleeping with him? I always intended to say no. Despite my mother's less-than-stellar example, I made it into my twenties still a virgin. When I turned twenty-five, I went through a promise-ring phase and vowed I would wait until marriage. I even kissed dating good-bye for a while. For thirty-plus years I did fine. Frustrated but fine.

Then I met Cole. He kept dangling an even better promise of an engagement ring in front of me. But I couldn't get to the ring without climbing into his bed. He said,

"I can't marry someone I haven't slept with. What if we're not compatible that way?"

Which made me laugh out loud and use words like "ridiculous" and "immature." Amazingly, we didn't break up after that. Then one night I was at his apartment and I stayed too late and he kissed me just right and two hours later I shame-walked my way out to my car.

All those years of waiting and anticipation and it was done and over in the amount of time it takes me to clean my bathroom. The experience was messy, painful, and disappointing. And just exciting enough to smash my resolve like a bird hitting a sliding glass door. I always had a hunch I would be weak where men and sex are concerned.

I wasn't prepared to lose the power to say no from then on. But, boy, I sure did. Now, it's simply something we do, like order a Netflix movie or fire up the grill for burger night. Every time I tell myself, "This is it. Not again. Not until he marries me."

If only. If only I weren't so pathetic. If only Cole didn't know how to push all the right buttons. If only God would help me out a little. Not that I've asked Him. I flip my pillow again because the blasted thing will not stay cool. I haven't talked to God in months. But I can feel His eyes on me, accusing me of breaking my promises.

He must be as disappointed with me as I am with myself.

I squint at the clock again. It's now 4:35. I can't keep tossing around here, letting stupid things keep me awake. Though I would prefer not to do it so late, I hunt down my box of sleep-aid pills in the nightstand. I nibble off half of one and swallow it dry. It will take about fifteen minutes to kick in.

So I turn on the light and pick up the generic romance novel sitting near the lamp. I need to do something besides think about how Cole won't do anything except take my dignity and how God won't do anything except point fingers at my guilt. And how all I can seem to do is make one stupid choice after another … which reminds me of my latest mistake. I'm several days late, and the thought I could be pregnant should terrify me, but it doesn't. I place my hand on my stomach and feel a rumble of hope. Hope of new life. Hope of a reason for Cole to make a lifelong commitment.

When I realize I've read the first sentence of the chapter I'm on five times and it still doesn't make sense, I shut the book, turn off the light, and let the darkness settle around me. The late night—make that early morning—traffic on the nearby streets rumbles through the partially open window. A faint golden glow whispers the inevitable dawn. I'm not going to sleep.

Guess it's okay to cry now.

◊◊◊

I must have finally dozed off around five. Three hours of sleep and, somehow, I manage to stumble through my day with only a few instances of sleep deprivation. Like throwing my phone away with my lunch trash. I didn't even know what I'd done until I heard Kelly Clarkson singing "Stronger" from the Wendy's garbage can after I tipped my tray into it. If someone hadn't called me at that moment, I probably wouldn't have noticed it was missing until I got home.

It wouldn't have been the first time I misplaced my phone.

The photo session skips along beautifully despite my blurry eyes. Thank God for cameras with automatic focus. I even manage to capture a few special moments, like the three-year-old daughter pouting in the corner as her mother tries to coax a smile with a Tootsie Pop, and a particularly sweet shot of Mr. Cobb gazing lovingly at his wife. The shots I get of the Cobb family, as a whole, are so fun I ask them to sign waivers to let me potentially sell some of the pictures to my stock photos client or use them in other projects. And, to my relief, they agree.

After lunch, I have just enough time to get home and take a decent cat nap before Jolene bursts through the door, putting soul into the tune she's singing as she throws her coat on the floor and grabs a can of Sprite from the fridge. One of the reasons we chose this apartment was because of its open concept living/dining/kitchen area. We also liked how the two bedrooms and bathrooms were on opposite sides of the common room. So we live together, share the rent and utilities, but still have our separate spaces.

Popping the top on her soda, Jolene stops singing long enough to take a drink before she notices me sitting at the table, checking e-mail. "Hey, you talk to Catie yet?"

"I've called several times but it keeps going to voicemail. What about you?"

"Same."

"Think we should go see how she's doing?"

"Don't you?"

I close my laptop. "Well, yes, I think we should. I know we should." Since I was laid off a few years ago, I don't have to imagine what Catie is going through. The whole experience devastated me, and I still haven't reached the same level of self-esteem I had before it happened. But for someone like Catie, whose identity is so wrapped up in her career, it has to be even worse.

"She gave so much of herself to that company," I say. "She must feel so betrayed."

Jolene throws her now-empty can into the recycle bin and snags another from the fridge. Two sodas in less than five minutes means my roommate is worried. I'm tempted to eat a Snickers myself, thinking about Catie, sitting home alone, in the dark, wrapped in blankets and sobbing into her two-day-old Folgers coffee.

Her second soda drained in practically one gulp, Jolene puts down her can and picks up her coat. "Let's go then. You ready?"

"I am. Why don't we grab some Chinese on the way?"

"A little Kung Pao?"

"I was thinking sesame chicken."

She hands me my purse. "Only if you chip in."

Humph. I guess that's fair.

◊◊◊

Twenty dollars' worth of Chinese later, we arrive at Catie's with bags of food and still unanswered phone calls. On the way, I also called Tess to see if she could join us, but, as the pastor's assistant, she's needed at tonight's church board meeting. She said,

"Give Catie a hug from me and tell her I'm praying for her, okay?" Then she belted out a semi-cheery "See you tomorrow night!" and hung up before I could say another word.

Jolene rings the doorbell of Catie's brick-front, two-story house and we hear Luna erupt in a fit of barking from inside. It's a familiar process: Luna barks like a mad dog every time the doorbell chimes then, as soon as she sees us, her tail starts wagging fast enough to fan a room.

Catie loves to entertain, and we love to hang out in her massive living area with its high ceilings, warm tones, velvety chenille couches, and, of course, big screen TV. Now that she's lost her job, I hope we don't lose our favorite gathering spot.

Sheesh, that was remarkably selfish. This isn't about you, Uli.

I'm hardly worried about her, though. Catie is talented and smart. She's sure to find a new position in no time. She has the kind of marketable skills employers look for. Unlike perpetually unemployed-and-struggling-to-survive graphic designers, which is why a small part of me might be happy about this turn of events.

Uli Odell, you are a horrible, self-centered human being. But is it so wrong to want someone to understand what I deal with on a daily basis? Especially when that person has habitually given me a hard time about not having a "real" job?

At that moment, said person answers the door, and I immediately regret my mean and selfish thoughts. Catie's dressed in jeans and a baggy, green flannel shirt and looks surprisingly cute. And young. She has wet hair from a recent shower, and her cinnamon scent is as inviting as a crisp, fall morning. Though she has only a minimum amount of makeup on, the one tell-tale sign she's had a few bad days peeks out from tired and watery light blue eyes.

"Well, you're here," she says. "You might as well come in."

I hold up the takeout bags as we follow Catie into the kitchen. "We brought dinner."

"Great."

Which I could interpret as, "Great! I'm hungry," if her tone of voice wasn't saying, "Great, now they'll want to stay."

After depositing the food on the kitchen island, Jolene and I take turns hugging Catie and offering our condolences. She doesn't say much, just starts pulling plates and forks out of cupboards. I take a seat at her dining room table, which is covered with resumes—one that is bleeding red from her edit pen, pages of scribbled notes, a book on writing cover letters, the help wanted section of the Gazette, and a laptop open to CareerBuilder.com.

Wow.

When I got the boot from my last full-time job, I spent two weeks in holey, old sweats, lying on the couch, weeping and watching *Little House on the Prairie* reruns. Then I used some of my severance pay to fly home to Iowa and let my mom pamper and placate me for another two weeks. Catie gets laid off and immediately turns job searching into a full-time occupation.

Uh, yeah. That's what you're supposed to do.

Mm-hmm. I'd rather be broke. Besides, I've got Cole to take care of me.

Before the stupidity of that thought can fully take

root, I turn my attention back to Catie. Though I already know the answer, I ask, "So … do you want to talk about it?"

Catie dishes out about a tablespoon of rice and, I swear, two bitty pieces of sesame chicken. No wonder she's about the same size as the wooden spoon she's holding. Jolene and I, however, intend to get our money's worth and load up our plates. We are, after all, just here to listen.

I slurp down vegetable lo Mein with sesame chicken while I wait for Catie to be ready to talk. She needs time. The woman has never been the eager-to-share type like Jolene or me. After what seems like half an hour of silence—though it must have been closer to five minutes—Catie sets down the still-clean fork she's been staring at and sighs. She says,

"It still seems so unreal."

"I know." Unfortunately.

And that opens the floodgates. Catie stands and walks around the table as she talks. "After all the years and work and dedication I gave to that company, they dump me without even a hint they were planning to let me go."

She stops, her face almost as red as her hair. I don't see her Irish temper often so it catches me by surprise. Her hands slice through the air like a hatchet as she talks.

"This last month has been exhausting. I put in twelve to thirteen-hour days trying to get those updates done … and they thank me by firing me?"

Jolene clears her throat. "I thought you were laid off."

Catie shoots her a glare, making Jolene jerk back in

her chair. I've never seen my roommate intimidated before. "What's the difference?" Catie asks, hands on hips.

"Severance pay?"

"You mean guilt money?"

Jolene glances at me and I shrug. She's on her own. "Um … okay."

Catie resumes her pacing. "Of course they feel guilty. They should feel guilty. I gave my life to that company. I sacrificed dreams and vacations. I came in whether I had cramps or a headache or my nose was so stuffed up I couldn't breathe. They counted on me for everything. And I always delivered." Catie drops into a chair. She suddenly looks exhausted. "They took what they wanted, and when they were done with me, they tossed me out the door."

Her comments so closely reflect what I went through when I was laid off from my graphic design job at a nonprofit a year and a half ago, I feel the tears well up. It sucks to be discarded, whether by a husband, a friend, or an employer. One tear slips down my cheek before I can stop it and I swipe it away. "I'm so sorry, Catie."

When her eyes meet mine she sighs again. "I know. What I don't know is how I'm going to get by. What if I can't find another job?"

Jolene says, "You'll find another job."

Catie pushes away from the chair and resumes her orbit of the table. "Maybe. Maybe not. I'm almost fifty and few companies want to hire someone older who deserves a higher salary. And they can't bring me in at entry level. I need money if I'm going to make my mortgage payment." She stops and her eyes widen. "I have a mortgage payment. I've never had to worry about paying my bills before."

I snort in a completely unladylike manner. "Welcome to the club."

"This is not a club I want to be in."

"Well, I don't see that you have much of a choice."

Catie rolls her eyes and, in fact, her whole head. "Really, Uli? You know, you almost sound like you're happy about this."

"Of course I'm not … happy about it. But this is life. And sometimes life stinks."

Jolene holds up her hands. "All right. Enough. The last thing we need is for you two to get in a fight. We all struggle with the insecurity of being single and on our own. But we have to trust that God has our back."

"Says the girl with the trust fund."

"Yes, Catie, you're right. I have some inheritance money." Jolene leans back and crosses her arms. "But that doesn't mean I feel safe all the time. Besides, don't you have a good-sized nest egg for emergencies?"

"I do. But it won't last forever and my mortgage isn't cheap."

"If things get too tight you could always move in with Jolene and me." I say it, but I don't know if I mean it. Where would we put her in our already-cramped apartment?

Catie smiles at me, her first pleasant reaction of the night. She knows exactly what I'm thinking. "Thanks, Uli," she says, coming over to where I sit at the table and putting an arm around me. "Actually … " She looks at Jolene, then back at me, as if uncertain whether to continue.

"Actually ... what?" Please, no secrets.

"Actually, things aren't all bad."

"Oh really?"

"Yeah, well, I ..." She shrugs, and I see a new Catie. One who's shy and sweet and hopeful and ...

"You're in love!" I jump up, put both hands on her arms, and look her in the eyes.

Catie grins again, her face flushing up to her hairline. "I wouldn't say 'in love' but in like, anyway."

Jolene seems just as stunned as I feel. "Who is it?"

"Brian Kemper."

"Brian Kemper!" My roommate and I say the name in unison, then look at each other and laugh. I ask,

"When did this happen?"

"Well, you know we went on that Pikes Peak hike, when I twisted my ankle? I told you all about that."

I sigh. "And he carried you all the way to your car. Lucky girl."

"Yeah, it was ... memorable. Then last Thursday we met for coffee. He's called a few times and we've had great conversations. And we're driving up to BV together."

Jolene's grin practically splits her face in half. "Well, there you go. I knew he'd fall for you."

"I don't know that he's fallen for me. But," she flashes another shy smile, "something might be happening there. It kind of makes losing my job not feel quite so bad."

She seems different—more confident in herself and more hopeful in love—and I tell myself I'm happy for her. But I'm not sure I mean it.

Chapter 11

Catie

My first jobless Friday seems to drag on forever. After pushing myself out of bed when the alarm goes off at six, I slip into jeans and throw on a beat-up Old Navy t-shirt over my laundry-day bra. Rain patters against the windows from the moment I wake up; the air is chilly and gray.

I turn on a talk radio station, throw a load in the washer, then go to work on cleaning my house. The whole thing gets a good scrubbing, top to bottom. Whether it needs it or not. All the while, I keep the laundry going, filling my suitcase as soon as items I want to take are clean and folded. My "to do" and "to pack" lists slowly get crossed off, one by one. But, try as they might, the work and the radio can't keep my mind off the fact I'm newly unemployed and have to spend the weekend trying to explain to friends and strangers what happened. It's a torturous, miserable, yet oddly satisfying day.

Finally, though, I'm packed, showered, and dressed in nicer jeans, a button-up, light-blue-and-white-striped shirt, jean jacket, and the cowboy boots Jolene talked me into at the state fair in Pueblo a few years ago. I really should thank her. They're the most comfortable shoes I own.

Once the house is locked up and everything's loaded, including my eagerly panting, "we're-going-on-an-adventure!" dog, I'm on my way to Brian's. We decided to take my SUV since it has four-wheeling capabilities, which might come in handy if we end up doing a little off-road exploring in the mountains. I arrive at his apartment a few minutes early, which is good since I need that much time to convince Luna to ride in the back. Many retreat lodges don't allow pets. A few years ago, though, we were fortunate to find one that did.

As I lift my hand to knock on the door, it pops open and there he is, all teethy grins and twinkling gray eyes, the handle of an Army-green duffle bag in one hand and a black coffee mug in the other. I should be so lucky as to find a man who's a stickler for punctuality like me.

"Ready?" I smile. I can't help myself.

"All set." He locks the door and follows me to the street. "Hey, any chance you'd let me drive? I love these twisty, mountain roads and haven't had much opportunity to explore them yet."

I hesitate for a second, then shrug and toss him the keys. "Sure." It's not an easy thing to do because I like driving too. It's a control thing, really. Still, having Brian behind the wheel of my car makes it feel a little more like we're together-together. An actual couple even.

Catie, don't get ahead of yourself.

Once we're on the road, we travel in silence for a while. The gloomy, drizzly weather doesn't bode well for a fun, outdoor weekend. Or so I think, until we crest the mountain ridge past Winter Park. That's just one of many things I love about Colorado: You can actually drive high enough into the mountains to get above bad weather. Much like being on a plane, we burst through the clouds into a gorgeous, blue-skied day. Heaven.

It's Brian's first time, though, and he murmurs a quiet, "Wow."

"I know."

"I wasn't expecting that."

With a sigh, I let silence fill the car again. Even though there's much to say. Three times, I open my mouth to tell Brian about my job loss, and three times I shut up before the words are spoken. He didn't get the mass e-mail. I didn't want him to think I'm pathetic or to feel sorry for me. Or to decide before the retreat even starts that he doesn't want to date a girl who can't hold on to a job. If I thought I could get away with it, I'd wait and tell him once I have a new job and I'm legit again. But since I'm sure the subject will come up at least once over the weekend, I'd rather he get the news from me. It's just finding the right moment.

As if he heard my thoughts, he asks, "So how was your week?"

"Fine." *Liar.* "How was yours?" *Coward.*

"Not too bad." Brian then tells me about a woman's allergic reaction to an antibiotic during an operation yesterday, which seems like it should be a more interesting story than it is. Maybe because he's a scientist, not a storyteller. I glance over at him, and he says something funny so I laugh. Or maybe I should say I laugh because he laughs. Okay, he's not the most fascinating conversationalist. Few men are. In fact, if I were to stack Brian against many of the guys I've known, he's positively riveting.

Still, it bothers me that I'm not hanging on his every word. Does it mean I'm not that into him? Men and women are so different. We're bound to have occasions where we're not completely engrossed in each other. Aren't we?

It's times like this I wish I had a better understanding of the male-female relationship dynamic. But my mom died when I was twelve and was sick for years before while she fought the cancer that eventually took her life. So I never really had a true model of how men and women interact day to day, though I certainly saw an example of sacrifice as my dad devoted all of his time and energy to her care. Their conversations focused on Mom's illness and what she needed. I don't remember discussions about work or favorite books or even what movie they wanted to watch.

Sure, I've known plenty of other couples throughout my life, but how they act in public is, for the most part, a shallower version of their relationship. What most fascinates me—and, at the same time, most frightens me—is the intimacy between a man and a woman in love. And I don't just mean sex. But all those private, shared understandings. The confidence they have in each other, to be open and real and to know the other person gets them at a deeper, more personal level than anyone else. The very idea of it captivates me.

Is that what I could have with Brian, even if I don't find his conversation particularly gripping? I have to believe it because I want to live it so desperately.

I ask if he wants to listen to Third Day or Over the Rhine and he chooses the latter, which is surprisingly quirky for someone as straight-laced as he comes across. Then he says, "You seem a bit distracted. Anything you want to talk about?"

Not yet. Unless, of course, I want our relationship to

delve a bit deeper. Which I do. "Well, actually, I got some bad news this week."

"Your aunt in Sandusky?"

Oh right. I forgot I told him about my dad's sister's sciatica. "No, no. She's actually doing much better. This bit of bad news was work-related."

"If they ask you to put in more overtime, you should say no. You don't want to fade out. The last thing you need is more stress."

I have to chuckle at that. Because I won't get more overtime, I'll definitely take a breather, and all I feel right now is stress. I say, "You're right. But since I lost my job, I don't think talking with them about overtime will do much good."

"What?" He looks over at me quickly then back at the road. "What happened?"

"They said finances were still low despite all the new upgrades I helped implement, so they had to make cuts in personnel. It's quite possible I worked myself out of a job."

"Oh man. That stinks."

"Yeah, it really does."

"So now what?"

"So now I find another job."

He slows the car down to make a sharp turn then glances my way. "Is there anything I can do?"

"Sure. If you hear of any great job openings where they don't mind candidates in their forties, let me know."

"If it helps, you don't look a day over thirty-five."

It does help. I gaze at the road stretching ahead of us and the mountains all around and the beefalo roaming the vast spaces between and I smile. It's possible I've overrated riveting conversations in my so-single mindset. Perhaps this is what's real and intimate—being there for someone when they need you. And knowing when to offer advice and when to just make someone feel better. Can I have that with Brian?

I hope so.

◊◊◊

Two hours later we arrive at the lodge a few miles outside of Buena Vista. I now know a little more about Brian, and he knows a lot more about me. As my perspective changed on how our conversation should go, we started to get into a fun rhythm. Fun, because we seem to have the same dry sense of humor.

Maybe we have more in common than I thought.

The A-frame lodge juts out from the side of Mt. Princeton, overlooking the hot springs below and a vast expanse of the peaks and forests and pastureland that make Colorado my favorite place. Every time I think about how much I love this state, I thank God for bringing me here.

About a dozen retreaters have already arrived and are wandering around, finding their rooms, unloading groceries in the restaurant-quality kitchen, or sitting out on Adirondack chairs, enjoying the view. Brian and I go our separate ways at the door—women down one hall, men down the other.

As I wheel my suitcase to the Blue Antlers room, which I'll share with Jolene, he calls out, "Meet me back here in thirty, okay, Catie? You can show me around."

"Sounds good." And I smile all the way to my room.

I should be in mourning due to the loss of my job, but all I can think is, *I'm going to spend the rest of my life with him.* Which sounds ridiculous and crazy. Hope does this, though. Makes the dreamer in me jump from, "Wow, that was a great conversation" to "Yes, I'll marry you," while the practical Catie wants to take a skillet and whack some sense into, well, myself.

Luna follows me down the hall to our room, always right at my heels, never needing a leash unless another dog is around. Since I'm here before Jolene, I decide to take the bed closest to the bathroom rather than the window. I am, after all, the early riser while Jolene typically sleeps until the scent of coffee finally makes its way down the hall and slips under the door. It works out for us. We never have to worry about who will shower first.

Our room, like the rest of the bedrooms, is decorated like you hope a lodge will be decorated: wood beams cross the nine-foot ceilings; décor in burnt orange, chocolate brown, and forest green warms the space and prominently features moose and deer; and, against one wall, two downy-soft beds so high I have to hop up onto mine.

First, I put Luna's pet bed in a corner. She immediately curls up into a ball and falls asleep. Then I shake out and hang up my clothes. I'm putting my toiletries away when my roommate makes her entrance, carrying an ergonomic pillow and small travel case. Just as I'm about to say something about how impressed I am to see her traveling so light for a change, Scott appears in the door behind her, pulling two suitcases. And neither belongs to him, obviously, since the two travel bags are covered with large, pink roses. If they are his, I don't want to know about it.

But they're definitely Jolene's. She instructs Scott where to put the luggage before ushering him out the door.

"Thanks, Scott," she says. "You're a doll."

"No problem." Before she can shut the door, he leans back in. "Just make sure you're all in the main room by eight. Uli's got some icebreakers planned."

Jolene winks at me. "Don't I know it. She's been running ideas past me all week."

"Okay. See you in a few." Scott heads off down the hall.

With a smile, Jolene hugs me—more of a whole-body shake, actually—and says, "My favorite retreat roomie! We are going to knock this weekend out, huh?"

"You know it."

My friend leans back, studying my face. "Oh, now what? I know you had a bad week, but can't you put that aside for three days and just have a good time?"

"That's exactly what I plan to do."

"Then what's with the face?"

I scrunch up my nose. "Sorry, Jo. This is the only face I have."

"Well, maybe tell it to smile once in a while. You're never going to win Brian's heart if you look like someone just ran over your dog."

Luna looks up and whimpers. She is one smart canine.

I wish this was the first time someone misinterpreted my facial expression but it's not. I pull away and cross my arms. "I'm not upset. I'm … pensive."

"Oh well, good. Go freshen up your makeup, Miss Pensive." Jolene opens the larger suitcase and unpacks four towels, which she sits on a small table in the corner, because that's about how many she needs to dry her mass of hair. Since most places only provide one towel per person, she learned long ago to bring extra. Then she rummages through her suitcase, finally pulling out a short-sleeved, black turtleneck. From her smaller case she chooses a bright, red-and-yellow scarf from a mound of colorful accessories. She looks at me and grins. "The games are about to begin."

Oh goodie.

Jolene strips off a plain, dark teal blouse to reveal what might be the laciest black bra I've ever seen. Great. Even her lingerie has more confidence than me. But since I have only a few minutes before I'm supposed to meet Brian, I do what she says.

I touch up my makeup, deciding to go all out by adding a hint of lipstick then comb through my hair with my fingers, bringing it back to life. After I tell Jolene I want to explore a bit, I hurry out of the room and down the hall, whistling for Luna as I go. Brian is already there, chatting with Tess. As soon as she sees me, she leans in and says something to him with a grin, before scurrying over to me.

"You made it," she says, the grin exploding into a full-on beam across her face. "I'm so glad you're here!"

"Well, of course I'm here. Why wouldn't I be?"

She stammers out a non-answer because she knew I would be here and that I was riding up with Brian. I take pity on her and say, "I really needed some time away from home."

"Oh sure."

We are then interrupted by an influx of retreaters who must have come in a van or convoyed up together. After hellos and hugs with the people we know and introductions to those we don't, the most recent arrivals mosey off to find their rooms. Tess tells us she needs to hunt down the new girl she's rooming with and skips away, leaving Brian and me alone. Well, as alone as you can be in a lodge housing over thirty people.

He says, "How's your room?"

"It's great. And yours?"

"Two beds and a bath. What more could a guy want?"

"Who are you sharing it with?"

He jerks his head toward the door. "Let's walk."

I nod, and Luna and I follow him outside.

As we wander off down the narrow gravel road, Brian asks, "Do you know Sean?"

"Short guy? Wears Star Trek T-shirts?"

"That's the one. And he doesn't just wear the shirt, he's got the Millennium Falcon on his pillowcase."

I laugh but don't correct him. He's not the first non-nerd to confuse Star Wars' most infamous spaceship with Star Trek's Enterprise. The fact he knows the name Millennium Falcon is impressive enough.

"Good for him," I say. "At least he wears his nerdiness loud and proud."

Brian laughs. "We should all be so courageous."

I lead him toward one of the many trails nearby. This particular one will give him a good overview of the area but won't be tasking or take longer than the fifteen minutes we have to get back to the lodge for Uli's games.

We spend the next thirty-five minutes enjoying the scenery and each other's company.

Which means we arrive at the main room twenty-some minutes after the games start. Not only doesn't it bother me to be late, but I'm kind of glad. More time with Brian leading to less time breaking the ice in full-on Uli fashion? Sounds like a good trade-off to me.

Chapter 12

Jolene

If Uli was a tornado, she'd be a category five. And when it comes to games, she tears through participants without mercy. I know this, but I go to the icebreaker part of the evening anyway. I'm supportive like that.

Besides, she'd kill me if I didn't.

I find a seat in a cushy armchair, trying to forget about the massive moose head mounted on the wall above me. At least this way I don't have to look at it. I smile at Trevor across the room, still surprised by his decision to join us for the weekend. He's never been a retreat kind of guy. When he said yes before I had a chance to finish my list of reasons, he could have knocked me over with a feather. Well, not literally.

He smiles back at me then returns to his conversation with Jim Espenshade, one of the older men in the group. I'm as sure they're talking about sports as I am that half the women in the room are wondering who the hot, black guy is.

Humph. Let 'em wonder.

Uli strides to the middle of the room, always aglow when she's the center of attention. In a striking, hot pink sweater—her signature color—she certainly grabs everyone's notice. She hasn't had a chance to be onstage for a while, so I'm sure she's eating it up. In her hands she holds a wide-brimmed straw hat she bought from a street vendor in Belize when a group of us vacationed there two summers ago. As far as I know, it's the first time she's found a use for it.

"Okay, everyone," Uli says, slowly spinning in a circle as she makes eye contact with the retreaters. "We're going to play my own Christian-ized, sanitized version of Truth or Dare." She pauses long enough to let people chuckle, and they do. I don't. She's just warming up.

"So, in this hat are slips of paper, each giving you either a task to perform or a truth to reveal." Several people groan. The introverts, I imagine, which I imagine makes up the majority of this group.

"Don't worry," Uli continues, "I've kept things simple and not personal. Well, not too personal anyway." She winks at Trevor and my stomach tightens a little. If she even *thinks* about moving in on. . . .

I stop myself mid-thought. Trevor's my friend, which means he's free to date whoever ... which means I shouldn't care who hits on him or what he might or might not do about it.

Uli reaches a hand into the hat and pulls out a handful of pieces of paper then lets them trickle out of her fingers and back into the hat. "To find out who goes first, I secretly taped a blue ticket under one of the chairs in the room. Everyone take a look and shout out when you find it."

No one shouts. But Amy, a tiny thing who is quite possibly the shyest girl in the group, turns three shades of red when she pulls the ticket out from under her seat. Since Uli knew where the ticket was, she's already next to Amy's chair, holding up the hat like a trophy. Amy, bless her heart, tries to reach into the hat, but Uli yanks it away.

"Oh no," my roommate says, and the evening has

now reached nightmare status for poor Amy. I'd do something, but it's probably best not to stretch things out or bring more attention to her. Amy will get through it, and Uli will move on to her next victim.

Uli says, "First, you need to introduce yourself." She looks around the room. "This goes for all of you. When it's your turn, tell us your name and your favorite thing to do on a rainy day."

Amy brushes a strand of blonde, fine, straight-as-paper hair behind her ear as a wince crosses her freckled face. "Well, uh, my name is Amy and, uh, my favorite thing on a rainy day is to, uh, play video games?"

With a dramatic raise of an eyebrow, Uli says, "Are you asking me?"

Ooh, that was harsh. Uli seems to be in rare form tonight. Maybe even a little on edge, which is unusual for her. Fortunately, Amy laughs, able to see the humor in Uli's question.

"No," she says. "That's it."

Good for her. Uli's grin doesn't quite reach her eyes, but she lowers the hat to let the younger girl reach inside.

Amy pulls out a slip of paper, scans it, and gulps three times. She reads out loud, "Describe your ideal first date."

Everyone chuckles, probably glad they didn't get that one. I glance over at Trevor. His eyes are wide, and I know he's wondering what on earth he's doing here.

Thanks, Uli, for playing into all those stereotypes people have about singles retreats.

As Amy hems and haws over her answer, I catch the quick look she throws at Sean, our group's favorite geek.

If I remember correctly, he even speaks Klingon. The expression on her face can only mean one thing and, as I look back and forth between the two, I wonder if it could be a match made in heaven. Maybe there's something I can do to push this love connection along.

Finally, Amy says, "I suppose dinner, of course, then maybe watch the extended version of, uh, *The Two Towers*." At this, Sean glances up and the two make eye contact for several seconds before both look away. He seems to know what she's talking about. Well, how about that. They might not need any help from me after all.

Now that her turn is done, Amy gets to pick the next participant. The evening races by as Uli continues to make her way around the room, forcing people to admit what they're allergic to or if there's anything they would stick their hand in the toilet to save. On the Dare side of the game, they end up performing tasks like karaoke-ing a Tears for Fears song or running around the outside of the lodge yelling, "The British are coming! The British are coming!"

Just a night of good, old-fashioned fun. A few people perform their tasks so well, I can't stop laughing and feel tears threaten to ruin my expertly applied makeup.

About half an hour in, Catie slinks into the room, Luna trotting alongside her and Brian trailing close behind. I'm trying to get over the unnaturalness of seeing her show up late to an event when she flashes me a smile so sheepish I could get wool off of it. She and Brian squeeze into what space is left on a couch, grinning, as the dog curls up on the rug in front of them. Brian whispers something to Catie, and they both laugh. Well, good for her. It's about time.

When I turn back to the game, Trevor has just pulled a command from the hat. He announces he has to use charades to help us guess what's on the paper.

"The only problem is," Trevor confesses, "I've never played charades." A few people chuckle, and we start laying out some of the basics. He catches on pretty fast. My boy is clever. After a little hit and miss, we determine it's a book with six words, the first is "love" and the fourth is "time." On a hunch, I shout out, "*Love In the Time of Cholera!*"

Trevor looks at me and grins, possibly as surprised as I am that I figured it out. Well, well, well. We're on the same page. At least, that's what I think until he tells Uli I'm next.

I stand up. Best to get it over with. "My name is Jolene, and my favorite thing to do on a rainy day is play Truth or Dare." I pause, then say, "Oh, wait, that's my *least* favorite thing to do" and several people snicker.

Uli, however, does not laugh but holds out the hat with a tight-lipped expression. She'll get over it.

But first, it would seem, she will have her revenge. I silently read my task: *You have two minutes to write and recite a love poem to someone in this room.* Ooh, she is a devil.

Reading the paper over my shoulder, Uli grins. "We'll come back to you when you're ready."

She moves on to Brian, the only person besides Catie who hasn't gone yet, and I find a piece of paper and a pen. While the new guy describes his most embarrassing moment—something about striking out during a Little League game, which really doesn't sound so bad—I take a seat over at the table and get to work on my masterpiece. I've always been good with rhythm and rhyme, but first, I need inspiration. Glancing around the room, I spy the perfect subject and quickly come up with the perfect poem. Uli will *not* love it, though everyone else will, which makes me smile.

Once Brian finishes his story, my roommate turns back to me and asks, "Are you ready?"

"Yes, I do believe I am."

"Great. Let's hear it."

Standing, I clear my throat and read:

"You're more than a neighbor,

Much more than a friend.

I can see how you like my caboose …"

At this point, I put a hand on my hip and pop out my tush on rhythm just to be clear.

Everyone laughs.

I continue, "With your vacant, brown eyes

You stare into my heart."

Then I look up and gaze adoringly at the giant head mounted on the wall above us.

"And that's why I love you, you big, ugly moose."

With a flourish, I high-step onto the chair and kiss that hairy beast right on the nose. This might be the most disgusting thing I've ever done but so worth it. The room erupts in laughter. I even get some applause and offer a little "oh yeah" dance of appreciation. I catch Trevor's eyes. He shakes his head, grinning. He knows how I am.

If Uli's theatrical training has taught her anything, it's to end on a high note. Though she had planned to keep the game going until everyone had a turn, she gives

Catie a much-appreciated break and announces it's time
to move on to the next activity: a video scavenger hunt.
This has become a retreat tradition, and it's something
we all look forward to each year.

After separating everyone into teams of three or
four, she makes sure we all have a smart phone or iPad
or something to record our performance tasks with. Each
team will start at a different spot on the ten-part hunt.
Once we find our location, we have to film our team
carrying out a related activity. Then we follow the clue
to the next place.

As soon as the rules are clear, Uli hands us our first
clue.

I end up with Trevor, Kate—a slightly overweight
but energetic twenty-something who's new to the class,
and clueless-as-corn Ellen. We find a spot in a corner of
the room and read the tiny slip of paper.

Everything I doe, I doe for you.

"Doe?" Trevor asks. "Is that a misspelling?"

"I doubt it," I say. "Maybe it's some place where
you might see deer?"

Kate snorts out a laugh. "We're in the Rockies.
There are deer everywhere."

"Aren't there two ceramic deer at the entrance to the
lodge?" Ellen glances around at each of us, as if worried
we'll dismiss her suggestion.

I grin. "I think you might be right. Let's check it
out."

We grab our jackets and Kate brings her iPad as we
head to the front door. Sure enough, we find two female
deer guarding the entryway. Nearby, we discover a stack
of envelopes in plastic bags. Opening one, we read our

task: sing *Do Re Mi.*

After Kate sets up her iPad on a bench and makes sure we're all in the shot, we start to sing. By the time we get to "La," we're in full-on competition to out-sing and outshine the others. I belt out "Ti" with gusto and am about to put jam on my bread with more heart than it deserves when Kate leaps in front of us, throwing out her arms and promptly losing her balance. She topples into Ellen who knocks into me. I desperately snatch at Trevor's jacket sleeve on the way to the ground, pulling him down on top of the women. We're all giggling so hard we can't find our feet and squirm over each other, a tangle of legs and arms.

Poor Trevor. He keeps apologizing, trying to get away from the scuffle without hurting anyone or putting his hands somewhere he shouldn't. I will never tell him how unsuccessful he actually was. Though I suspect he knows exactly what he touched. He is, after all, a man.

Once we pull ourselves together, we gather around the note with our next clue. Kate reads it out loud:

Tiptoe through the tulips. With me.

"Tulips," Trevor says with a groan. "Do we even have tulips in Colorado?"

I shrug. "Not that I know of."

We linger in silence for a few moments, thinking. Then Kate says, "*With me* is set apart. It could be significant. Maybe we need to find Uli."

Ellen nods. "She was in the main room. Do you think she's still there? Though I don't know what that has to do with tulips."

"Or she could be referring to a garden." I pause for a moment. Then I remember: "There is a cute little prayer garden down the road a bit."

"Well, we might as well check out the main room since we're here." Trevor nods toward the lodge. "If we don't find her, we'll go to the garden."

We're all in agreement and, after not finding Uli inside, start the short trek toward the prayer garden. Though Uli doesn't want her clues to be too hard to figure out, I can't imagine her making it so easy we'd find her just hanging out in the great room. She prides herself on being clever. Especially if it means shattering the dumb blonde stereotype. Uli does *not* like being lumped into that group. At all.

Kate and Ellen forge ahead, apparently in more of a hurry than Trevor and me. Ellen asks Kate for her slow-cooker recipe for chicken and noodles. I strain to listen, at first. But Trevor is taking it slow, staring at his feet and being his usual quiet self. I shouldn't leave him behind.

"So," I say, making a mental note to get the recipe later, "are you having fun?"

"Sure."

"Really? You're glad you came?"

"Why not?"

I stop walking and look him in the eyes. "I know this isn't your thing, Trev. I know you're only here because I … persuaded you."

He grins. "You can be very persuasive."

"When you're a social worker, it comes in handy."

We start moving again. And then, in the dark, under a sky punctuated by stars, on the side of a mountain dotted with snow, his hand brushes mine. One of those quick, accidental moments. It's nothing. Less than something. But Trevor takes a sharp, quiet breath. All of a sudden I want it to be intentional. And I want it to happen again. It's like someone flipped a switch I never knew existed.

"This will never do."

He looks at me.

Yep. I said it out loud.

"Why not?" His fingers curl around mine.

It was definitely intentional. *Oh boy.* This is all so unexpected and confusing and ... dreamy. Still, in a move that shows I'm more clueless than Ellen, I say, "We're friends."

"Yeah. Good friends."

I slow to a stop but can't look at him. Not yet. With most men I'd be coy and flirtatious, but Trevor is different. "The best." It's barely a whisper. I'm not even sure he heard me.

He glances ahead to Ellen and Kate, who disappear around a bend. His grip on my hand tightens as he pulls me off the road and behind a tree. I do a skip and a jump to keep from falling over. Stumble against him. Grab his arm and look up. In the star-lit silence he stares down at me. I can see the hope in his brown eyes. "Who better to fall in love with than my best friend?"

I barely squeak out, "In love?" and he kisses me. Lord have mercy, he kisses me. It's short and sweet and my whole body melts. My hands clutch at his shirtfront. He pulls back, his eyes searching mine. For some reason I whisper, "Heaven," but in truth it's a miracle I can speak at all. So he kisses me again. I might as well kiss him back.

Time slows until it moves as languidly as a lazy

river. I'm not sure how long we're there, making out like two teenagers in the back of a station wagon, only this is so much better. We float under a starry sky, surrounded by the scent of pine trees and the rhythmic sounds of a forest at night. His hands pull me closer. Then Kate calls my name, and I push him away. For several seconds we just stare at each other as Kate and Ellen head back our way, getting dangerously close to our hiding place.

"So," Trevor says, a grin I've never seen before lighting his face, "we'll talk about this later?"

I take a deep breath and somehow manage to smile back.

"Oh, absolutely."

Chapter 13
Uli

No one appreciates me. I spent weeks putting these stupid games together and does anyone care? Does anyone thank me?

Nope. I'm just bits of red cabbage in a cobb salad.

Yet still I sit on a bench in the prayer garden, waiting for one final group to make their way here. In retrospect, I shouldn't have made myself part of the game. Now here I am, in the dark, listening to animals rustle through the grass, hoping it's only a deer, bored out of my mind, wondering how I got here, trying not to cry. Yep. Just another normal Friday night for Uli.

Though I begged with far more earnestness than I should have, I couldn't convince Cole to come with me. Which, I suppose, is a good thing. I can't say I'm exactly proud to be seen in his company, even in the role of girlfriend. Especially in the role of girlfriend. He can be a bit of, well, a jerk. And sexist. And crude.

Boy, can I pick 'em or what?

The sound of voices and footsteps coming toward the garden interrupts my thoughts.

Thank goodness.

◊◊◊

I'm rooming with Ellen this weekend. Tess and I had planned bunk together originally, but then one of the new girls asked her to please share her room, and Tess couldn't say no. It's possible turning down someone in need would actually cause her physical pain. She has a heart as big as the Rockies and would give a liver or a finger or an eye to anyone who had a good reason. Or a bad one. Or, very likely, no reason at all.

When Ellen asked me if I wanted to room with her instead, I hesitated. I knew I should agree, but I didn't want to. Ellen has a tendency to invade my personal space and ask a lot of questions I don't feel like answering. Instead of reaching out and loving her, I back away. Then I see Tess being her sweet self to everyone, and I know I'm a horrible person. So I said yes to Ellen.

And she's been driving me crazy since we unpacked our overnight bags. She wanted to talk for half of the night then snored for the rest. Now it's sometime after eight on Saturday morning. Everyone's supposed to meet for breakfast at 8:30, but I'm still waiting for Ellen to get out of the shower. It's not her fault, really. We both overslept. It's a miracle I'm awake now.

Ellen finally finishes, leaving the bathroom steamy and stifling. I stand up. Too quickly, apparently, because a wave of pain and queasiness pounds through my abdomen. Dropping back onto the bed, I groan and put a hand on my stomach. Ellen's standing at the closet, picking out a shirt from the suitcase she stuffed in there and, apparently, doesn't notice my distress. Or, if she did, she's not even remotely interested or curious. Just as well. It's not something I want to talk to her about.

The feeling passes but still I lie on the bed. Sweat drips down my forehead and the back of my neck aches with heat. The last place I want to be right now is in that bathroom. I'll just rest and give it a little time to cool off.

Since Ellen prefers a low-maintenance lifestyle,

fashion-wise—she usually wears jeans, a T-shirt, and old-lady sneakers and claims she's allergic to makeup—she's ready in no time. Grabbing her small camera bag and Bible, she takes a few steps toward the door before turning back to me.

"Are you coming to breakfast?"

The thought of eggs or bacon or pancakes or even a fruit cup makes me want to hurl, so I just shake my head. But I don't want to be left behind. "Could you ask Jolene to come see me, please?"

"Sure." Then she's gone, slamming the door behind her.

The noise pounds through my skull. I need some relief, even if it's temporary, so I stumble to the bathroom and soak a washcloth with cold water. Once I'm back on the bed, I lie down again, rest the cool cloth on my forehead, and let it work its magic.

"Just a few minutes," I whisper to no one. "I'll be fine in a few minutes."

◊◊◊

"Uli. Uli, are you okay?"

I wake up to see everyone I've ever known hovering over me. Is this heaven? *I sure hope not.*

Jolene smoothes the hair off my forehead. "Welcome back, sleepyhead. We were starting to worry."

All right, so it's just Jolene, Catie, and Tess, but in a room this size it seems like a lot more people. All staring at me like I'm face up on the ice after botching a triple axel in the Olympic long program.

"I'm fine." I struggle to sit up. "Just needed to rest my eyes for a few minutes."

"A few minutes?" Tess sits down on the bed and puts a hand on my arm. "Uli, we tried to wake you up three hours ago, but you mumbled, 'I'm sleeping' and wouldn't budge. So, we all went on a hike."

I look at Jolene, stunned, but she nods. "Yeah, we just got back. And here you are, still snoozing the day away."

Now I'm awake. "What time is it?"

"Eleven-fifteen," Catie says. "We're going to have lunch soon, if you're hungry."

My stomach rumbles in response. At least the nausea has passed. "I could eat."

"Glad to hear it." Jolene stands and puts her hands on her hips. Now that she's not worried about me, I get the distinct impression she wants to paddle me or, at the very least, slap me upside the head. "We're heating up the leftover chili from last night and making grilled cheese sandwiches."

"Sounds good." Not really, but I'm sure I can find something. I still feel groggy, and my only thought is to follow them to the kitchen. But as I start toward the door, Jolene stops me.

"Um …" She gives me a once-over. "Sweetie, why don't you take a shower and get cleaned up, then meet us in the great room. It will take about that long to get everything ready anyway."

Oh right. I catch a glimpse of myself in the dresser mirror. My hair has the wonky charm of Pickup Sticks, I'm still slumming in my oversized, Tweety Bird nightshirt, and the circles under my eyes make me look like I'm about to wiggle my way into a football huddle. Facing the mess that is me, there's no way I can make myself presentable in the time it will take them to warm a pot of chili and fry up some bread and cheese. I typically need at least an hour.

Somehow, though, I manage to make it to the great room in just over forty-five minutes. After putting on the basic minimum amount of makeup needed by a woman my age, I slipped into jeggings, a lightweight, periwinkle-blue knit shirt, and a soft and cozy gray sweater that's long enough to cover everything I want to cover. My hair even looks halfway decent—just scrunchy and messy enough to look deliberate.

Right before I leave the room, I slide on a pair of fuzzy-cool slippers. Not only do I take slippers pretty much everywhere I go, but I brought four pair on this trip alone. Today I choose the off-white ones with beaded laces. It's just how a girl on a mountain retreat should dress, right? Comfortable but stylish.

I take a deep breath and hush up the voice saying I'm trying too hard and there isn't a single person in this lodge who will think I'm stylish or even care a whit what I wear. So I grimace at my semi-satisfied reflection then join my friends.

With their morning exercise taken care of, the group has gathered for a relaxing afternoon. After lunch, we talk about what we want to do with the rest of our day. Some decide to head into town for sightseeing and souvenir shopping, others will take advantage of the Mt. Princeton hot springs, and the rest will explore the immediate area, find a perfect spot to read, or even take a nap. We have plenty of time to take it easy before a night of make-your-own-pizzas, salads, and sundaes, hot-tubbing, and Hitchcock movies by the fireplace. It's a rough life. The only thing that could possibly make me happier would be someone to hold my hand. I'd even take Cole. My belch-in-your-face boyfriend. It's better than being alone.

As I ramble around the room, chatting with friends and dismissing every "Are you okay?" or "How are you feeling?" with a quick "Guess I just needed a good night's sleep," I try to figure out the kind of stuff people are leaning toward doing. I have to choose the right activity with the right group. This is a key decision on a retreat. If I pick the wrong thing, I could end up stuck in a situation I can't get out of. Like the time I spent three hours trapped in a car with Dave Reynolds while he told dumb blonde jokes and tried to find cheap, used tires, which he had no intention of buying. He just wanted to make sure he wasn't "gettin' scammed by doze guys in da Springs," as he put it. No, he's not gangster, but he thinks it's cool to talk like Joe Pesci. We call him Mafia Dave.

I skirt around the side of the room where Dave and a few of the other guys are talking about the World Series. My best bet is to hover as close to my girls as possible. Then, whatever we do, at least I'll be with friends.

So I join them in a corner cluster of furniture. Catie sits next to Brian on a sink-into-it faux-leather couch while Jolene lounges on a rustic-looking hickory chair. Trevor has taken a spot on another one just like it, which faces Jolene on the other side of a big, glass coffee table with antlers for legs.

I fall onto the leather loveseat that completes the set,

fling my feet over the cushy arm, and ask, "What's the plan? Is there a plan?"

No one answers. No one looks at me either. Heat rushes up my chest and into my face. Have they been talking about my dead-to-the-world, over-sleeping incident? What did they say? Did they come to any conclusions? The tension is as thick and heavy as a wool blanket on the Fourth of July.

Catie clears her throat. "We haven't decided yet. Do you have a preference?"

Okay, I can get through this. I'm an actress, after all. "I'm totally flexible. But I would definitely like to go somewhere. It's so nice out, and I could use the fresh air."

More silence. Trevor glances over toward Mafia Dave's crew, probably wishing he was with them, talking about RBIs and grand slams. At least, I think those are baseball things. Everything I know about sports I learned from Cole.

It's not a compliment.

What's also not a compliment are the awkward silences and stares I'm getting from my friends.

Dear God, what did Jolene tell them?

Brian says, "Well, why don't we drive into town and see what we can find?"

"Whatever we do, I say we include a stop at that ice cream place on Highway 24." Usually I wouldn't bring attention to my yearnings for the sweet stuff but today I don't care. It's not like they can't tell by looking at me that I have a tendency to overindulge my sweet tooth. And if I'm pregnant ...

I shake the thought away and turn to Jolene. "You

know the one I'm talking about, right, Jo? Where you place an order and they give you a famous person's name instead of a number?"

Jolene grins. "Oh, yeah. Last time we were there I was John Wayne, if I remember right."

This catches Trevor's attention. "Really? I've never pictured you as the cowboy type."

With a smile that could intimidate the sun, Jolene says, "Is that right? How do you picture me?"

He beams back at her but doesn't reply. The heat between them practically sets the coffee table on fire. I'm glad I'm not standing in the way. Something definitely happened, that much is obvious. Well, hopefully, they're actually moving forward with whatever it is.

Why anyone wouldn't jump all over a potential love interest with the unashamed enthusiasm of Winnie-the-Pooh clinging to his honey pot, I will never understand. But the two have been avoiding a romance under the guise of friendship for as long as I've known them. It might be one of the most depressing things I've ever witnessed, and I hope it's finally over.

And that's when I realize there is something more depressing. I'm the fifth wheel. Besides the electricity crackling between Jolene and Trevor, Catie and Brian are practically cuddling on the couch as they sip lattes. I've been dating someone for a year—someone who might have gotten me pregnant—but here I sit, surrounded by people yet alone, just like when I was the fat girl at the junior high spring dance. As the two couples discuss whose car to take into town, I wonder if it's worth going under the circumstances.

Then, to my forever relief, Tess joins us with a happy, "What's up?"

Thank goodness. Anything that evens up the numbers. I smile at her and she grins back, looking as cute as a college student. Though Tess's fashion sense never extends much further than a cardigan or crewneck sweater over a turtleneck and jeans, she's still the prettiest girl in the room. And there are several attractive girls here, including Jolene and, when she puts effort into it, Catie. But Tess's beauty hasn't been affected by age. She glows from within, and half the men here have a secret—or not-so-secret—crush on her. They all know where she stands on the whole marriage thing, though, and no one's had the nerve to pursue her.

The thought hits me that maybe Cole would, and maybe that's at least part of the reason I didn't try too hard to convince him to come. How pathetic is it to worry I could lose my man to the next sweet, young thing to sashay past him?

And just like that I don't feel like smiling at Tess anymore or going into town or being, now, a sixth wheel. I still want ice cream, but that's about it. I sit up, ready to tell the group I've changed my mind and will spend the afternoon reading … when a black, hairy spider the size of a quarter drops down from the ceiling and dangles two inches in front of my face.

Every nightmare I've ever had tackles me in a gulp of air. Fear hits me full-force, stopping my heart. I can't escape. I can't move. All I know is it could land on my leg or my arm or, heaven forbid, swing forward on its monster-web of evil and launch itself onto my nose before skittering across my face and into my hair and—

"Oh, help me," I whisper, afraid to breathe. "Just get it away from me."

Knowing how all my friends feel about spiders, I look to Brian. The new guy. My only hope. His eyes are wide and I realize, to my dismay, he's as scared as I am. "Don't look at me," he says, pushing back into the couch. "I can't stand those things."

I'm about to lose all hope of rescue when a hand holding a plastic cup appears in my field of vision and scoops up the spider into it. Hauling her captive over to the double, glass doors leading to the back patio, Tess exits and graciously flings the creature into the grass. I would have killed it. She comes back in the room, a satisfied look on her face.

"Well," Tess says, "if I'm going to live in a third-world country, I figure I should at least be able to handle a little spider."

Everyone laughs but me. I'm still recovering. "Little? That thing was the size of Rhode Island!"

Brian shudders then smiles at Tess, "You're braver than I am."

Well, isn't that charming? What kind of guy wants to be rescued by an itty bitty girl like Tess Erickson? For his many shortcomings, Cole has always dispatched any creepy crawler threatening my well-being. I don't even have to ask. If a spider scurries across the carpet or up a wall, Cole grabs a shoe and smashes it into oblivion. Maybe he enjoys the kill a little too much, but the important thing is he protects me. Unlike Brian, who backed into the couch as if the creature had dropped in front of *his* face.

"That spider was huge. You're our hero, Tess,"

Catie says. "But, Uli, I wish you could have seen your face. Other than the fact you were horrified, it was pretty funny."

"Okay, I'll give you that."

They chuckle again, and I try to join them. I really do. But, "What you all have to remember is this will keep me up for weeks. Every time I close my eyes, I'll see that thing coming toward me."

Jolene reaches over and puts a hand on my knee. "I know. You poor thing. I'm actually impressed by how calm you were." I smile my gratitude. Then she ruins it by folding her hands over her heart and whispering melodramatically, "Oh, help me. Help me! Get this monster away from me!"

Which, of course, gets them going again. And it hits me wrong and hard and all I want is to get away from *them*. "Well, I'm glad I could entertain you all. But if you don't mind, the show's over."

I stand up so quickly, I almost knock Tess off her perch on the arm of the loveseat. She catches herself, then says, "Uli, don't be like that. We're just having fun."

"At my expense."

Jolene tilts her head at me like I'm a child who doesn't want to eat her broccoli. "If you could see the humor in this, you'd be laughing with us."

"Yeah, Jo, it's hilarious." *Oh, hush, you grumpy, old sourpuss. It's one thing for them to think you're hormonal, you don't have to prove it.* Sometimes, my sinful nature gets the best—or worst—of me. Now all I can do is try to escape before the real spider in my life lands on the coffee table and spins a whole new set of problems.

My friends stare at me like a zombie took over my body. Any minute, someone's going to say, "Who are you, and what did you do with Uli Odell?" I take a deep breath. I can fix this.

I have to.

So I laugh. "Come on, guys, you know I'm just kidding. Besides, I didn't have to see my face when it was far more entertaining to see all of yours. Seriously, Brian, I think you were more scared than I was."

It's a small enough dig, and I might have gotten away with it. Until I add, "Do you need to change your underwear before we go?"

Silence. Catie looks more horrified than I felt when I first saw Charlotte dangling in front of my face. Jolene's eyes narrow, and she shakes her head. "Really, Uli?"

"What's the matter? I thought we were all trying to see the humor in this? Or is it only funny if you're laughing at me?"

Heat floods my face. I don't know how to salvage this situation. If I stay much longer without getting a grip on things, I'll find myself completely friendless. Then my stomach tightens in a twist of pain and I have an out.

"Hey, I'm sorry. I know I'm in a bad mood. I'm not sure why." Well, I am, but they don't need to know that. "I think it's best if I spend a little time reading and … praying this afternoon."

"Are you sure?" Jolene glances at Catie then back at me. "Maybe some fun time would do you good."

I muster up my best smile and flash it at my roommate. "No, no, you guys just go. It's fine. But if you want to bring me something chocolate, I won't complain." I start to walk away then turn and wave. "See you all later!" So cheerful. So fake. To my amazement, I'm able to hold this façade until I reach my room.

It takes me an hour and a half to cry myself to sleep.

◊◊◊

Well, I'm not pregnant. Just late. I found that out the hard way when a familiar and unpleasant feeling woke me from my tear-induced slumber. After spending ten minutes rinsing blood out of my jeggings and under things, I try to figure out what else I can wear. Why, oh why, haven't I learned to always, *always*, bring extra clothes on a trip?

I fret over what to put on for five minutes before it occurs to me I only have to change the lower half of my outfit, so I simply pull on the jeans I wore last night. I run a pick through my hair and stare in the mirror while I touch up my makeup. I'm relieved at this turn of events. Of course I'm relieved. And I'm glad I didn't say anything to Cole. Now I won't have to come face to face with his gut reaction. Because a gut reaction is about the best you will get from Cole Moretti.

So, there it is. All of my emotions and pain were nothing more than premenstrual symptoms. Strange how I was able to fool myself into thinking otherwise. The longings of my heart took over all reason, momentarily. Now everything is back to normal. This is how it should be. What on earth would I do with a baby anyway? I can't even take care of myself. And I certainly can't count on Cole to step up to the plate. It's better this way.

My hand slips and the mascara brush jabs against

my eye. Pain shoots into my brain. I want to hit myself for being so clumsy. But since my eye smarts and waters from the sting, that's punishment enough. Once I can see again, I glance into the hand-held mirror to assess the damage. The brown-black mascara smeared across my eyelid makes me look like I just took a punch from the neighborhood bully. Using a tissue to clean myself off, I try to blot the tears. Tears that won't stop even after the agony in my eye fades away.

You're still a fool, Uli.

Isn't it funny how we don't always know when we're lying to ourselves? But sometimes we do—when all our insecurities and mistakes are laid bare. And my inward insistence that I'm happy or even content with this outcome is pure bull. I want to be pregnant, blast the consequences. Now. Before it's too late.

For all I know it's already too late, and I'm doomed to spend my life childless and alone.

Slowly, I breathe in and out, staring at my sad, bloodshot eyes in the mirror. I know it's almost dinnertime and all my friends are gathered in the great room, laughing and making pizzas and creating memories and enjoying each other. Yet here I am, in a dungeon of my own making, trapped by what I want, surrounded by four dank, stone walls keeping me from hope: Cole's unwillingness to commit, good Christian boy-men who won't make a move, the fear and loneliness I fight on a daily basis, and my own ticking biological clock.

A loss knocks on my heart, and it's not my dreams. It's God. He wants me back. He wants me to stop trying to do things my way. A lifetime of Sunday school and church has taught me everything I need to know about what I'm doing wrong and how everything I'm going through is the immediate result of my stubbornness and rebellion. But I don't care. I can't feel Him anymore. I haven't felt God's presence in my life in so long.

Years ago I was in church, worshiping and crying and begging for the assurance of His love when, in the middle of the song "In Christ Alone," I felt warmth and love surround me in an invisible hug. I'd never felt His presence so keenly before. It poured over me like perfume from a jar.

For years, I hung on to that as evidence of God's love. But time and frustration and regret wore me down, pushing that memory into a vague dream of something I hope happened but I'm not sure ever really did. Sometimes, I can't feel anything but disappointment.

"God, I feel so abandoned. So helpless. So … unsafe." I whisper the words into the room, but they seem to bounce off the ceiling and hit me in the face. Just like every prayer I've attempted over the last ten years.

"Fine," I say, as the realization that no one's actually listening floods my mind and breaks my heart.

"I'll just do this on my own."

Chapter 14

Catie

Trevor and Jolene offer to drive into town, which means Tess, Brian, and I crowd into the backseat of Trevor's Jeep Wrangler. Since I'm the shortest—whether I like it or not—I volunteer to sit in the middle. Which means my entire right side is pressed against Brian. Now this, I like.

I am completely surrounded by the truth that something is happening between this man and me. It feels wonderful. And amazing. And too good to be true. I shift a bit, loving the sensation of his arm grazing mine. I feel brazen and impulsive. Ready for anything.

As if she heard my thoughts, Jolene turns around and says, "Would you all be up for a little four-wheeling instead? Trevor's been wanting to test this Jeep out, and there are plenty of paths around here that are perfect for it."

We all quickly agree, and soon we're on our way to some back mountain road with big rocks and steep terrain, which means plenty of snow and mud to avoid. Good thing I wore sturdy hiking boots.

On the way, we call Doug and Lindsay, who also enjoy four-wheeling, because it's best to travel with at least one other vehicle in case you get stuck. They agree to meet us at the trailhead for Buckeye Gulch Road, just north of Leadville. Doug brings along his brother, Matt, and Matt's girlfriend, Stacy, who's new to the group. We all meet up at the designated spot and, after some discussion, hit the trail.

The route Trevor chose follows a stream for about two miles. It's sufficiently treacherous, but our drivers have years of experience in off-road maneuvering. Still, no matter how many times I go rock crawling, I'm bound to spend the entire journey with my nerves in my throat. All it takes is one bad turn.

We start off slow and easy, carefully crossing some private property before hitting the climb. Every jolt rocks me against Brian or Brian against me. It's a leisurely, terrifying, delicious torment.

After about half a mile, Trevor stops the Jeep and everyone gets out to walk around while the drivers scout a particularly uncertain rock formation ahead of us. Brian sticks with the rest of the men; Jolene, Lindsay, and Stacy stay close to their significant others; and Tess and I scurry off into the woods to explore a bit before they call us back. I whistle for Luna, who jumps out of the Jeep's back storage area and obediently trots along beside me.

"Are you having a good time?" Tess stumbles over a rock, recovers her balance, then looks back at me. "You seem like you're having fun."

"Well, it's nice to have something to get my mind off the fact I won't be going to work on Monday."

"Oh right. I'm so sorry about that, Catie. I know you gave a lot of yourself to your job."

I stop walking and lean against a large rock. Always sensitive to my mood, Luna scampers over and sits on my feet. Tess means well. I sigh. "I'm trying to get a good perspective on it and see God's purpose in the whole thing. But it's hard. I feel like ... like ..."

Tess sidles up next to me on the rock. "Like what?"

"Well, I've never been married, so I'm only speculating here but ... I think it's like a divorce. And not the mutual, this-isn't-working-out kind of divorce, but the one where he throws you out of the house and says he never wants to see you again, and you don't know why."

I glance over at the girl next to me. She's really trying to sympathize, but her sheltered life makes it hard for her. Well, we all have to grow up sooner or later. I continue,

"When you've been in a ... relationship for fifteen years and, suddenly, it's over, does it really matter what kind of relationship it was? I feel like the company I gave so much of myself to just kicked me to the curb without a thank you or we'll miss you or we wish we could make this work. Just 'Get out. We never want to see you again.' At least, that's how it feels."

Wrapping an arm around my shoulders, Tess leans her head against mine. "I honestly can't imagine how awful that must be."

No, I suppose she can't. At least she can admit it "The worst thing is—" I turn away and press my fist against my heart. "I can already feel the bitterness sitting on me. That on top of being single, now I have to deal with this. What if I become so angry I blame God for all the bad stuff in my life and forget to thank Him for the good?"

I pause. Why do I feel so hesitant to tell her about Brian? Tess is one of my best friends and might even have some good advice, despite her age. So I say, "I'm just glad He brought Brian into my life. The timing is perfect and reminds me how much God cares."

"Brian?"

"Yes, I ... think something's happening there."

She stares at the ground and scuffs at a rock with her boot. "Really? What's going on?"

"I'm not sure." I grin, then bump against her with my arm. "But it's something. I haven't felt this hopeful in ..." How long *has* it been? "I don't think I've ever felt this hopeful."

"But, Catie, wouldn't it be better for your hope to come from God? You *know* He loves you. Men can be so ... unpredictable."

The comment makes me laugh. Out loud. "Brian? Unpredictable? He's more reliable than the sunrise."

"Hmm. Maybe you're right. Still," she finally looks at me, "how does that Psalm go? 'And now, O Lord, for what do I wait? My hope is in *You.*' And in Second Corinthians, Paul said, 'On Him we have set our hope that He will deliver us again.'"

I can always count on Tess to have the right verse for every occasion. I'm about to break into a discourse about another significant hope verse—this one from Proverbs—when Trevor honks the horn, signaling it's time to return to the vehicles. It's just as well. Talking or even thinking about that particular verse usually ends with me sobbing into my shirtsleeve. This is not the time or the place. I can cry all next week, alone in my house, unemployed and pathetic.

But today, I have hope that something can, and will, happen. So, I nod and say, "You're absolutely right, Tess," and then, with a grin, I race her back to the Jeep.

As we break out of the trees, I spot Brian scanning the area, a worried expression on his face. When he sees me, he grins. "I was about to send out the search team."

Tess, who's following close behind me, giggles.

I say, "Don't kid yourself. If we get lost, you *are* the search team."

He laughs as we climb back into the Jeep and renew our slow crawl. We rock and tilt over one huge boulder after another. The farther we go, the more confident I feel. At one point, when the right wheels go up so high it seems like we're on a ninety-degree angle, I grab Brian's arm. The whole moment feels suspended in the air. Then the wheels come down again, and I let go.

Shortly after, Trevor stops the Jeep again. "All right, folks," he says. "Let's take a look."

A large crevice stretches ahead of us before it curves around a bend. The guys and their women tramp off in that direction to see what's to come. This time, though, Brian opts to hike with Tess and me and the dog. We trek a good distance into the forest at a fast clip, without the distraction of conversation. It's a friendly silence, broken only by the sound of twigs and leaves crunching under our boots. I take the opportunity to enjoy the blue sky and the stark branches silhouetted against it, to breathe in the smell of snappy pine trees and fresh air. Luna trots along beside me, her senses on the alert. Seeing any kind of animal would just make her day.

I take each step carefully. It's one thing to let a guy carry you down a well-defined trail; quite another to ask him to do the same when you're blazing your own pathway through the woods. I wouldn't want to—

Great. After years, decades even, of hiking around Colorado, I'm suddenly worried I'll twist my ankle. Good grief.

Stepping around a fallen tree, I glance up and realize Brian and Tess are no longer right ahead of me. I'm not sure where they are. I wait a few moments but hear nothing. Where did they go? At least I know where I am. All I have to do is turn around and head back down to the Jeep. But though I keep walking for another five minutes, I still don't come across my friends.

Now I'm even more annoyed. I should be the one lost in the woods with Brian. What are he and Tess doing? Are they talking? Knowing the two of them, they're discussing Tess's plans to head to China next summer for a short-term missions trip. But even though they're not enjoying a romantic moment, I'm still jealous of any time someone gets to spend with Brian that I don't.

The horn blasts through the trees, sounding farther away than I would have thought.

"Come on, Luna." We turn around and cautiously hurry back down the hill. I'm at the Jeep, chatting with Jolene, for several minutes before I see Brian finally come into view. And, what do you know, he has Tess in his arms. Apparently, he has a thing for carrying fragile women down mountainsides. They draw closer and I see Tess's cheek rests against Brian's neck, and her face looks flushed.

I remember it well.

But was I red and clingy and helpless-looking when he carted me down Pikes Peak? Pushing aside my emotions, I race over to them. "What happened?"

Brian says, "She fell."

"I'm fine." Tess shrugs. "Just clumsy."

After setting her down on a low rock near the Jeep,

Brian goes to the back of the vehicle to get bottles of cold water out of the cooler.

Jolene kneels down beside Tess. "Are you hurt?"

"Nothing serious," Tess says, shaking her head. "I bruised my wrist and scraped my knee. I'm more embarrassed than anything. I'm just glad Brian was there."

The two share a smile and he says, "I seem to have a gift for being around when women trip on mountains."

He grins at me then, and everything is good again. I wouldn't mind having a heroic boyfriend one little bit.

◊◊◊

As is tradition, our retreat time wraps up Sunday morning with a big breakfast of waffles and all the toppings you could possibly want, plus pan-fried potatoes and thick fruit smoothies. It's my turn to help out so I spend the morning chopping, mixing, frying, and serving.

Once everyone's appetite has been taken care of and the kitchen is spit-spot clean again, we fill up spiritually by gathering in a circle in the great room for a time of prayer and praise. After spending the weekend in such close proximity, people have a tendency to open up. A lot. Which means the morning can turn into something of a weep fest for the women. The guys hang in there, to their credit, while the girls sniffle about forever friendships, broken dreams, and answered prayers.

One of our newer couples, Piper and Jim, provide the highlight of the morning when they announce their engagement. The women pass around a box of Kleenex while admiring the ring. I smile along with everyone else, genuinely happy for them. But I don't cry.

I admit I'm kind of with the men on this one. It's a bit too emotional for me. I understand wanting to open up, but can't we keep the tears under control? There's such a thing as showing restraint when you're in a big group. This kind of deep sharing should be reserved for intimate gatherings with close friends.

And some things should be kept secret, period.

All of which puts me in a bit of a bind. On the one hand, I want to ask for prayer in my job hunt. If I knew it would be that simple, I wouldn't hesitate. But, on the other hand, I know how these things go. Someone will tilt her head and say, "How are you doing, Catie?" Everyone—okay, the women—will look at me with tear-filled eyes and, before I know it, I'll spill every last drop of grief this jobless situation has dumped on me. Right here in front of God, my singles group, and Brian Kemper.

So, I decide to keep it to myself ... until Jolene looks me right in the eyes, tilts her head, and—I'm not kidding—asks, "How are you doing, Catie?"

The glare I send her is for Jolene alone. She knows I do not like having attention steered my direction. "I'm fine. Though yes, I would like prayer about my job situation."

Someone asks, "Do you have any leads yet?"

"Well, no, not yet. I'm sprucing up my résumé, though, and have started researching what's out there. Mostly I'm still just trying to get used to the idea."

"I know what you mean," Ellen says, then proceeds to bore us with a five-minute story about being laid off from her secretary job two years ago. The tale should have ended sooner since it didn't take her long to find a similar position at a different company. But it didn't. From what I can tell, Ellen has made a career out of hopping from one job to another, which means she has no savings or retirement money. I honestly don't know what she'll do to get by when she's older. But she doesn't seem too worried. Maybe I could give her career advice. Become some kind of life coach. Not that anyone would want advice from can't-keep-a-job, can't-get-a-man me.

Anyway, Ellen's taken the attention off of me, so for that I'm grateful. It would bother Jolene and, especially, Uli, to have someone hijack their prayer request, but I see it as a blessing.

Glancing around the room, I discover one other woman who's not a mess of tears. Uli. I've been worried about my younger friend since her meltdown yesterday. She was quiet at dinner last night and spent the evening curled up on a recliner, wrapped in a soft, brown throw while we watched *Rear Window* then *Notorious*. She barely spoke, just munched on popcorn and drank an entire two-liter of Diet Coke. Adding to my concern, her eyes were red and her face scrubbed clean of makeup. After the movies, she shuffled back to her bedroom without saying a word to anyone.

Today, however, she seems more like her old self. Though she's wearing flannel, pink-plaid pants, a white, Berber-fleece pullover, and another frivolous pair of slippers—this time they're white with pink pom-poms—she looks casual but put together.

At breakfast, Uli laughed and flirted with every man

at our table. She told jokes. She covered her waffles with chocolate chips and syrup and whipped cream. She belted out the Happy Birthday song when we discovered one of the girls, Beth, was celebrating her fortieth birthday. Uli's enthusiasm was especially impressive considering she turns forty in less than a month. She doesn't talk about it, but I have a feeling it's all she thinks about.

Now she's sandwiched on a couch between Mafia Dave and Star Trek Sean. She's spent almost the entire share time slumped against the cushions with her legs stretched out in front of her, texting and taking random pictures with her phone. And looking bored out of her mind. Still, she's somehow managed to ignore Jolene's glares of disapproval. It's a miracle of polite protocol that Jolene doesn't stomp over and snatch the Droid right out of Uli's hands.

Most telling, Uli hasn't shared a prayer or a praise or launched into one of her typical, end-of-the-weekend, you-are-all-so-great speeches.

And then she raises her hand.

"Uli," Scott says, "you have something you want to share?"

"I do." She slides her fuzzy feet off their perch on the coffee table and sets down her phone. With a smile that drips insincerity, she continues, "I just want to thank you all for a great weekend. It's knowing I have people like you in my life that makes getting up every morning worthwhile. You've all encouraged me more than you can know, and I'm just so glad I can call you my friends."

Several of the women grin back at her, not knowing

Uli good enough to hear the sarcasm. A few people seem unsure what to think, so they just nod with tight-lipped smiles.

But Jolene knows. She looks my way, her eyes wide and a little angry. We're both wondering the same thing.

What is wrong with Uli?

◊◊◊

As Brian and I load our luggage into the SUV, I push Uli out of my mind, at least for the time being. I have two-and-a-half hours of alone time with Brian ahead, and I don't intend to waste it worrying about something I can't, at the moment, do anything about. We'll have plenty of time to talk over Uli's issues at our next Accountability Monday. Since she drove up with Trevor and Jolene, though, I suspect she'll have to explain herself on the ride home.

What I'm hoping for, at the moment, is that Brian will take the next step and ask me to go on an official date. Before heading out of town, a group of us meet up at the ice cream place on Highway 24, at Uli's insistence. After fifteen minutes of waiting in line and twenty minutes chomping down cones and establishing our memories of the weekend just past, we finally hit the road.

I didn't get to spend as much time connecting with Brian as I had hoped. We didn't have that moment when everything clicked and we became a couple. If only I had a single, simple clue as to how to close the deal. Should I say something? Or just reach over and cover his hand with mine? Could I be so bold?

Unlikely. But I'm not entirely clueless. Last night, while most of the group was watching movies or enjoying the hot tub, I pulled Jolene aside and asked her for advice. Now, I click off all her suggestions in my head and get down to business.

One: *Let him do most of the talking.*

Easy enough. I can keep him busy with questions all the way back to Colorado Springs if I have to. But I don't have to because I start off by asking him about his relationship with Christ, which leads to a forty-minute testimony. His passion for the things of God is infectious. And intimidating. Am I spiritual enough for him? Would he want to date a woman who's angry at God 75 percent of the time and only talks to Him reluctantly the rest? And who's apparently more concerned with how her faith can help her win a man than she is in mending her broken and bleeding relationship with God?

We stop for gas and sodas at the Badger Basin Country Store near Hartsel then zip back on the road toward home. It's my turn to drive. Once we're heading east on Highway 24 again, I push my doubt and guilt aside and continue with the task at hand.

Two: *Compliment him.*

"You know," I say, "I'm surprised you're not a preacher or in some kind of full-time ministry. You have a gift for sharing the Gospel."

He grins. "You really think so?"

"Definitely." I take a sip of Sierra Mist, then set the cruise control since we're on a long, flat stretch before we get into the mountains again. "Have you thought about going to seminary?"

"Thought about it, sure, but I don't know how realistic it is." He scratches his chin for a moment and shrugs. "I like my job. I have plenty of opportunities to talk about God with the people I meet there."

"You can minister anywhere."

"Exactly!"

We share a look and a smile. Time for the next step.

Three: *Never underestimate the power of physical touch.*

Taking a deep breath, I reach over and put my hand on his arm. In my mind I'm about to say something encouraging, uplifting, and so perfect he'll ask me out here and now. But my brain betrays me and all I can stumble out is, "Well, I'm sure you'll be … great … at whatever you do."

He clears his throat and says, "Thanks, Catie. That means a lot to me."

How wonderful would it be if he's as uncertain as I am?

I slide my hand away and switch off the cruise control as the road starts to climb into the mountains again. He makes me so nervous I can barely breathe.

It's all right, Catie. Have faith.

Just as I'm about to ask my next question, Brian says, "So, did you enjoy yourself this weekend?"

"I did. What about you?" And I hold my breath.

"Oh, I had a great time. Even better than I thought it would be."

"Really? What did you like the most?"

He smiles at me. "The company, of course."

In those four words, my confidence grows. Then he asks to hear how I came to know Christ. So I tell him. I tell him about the strong Christian heritage from my mom's side of the family versus the Delaney's strict Catholic background. And how Dad converted just a few months before meeting Mom. All of which led to me being raised in the church and choosing faith in God at the age of five.

As I reach the end of my story, we crest a hill about twenty miles from Woodland Park.

I say, "It looks like a storm."

Brian glances at me then out the window at the clear sky stretching like a frosty-blue canopy over our heads. "A storm?"

"Up ahead." I point toward an ominous line of dark clouds on the horizon in front of us. Apparently, the bad weather never left Colorado Springs. After three days of sunlit perfection, it's now time to drive back into the real world.

One where I don't have a job, and I don't have a plan.

But I might soon have a boyfriend.

Chapter 15

Jolene

Four hours. That's how long I've been on the phone. Every time I hang up, it rings again. At the sound of the most recent trill, I look down and see Trevor's come-hither gaze peering at me. Funny. I never saw the picture that way *before* he kissed me. Well, he's not going to sway me so easily. I click *ignore*. I've been ignoring his calls since we got back from the retreat two days ago.

And then I think about that kiss, and my body sets to tingling from head to toe. This is exactly what I didn't want to happen. He's moony-eyed and more than ready to pucker up, as far as I can tell, and someone has to put her perfectly pedicured foot down. I'm still a bit stunned at how eager he is to jump into a relationship. Oh sure, it will start out great—Friday night's smooch-a-thon proved that much—but eventually it's doomed to end in disappointment. That much I know. I can't give him what he wants. Then, after it's all over, I'll have lost my best friend. Better to put the brakes on now before it's too late.

My phone beeps a text message, and I click on it. DON'T MAKE ME COME OVER THERE. ☺

It might already be too late. Bless his heart. But I'm not ready. *God, You know I'm not ready. You know I have too much baggage to ever be the kind of woman Trevor deserves. I need Your approval on this before I even think about moving forward. I really don't want to hurt him. You know how good I am at hurting people.*

Laughter from the Cocoon House family room drifts

toward me. I haven't interacted with any of my girls all afternoon. My day was pilfered by the need to work through issues with a couple of the people who employ our residents. I also had to call a few vendors to order bulk items for our pantry and suffer through a rather long and confusing chat with Sara's mother. Who was clearly drunk when she called.

Sara Bailey has been part of our house family for only a few months, and her mother thinks it's time for her to come home. But Sara's mom puts all the responsibility for her welfare on her daughter's shoulders. She's a lazy, bitter woman looking for a free ride, and the last thing I will do is put one of my girls in a no-win situation like that.

But I will help Sara grow stronger and more confident, so when she does go home, she can be there for her mother while still setting up good, firm boundaries. In the meantime, I'll do all I can to keep her here until I know she's ready.

Another reminder to put my girls first in everything, including my personal life. Trevor can wait. So, I text a quick I'LL-CALL-U-LATER to my fine friend, then head to the family room. I stand in the large, arched entryway for a moment and take it all in. Three women circle a small table, playing cards. Benita and Jillie—who became friends almost the minute they met—chat quietly on the couch. And Sara sits in a corner, reading a Beth Moore devotional book. Three months ago, Sara laughed when I suggested she pass the time by reading. Silly girl. Eventually, they all figure out I have a few good ideas.

"So," I say, drawing their attention to me as I take a

seat on a faded, green-and-white-plaid glider, "who wants to start?"

Everyone except Jillie and Benita, who are fine where they are, moves to a new seat, forming our inner circle of safety and honesty. I try to have these spontaneous updates three times a week. It gives the women a chance to share what's going on in their lives. This lets me know where they are in their journey and where they could use help.

Having set a pot of Mexican tortilla soup to simmer on the stove in anticipation of supper, SueAnn joins us. Her calm and loving demeanor always comforts the girls and makes it easier for them to open up. And she's a prayer warrior, something they all need.

To no one's surprise, Davia, our resident extrovert and reformed con artist, gets things rolling by telling about her first week answering phones for a local veterinary clinic. Yep, a girl who doesn't like animals now works with them on a daily basis. I love God's sense of humor.

"I like it," she says. "More than I thought I would. You know what I'm saying?" She holds a finger to her nose then fakes a sneeze. Well, it certainly seemed fake. Davia always thinks she's playing a role. "Now if I could just get over these allergies. I'm not really fond of having to breathe through my mouth. You know what I'm saying?"

I tried for six months to cure Davia of her habit of adding "You know what I'm saying?" to every sentence, to no avail. It's nearly impossible to get someone to quit doing something they don't realize they're doing. Eventually, I had to let it go. It's finally reached a place where it feels like one fingernail scraping down a chalkboard instead of all ten, so that's a plus.

Next up, Jillie—a petite, former prostitute with short, bleach-blonde hair—asks us to pray for her recurring migraines. After being with us for almost a year, we finally decided she was ready to take a job. But working at a Subway down the street hasn't been easy for her. "It's just so hard to get anything done. I feel like I'm always working at less than my best" She grabs a bit of her hair and begins twisting it between her fingers. Since she always works the same section, she's starting to get a bald spot in that area. "Some days, I just don't know if I'm gonna make it."

Benita puts an arm around her friend and turns sad but hopeful eyes to me. In the short time she's been at Cocoon House, Benita has knocked me over with her sweet compassion. But she's holding something back. Her eyes speak of loss and pain, yet she remains cheerily optimistic. It's further evidence of her good heart, which makes the news I have to give her later tonight that much harder. My shortest phone call today—all of two minutes, if that—also threw me the biggest curve ball. It's all I can do not to cry just thinking about it. Instead, I turn my attention back to Jillie and her migraines.

"I think we need to pursue treatment a little more aggressively, Jillie," I say. "I'll call Dr. Saunders and see about getting you an appointment."

"Thank you, Miss Woods. That'd be great." Then her mouth lifts in a half-grin. "My sandwiches are starting to suffer."

As the girls laugh, Sara clears her throat. "I have something new I'd like to run past everyone."

"All right." I turn my attention to Sara, a tomboy through and through with a plain face and curveless figure. But simple honesty and a sense of humor spark from her light gray eyes, and I see the beauty within. "What's up?"

"Well, y'all know I'm pretty handy with tools and stuff like that, right?"

Everyone nods. Sara fixes all kinds of things around Cocoon House, from malfunctioning light switches to clogged toilets. SueAnn's husband, Ralph, is our official handyman but having Sara around lets him focus on the bigger stuff, like re-tiling the roof.

Sara continues, "So, I was thinking I could fix up some of that junk in the basement. Fix it up, re-purpose it, bring it back to life. And, if it looks good, maybe sell it?"

This immediately catches my attention. My love for antique-hunting and finding hidden gems in old stuff draws me to the idea. Taking junk and fixing it up for resale? How much fun would that be? Sara's suggestion has fabulous potential. I lean in but try to not seem too enthusiastic until I'm sure it's something we can move forward on.

"I think that's a great idea, Sara. We could get some paint and material and really go to town. There's definitely a ton of stuff around here to work on, but ..." My mind races ahead as a plan formulates. "What if we got word out that we're taking donations of old furniture and knick-knacks and stuff?"

Sara scratches her head. "You mean, make it a kind of regular thing?"

"Why not?" I stand and start pacing around the

circle. "We could take donations of junk, fix it up, and then have sales here, like, one Saturday a month."

"I could help," Benita offers. "I've worked with fabric a lot and could do upholstery stuff."

Jillie nods. "And I could do something too. Maybe paint, if the fumes aren't too bad."

The other three women are clearly not into the idea, but that's okay. The four of us could do quite a bit. It would bring in some extra income for Cocoon House and provide the women involved with a little spending money.

I stroll to the glider and sit again. "All right. I'm liking this. But what should we call it? I think we need a fun name. Over time, hopefully, we'll build a reputation and people will know they can buy cute, well-crafted girlie stuff at Cocoon House. I think it has tons of potential. But we need to call it something."

The residents are silent for a few moments, then Benita says, "How about Girl Stuff? Keep it simple?"

"That's close, but ... I don't know." Sara taps a fingernail on her teeth for a few seconds. She pops the same index finger up like a light bulb just flicked on over her head. "What if we spelled it g-r-r-l instead of g-i-r-l? Grr-l Stuff. You know, give it a slightly tougher quality."

I nod. "That might work. Grr-l Stuff Saturdays. I like it. I'll come up with some marketing ideas and see how it looks. I'll let area churches and some of the people who support Cocoon House know what we're looking for so, hopefully, the donations can start coming in."

Sara says, "And I'll take an inventory of what we

have to start with. We'll need some supplies before I can do much, but I can at least come up with a few ideas. I mean, I know there's a headboard down there that I think would make a great bench. It'd be cool to paint it light green then add black and white plaid cushions."

"Ooh, that sounds gorgeous. I might have to buy it myself." I smile. "This is gonna be fabulous."

"And don't worry about paint and wood, at least not right away." SueAnn bobs her eyebrows at me. "I happen to know where I can get my hands on a bunch of leftover stuff from a very handsome contractor." She's talking, of course, about Ralph. "And I can probably get a few other things like nails and glue and whatever else you think might be helpful."

"That would be great," Sara says. "How about I make a list?"

"You get started on that." SueAnn gets to her feet. "And I'll go finish supper."

Benita jumps up, always ready to lend a hand. "I'll help you, SueAnn."

"Thanks, sweetie." The two leave, and I finish our share time with a short prayer. But I can't stop thinking about Grr-l Stuff. It has so much potential, I want to get going on it right away.

But it's not the only thing on my mind tonight.

◊◊◊

After dinner, I ask Benita to come to my office. I can't avoid it any longer. She needs to know.

"Close the door behind you, Benita, and have a seat."

Now she realizes it's serious.

"Is everything okay, Miss Woods?" She stays standing. So do I.

"No, I'm afraid not. I—"

"If it's something I did, I know I can fix it. Was it the scratch I put in the floor? Because maybe Sara—"

"Benita—"

"—can help me refinish it."

"Wait," I say, holding up a hand. "Just hang on. It's not anything you've done. It's worse than that."

She must see it in my face because all the color washes out of hers. "Diego."

"Yes, Diego. He's been released."

Benita starts panting like she just ran a marathon. She shivers and shakes her head, saying, "Oh no, oh no" over and over.

I put an arm around her and lead her to a chair. "Now, it's way too soon to panic. He doesn't know where you are. And we certainly don't know what he's planning to do now. Since he's on parole, I imagine he'll have to stay in the area but … Benita, do you even know if he'll want to see you?"

"He wants … I mean, I testified against him. And Diego tends to hold a grudge."

"All right. Well, we will certainly need to be on the lookout. In the meantime, we'll keep praying and trusting that God has everything under control, okay?"

She looks up at me with trusting eyes and nods. Once again, I'm struck by her naiveté.

God, please protect her. And give me the strength and wisdom to know what to do.

◊◊◊

On the way home, I call Freddie. It's the first chance I've had to tell her,

"Trevor and I made out at the retreat."

Silence. Then I hear a deep breath or a sigh of relief. "Was it your idea or his?"

"Well, I don't know. Our hands touched and the next thing I know he's dragging me behind a tree and kissing me like he just got home from war."

"Ooh, nice. The first time Sam kissed me like that, I knew I'd spend the rest of my life with him. How was it?"

"It was okay." I bite my lip. I can just imagine the look on her face.

"Jolene!"

"Well, what do you want me to say? That I've never been kissed like that before?"

"Have you?"

"Freddie, I'm still trying to get my pulse back to a regular rhythm."

She sighs. "Yes, that's what it's like."

"It's a powerful thing." I pull up to the Academy intersection, where a long line of traffic tells me I'll be late getting home. "So, how do I forget it?"

"Why would you want to forget it?"

"Because Trevor deserves better than a mess like me."

Another breath but this one is more of frustration than relief. "Shouldn't you let him decide that?"

"He doesn't have all the facts, Freddie."

"So, tell him."

"Then I'll lose him for sure."

"Jolene." I hear a tinge of pain in Freddie's voice. "We all have histories and every one of them contains mistakes and regrets. Trevor is a good man. He'll understand."

"But will he forgive me?"

"A more important question is: God has forgiven you, so why haven't you forgiven yourself?"

◊◊◊

I can't avoid Trevor any longer. Now it's Friday and guilt washes over me for the five days I've put him on hold. Which makes me "that girl." The one who whimpers on and on about how much she wants to reel in a man then scampers for the hills as soon as she gets one on the hook. I never thought I was the scared-of-commitment type. But this thing with Trevor has me re-thinking a lot of previously held assumptions.

Time to face my fear and get this taken care of. Tonight. Through a series of texts earlier today, we decided to meet at The Elephant Bar for dinner. Just Trevor. Just me. Just so much to get all worked up about. What if he's the one? The man I've been waiting for all my life? My talk with Freddie gave me reason to hope we might be able to work through all my baggage after all. Out of the many men I've known and dated over the years, could it really have been Trevor all along? It's just too weird.

Then again, maybe it's not him. The last thing I want is to spill my guts and let myself fall and end up with a broken heart. What if I fall so hard I can't get back up again? I've done such a good job of convincing people how strong and confident I am that they often come to me for advice. If I mess this up, they might learn what a complete mess I really am, and it could change the whole course of my life.

So, is that what you're afraid of, Jolene? You don't want anyone to know you have weaknesses? It's all an ego thing? You don't want people to know you're just as troubled as the girls you minister to?

All of this skips through my head as I dress for my date. I decide on a silky, black-and-white, reptile-print dress and my favorite black pumps, and finish the look by tying my hair back with a pink scarf. It occurs to me that, perhaps, I should dress down a bit. This outfit really shows off my curves, and if I want to put the brakes on things a bit, this is not the way to do it.

Of course, if I want him to kiss me again …

I walk through a spritzed cloud of Cashmere perfume and try to breathe like a normal person who's not falling for her best friend.

Oh Lord, help me. Because I definitely want him to kiss me again.

◊◊◊

"So, why have you been avoiding me all week?" Trevor cuts right to the chase as he bites into a pre-dinner mozzarella-and-tomato appetizer. His eyes meet mine, and though he tries to hide it, I can't ignore the hint of sadness. I don't want to hurt him. Ever. Another reason why this will never work.

"It's been a crazy-busy week." That's only a mild

exaggeration. Cocoon House is always crazy and usually busy.

"Mm-hmm." Trevor knows exactly what my work is like and that I've always had time to call him before. He takes another bite and waits.

"I just … I don't know what to think about all of this." I lean forward, though the tall-backed booth we're sitting in does a good job of shielding us from the dozens of diners enjoying a Friday night out. It also buffers some of the noise. I whisper, "You can't tell me you're not a little freaked out."

"Freaked out? About what?"

"You and me. And … and … last Friday." *Don't blush. Don't blush. Do. Not. Blush.*

He grins. The tease. "Oh. Are you talking about when we kissed?"

I don't reach across the table and smack him because I'm pretty sure people would notice. "Yes, of course I am."

"And that scared you."

Humph. "I didn't say scared. Freaked out. And I'd appreciate it if you'd stop acting like it was nothing."

His eyebrows leap up toward his nonexistent hairline as the waitress approaches our table. After ordering the rainbow trout for himself and a Japanese Ahi rice bowl for me, Trevor turns his full attention back to me. The waitress leaves with a promise to refill our drinks. I should have asked more questions about the menu or told her my life story or anything to get her to stay. To have a buffer for a few more minutes might ease some of this tension. Because it's quite possible Trevor wants to devour me instead of the fish. And that makes me all tingly and sweaty at the same time.

"So," he says, "you think I'm acting like it was nothing?"

I nod and bite my lip.

"I called you at least once every day this week and sent you about a dozen texts, and you think that was nothing?"

"Well, you just seem very casual about things. Tonight anyway."

He sits back and crosses his arms. "Jolene."

"Yes?"

"I'm not freaking out because this feels very natural to me. I love being with you. I love your heart and your smile. I can't stop wondering when I'll kiss you again." He leans toward me and covers my hand with his. "I hope it's soon. Like tonight."

My heart stops beating. Just for a second, but when it starts back up again I'm sure it's to the rhythm of "Be My Baby." Of course, since that's the song currently streaming through the restaurant, I can't make too much of it.

His thumb slides over mine as he whispers, "In fact, if you want to run out to the car right now …"

Trevor lets the words hover over us like an alien spaceship. For a second, I don't know whether to hide from its death rays or skip blindly into the oh-so-welcoming light. But common sense wins the day, and I jerk my hand away and gulp down half of the sweet tea in my glass.

Then I look him square in the eyes. *I can do this.* "Trevor …"

"Uh-oh." He runs his abandoned hand over his scalp

and massages the back of his neck. "That's your serious voice."

"I am serious. I want to be smart about this."

"Smart *and* serious? Come on, Jo, what fun is that?"

"One of us has to keep their head on straight. Otherwise, we'll end up jumping into something we'll regret later." Wow. It's like I read *How to End a Romance Before It Starts for Dummies*, and I'm working my way through the clichés one by one. I'm about to add, "It's not you, it's me" for good measure when he interrupts.

"Why would you think we'll regret anything? You don't think I've thought this through? Prayed about it?"

He's prayed? About us? A drop of sweat beads down the back of my neck and trickles along my spine. I was wrong. I *can't* do this.

Then the food arrives, and I don't have to. The conversation stalls as we chew and sip and I try not to look directly at him. Otherwise, I could very well become distracted by his death-to-my-resolve rays. Why does he have to rock the spaceship? Why can't things just stay the way they are? And why in the name of cheese and crackers does this upset me so much? Have I really waited forty-six years for my chance at love only to run screaming at the first hint of something real?

Breathe, Jolene. Just take a deep breath and chill. It's not like he's proposing. You're taking this way too seriously. So I push out my breeziest laugh, throw my hands in the air, and say, "Okay."

Trevor finishes his last bite of rice pilaf and licks his lips. Blast him to Jupiter, he did that to punish me. I don't know whether to punch him or kiss him. Though the notion of both merits consideration. As if he can read my thoughts, he grins. "Okay ... what?"

"Okay, let's see if ... you know ..." I wave my hand between us, clearly the international signal for "figuring out you and me and whatever that means."

He crosses his arms again. "I'm gonna need to hear you say it."

I can play his game. He should know by now not to mess with me. Folding my arms to mimic his move, I say, "I'm this close to changing my mind again."

"Well, we wouldn't want that." The secret smile he sends my way melts my bones, and I'm glad I'm sitting down. Tension stretches between us—an intense physical attraction radiates through the pit of my stomach. How was I able to fool myself into thinking I wasn't attracted to him for so long? Things have officially moved into dangerous territory between us. I take several deep breaths, trying to get the sudden wave of desire under control. Then the waitress arrives with our check. God bless her gift of perfect timing.

I'm aware of Trevor's hands as he gives the woman his credit card. And my mind drifts to his Jeep, sitting in a dark corner of the parking lot, with its warm leather seats and Norah Jones album on deck. It would be so good and so easy and so amazing to follow him out there and pick up where we left off a week ago.

Which would be the biggest mistake I could make right now. Since I drove separately and met him here, it's a mistake I can avoid. It's a mistake I *have* to avoid. I silently thank God for His grace and say, "So, do you want to get together tomorrow?"

He raises his eyebrows. "What about tonight?"

"I'm tired. I think we should call it."

"Really?"

"Yes."

"Are you sure?" His eyes twinkle all kinds of promises. *Lord, give me strength.*

"Trevor."

"Yeah, I know. As much as I want to … be alone with you, I know it's not the best idea. Okay, it's a great idea, but we need to take this slow."

"Exactly."

"One step at a time."

He takes my hand again, his thumb drawing lazy circles on mine, shaking my resolve. It's definitely time to leave. Not just leave but get away from him as fast as my un-athletic legs will carry me.

I pull away and stand up. "So, tomorrow then? How about a matinee?"

"I'll pick you up at one."

"Sounds great."

Then I dash for the door as if the hounds of hell were after me. This reminds me of the day Benita entered Cocoon House and optimistically declared she would run like Joseph if she ever saw Diego again. I chuckled at the time, feeling I would never have to physically escape temptation.

Yeah, now it's not so funny. But I do smile all the way to my car.

Chapter 16

Uli

Tomorrow is my birthday. Four-oh. Thirty-nine plus one. Ten years from fifty.

Nope. There's just no good way to say it. And no way to avoid it. The clock will strike midnight, and I will turn forty and still be as unmarried as the day I was born.

Unless I jab an ice pick through my eye.

Once again I find myself lying on my bed, staring at the red numbers on my alarm clock as they tick away my life. I dangle the ice pick possibility around in my mind for a few moments. If only I didn't have such a strong aversion to pain. Or such an intense desire to cling to whatever hope I have left. Hope has been my lifelong blessing … and curse. When I was thirteen, I was so desperately lonely, I actually thought about suicide. I'd run razors along my fingers and watch them bleed and think how easy it would be.

But I never could because I couldn't shake the feeling that someday—maybe tomorrow!—*he'd* come along. My soul mate. My Prince Charming. My best friend and the love of my life. He would ride into my heart and carry me away. From that day on, I would never be lonely again. So, if I could hang on a little longer, God would answer my prayer. At least, God as I understood Him to be: an invisible, benevolent Santa-Genie who longed to grant my every wish. I just had to believe.

While my dad was alive my family attended church fairly regularly. He passed away when I was only seven, though. After that, my spiritual growth was limited to sitting in a church pew on the occasional holiday or whenever Mom wanted to impress her latest meal ticket with her pseudo-piety. The rest of the time, she was more interested in instructing me on how to get a man than guiding me to a greater understanding of God.

Well, look where that got me: stuck in a relationship with someone who doesn't love me enough to make a commitment. Who's never carried me away, or anywhere else for that matter, not even metaphorically. Sometimes when I'm with Cole I feel as isolated as I would standing at the top of Pikes Peak on a dark night, after everything has been shut down and the only light comes from the stars above and the city below. Waiting for someone to rescue me.

Always waiting.

So here I am, about to turn forty without a ring, without a husband, without children. And no money. And—

Ugh. This is getting me nowhere. It is what it is. I need to accept it and move on.

I'm so not good at moving on. But I am good at recognizing when I have insomnia. So I take a sleep aid and push all the pessimism aside until morning. Who knows? Maybe I'll feel better once the sun comes up tomorrow. If such positivity worked for Little Orphan Annie, surely it can work for me.

And that's how I go from standing alone at the top of a mountain to singing myself to sleep.

◊◊◊

My birthday promises to be a typical November day in Colorado—sunny and cool, but the sun makes it warm enough to wear shorts and sandals, if you're so inclined. I am not, thank you very much, but more power to those who are.

I spend the day working, determined to finish editing the photos for at least one of my clients before the partying begins. We'll meet at the Macaroni Grill for dinner then head over to Catie's for cake and games. She hasn't been around much since the retreat, and I still haven't asked her how things went with Brian. It would be great if a new boyfriend was keeping her away. Well, I should know how it's going tonight.

And then there's Jolene, who's been out with Trevor almost every day for the past week. On the rare occasion she's been home, she's berated me for my "shameful behavior at the retreat." She's about as up in arms as I've ever seen her, and Jolene knows how to get up in arms over just about anything.

It's hard to explain what happened in Buena Vista. I was so frustrated. And hurt. And angry. I rarely let myself get angry. But the way they laughed like I was some colossal punch line ate at me like hyenas picking apart a carcass. The emotion had to go somewhere, so I released it in a torrent of sarcasm. In retrospect, I handled it about as well as I could have in that situation. So every time she brings it up, I say, "Let it go, Jolene," then stomp into my room and shut the door.

Anyway, back to tonight. We now have Catie and Brian and whatever they're up to plus Trevor and Jolene. Couples to the left of me. Couples to the right of me. Well, two couples but that's enough reason for Cole to go along as my date, whether he wants to or not.

After I get out of the shower, I call him to make sure he'll be on time. He won't like it—because it's "nagging"—but I don't care. I'm not going to be late to my own party.

He answers on the fourth ring. "What?"

"Are you ready?"

"Yeah. Just about."

"I don't want to be late tonight."

"I know." Did I actually hear him roll his eyes? Maybe the heavy sigh gave it away. "You only told me a million times."

"Cole, please. This is important to me."

"Hey, it's your birthday. And …" There's a pause, but is it because he's thinking about how much he loves me or because he just guzzled down half a bottle of beer? "I want you to have a great night, Uli."

"Really?"

"Sure, baby. I want you to be happy. And I want to make you happy."

It's the first time in months that I've remembered why I fell for him. He used to treat me like a princess. He would bring me Milky Way Midnight candy bars and diet Mountain Dews just because he knew they were my favorites. He gave me red roses on Valentine's Day. Sure, I've always preferred pink ones, but roses on the day of love always count for something.

So maybe it's a warped, Shrek-like view of how a princess should be treated, but at least he tried. Until I slept with him. Things have been different ever since. Like now, when he says he wants to make me happy then burps a good-bye and hangs up.

Just when I think my day can only get better, my mother calls to wish me a year of happiness. It's sweet, at first. But she really can't help herself. It takes her about five seconds to threaten me with a lifetime of barren loneliness if I don't find a man soon.

"Can we talk later, Mom?" I say. "I'm getting ready to go out."

"Well, that's good." She sounds disappointed.

"There will be single men, if that helps."

"Uli—"

Here we go.

"I know you don't like my … interference when it comes to your love life."

I grunt, and decide to wear dangly silver earrings instead of hoops with my knee-length, silver, white, and mauve sweater.

"But as someone who's been widowed once and divorced twice, I certainly know what I'm talking about."

"Mm-hmm."

There's silence and, for a second, I hope we might have been disconnected. No such luck.

"Uli," she says, "why do you fight me on this?"

"I'm not fighting you, Mom, I just have other things on my mind."

"Why is there always this wall between us?"

Wow, I so don't want to get into this tonight. I sigh. I can't help myself. Apparently, Mom not only heard my audible reaction but figured out exactly what it meant because she says,

"Fine, sweetheart. We'll talk about it another time."

"Thanks, Mom. And … I love you."

"I love you too."

By some miracle, I still managed to *not* tell her about Cole. I know it would make things easier between us. Except, in the end, it wouldn't. Instead of the constant you-need-a-man harassment, she would, no doubt, light into me with great enthusiasm, pushing me to seal the deal with Cole, marry, and start a family. A whole other kind of harassment.

Having a boyfriend would never be enough. Not telling my mom about him is the lesser evil.

To my surprise, Cole actually shows up on time, and we drive to the restaurant in his beat-up black truck, which smells like wood and metal and beer. Dinner ends up being about what you'd expect when a dozen or so singles eat pasta and don't drink. Besides my chicken parmesan, the highlight of the evening is when our waiter stands on a chair and belts out "Nessun Dorma"— which is now my favorite aria—to a roomful of captivated diners. The waiter looks like Antonio Banderas and sings like Andrea Bocelli, which makes the evening memorably sweet. And if Cole had remembered to hit play when I asked him to record the moment on my camera, it would have been something I could cherish for the rest of my life.

After dinner, those who consider 9:30 p.m. too late to stay out on a Saturday night head home while the rest of us caravan to Catie's house for dessert and games. She's festooned the living room with black streamers and balloons, which I don't appreciate, and made a devil's food cake layered with chocolate mousse and whipped cream, which I do.

I'm especially glad my single mom friend, Audrey,

was able to join us. Though she's quiet, she fits in with the group quite nicely. They sing "Happy Birthday" to me as I blow out the candles. Then we heap cake onto black paper plates and find a place to sit in the living room. Trevor and Jolene are together but not. They seem awkward and uncertain, sitting next to each other yet not looking at each other, like they're on their first date. I'll have to ask Jolene about that later.

Catie and Brian seem just as tense and, as far as I can tell, haven't said two words to each other all night. I feel sadness radiating off of Catie, but I don't know if it's because of her job situation or Brian. Probably both.

And that's the gist of the evening—silent intrigues covered by laughter and a few rounds of Apples to Apples. Tess seems more effervescent than usual, giggling at everyone's jokes and making a few of her own.

Near the end of the game, it's Tess's turn. She flips over a card, revealing her word, "lovable."

She reads aloud: "Adorable, enchanting."

Then, a strange thing happens. Brian clears his throat and laughs, but it's self-conscious, short, and doesn't make any sense. Except, apparently, to Tess, who glances up into his eyes and flushes cherry red from neck to forehead before looking away. The moment tells me everything I need to know.

As Tess blushes like a new bride, Catie's face blanches white, and the party is over. Tension troubles the room, and those who feel it but don't get it suddenly respond to an urgent need to go home. We shoo everyone out the door, including Cole, who doesn't seem to mind as much as I wish he did when I tell him I'll ride home with Jolene. But then, he's always been practical.

Catie shuts the door and leans her forehead against it. Only the four Accountability Monday girls are left, yet it feels like three against one as we all turn to look at Tess. Her eyes shimmer, and she takes a step toward Catie. For a moment, we just stand there in the entryway, each of us silently realizing this is going to hurt.

Jolene finally breaks the quiet. "What's going on here?"

She directs the question to Catie, whose face has hardened to white ice. At first, I don't think she'll respond. Then, in a voice hoarse with pain, she says, "Ask Tess."

Tess seems to slump into herself as Jolene lays a hand on her shoulder. "It's all right. Just spill it."

I can't take it anymore. "You're dating Brian. Aren't you." I already know the answer. We all do.

With a nod, Tess looks at Catie for the first time. "I'm sorry. I should have said something."

Catie shrugs. "Why? You don't owe me—or any of us—an explanation. You're free to date anyone you want." She says the words flippantly, but her voice cracks, just a little.

Jolene's the only one who's surprised. "How long has this been going on?"

"He asked me out after the hike."

"Wait. What hike?" Glancing at Catie, the truth dawns on Jolene's face. "You mean the hike we went on after church that Sunday? The first day we met him?"

Tess nods again. Catie groans and marches into the living room. Luna, apparently sensing her owner's distress, scampers down the stairs from the bedroom and trails close at Catie's heels. We all follow the two of them.

"I'm so sorry, Catie. I know I never should have kept this a secret." Tess lifts a hand toward our friend, then drops it. "It's just I ... I didn't think anything would come of it. I wasn't interested, at first. And I knew you were—"

"But you went out with him anyway."

"Yes. I don't know how it happened. But the more time I spent with Brian, the more ... right it felt. You know?"

Catie looks Tess square in the eyes. "Yes, I do know."

Tess goes pale, her mouth hanging open like a dead mackerel. So Jolene, ever the negotiator, steps in. "Tess, you should have said something from the very beginning. Or at least brought it up at our last Accountability Monday. You knew what Catie was feeling and, whether you thought what you had with Brian would last or not, you should have told her. Can you see how this hurt her more than your silence?"

The regret Tess feels drops tears that streak down her cheeks. Everyone will forgive her—even Catie, I imagine—before she forgives herself.

Catie says, "What I don't understand is everything that happened the weekend of the retreat. Why did Brian ride up with me and spend so much time with me? Did you give him *permission* to test the waters or something?"

"No, of course not." Tess gulps. "We ... I ... I told him I didn't think things would work out because of the age difference and he should ... consider other possibilities."

"So, for the brief moment you didn't want him, you thought he should give old Catie a shot?"

"It wasn't like that."

Catie stops her with a look. "When did you decide to take him back? Right after the retreat?" Her eyes widen as realization dawns. "No, it was when we went four-wheeling. When you and Brian ditched me in the woods. Did you really fall down or was that all part of the scheme?"

Tess gasps. "That's not fair, Catie! I didn't mean for any of this to happen."

It's time to step in before it gets too confrontational. "Of course you didn't do it on purpose, Tess," I say. "You're hardly the first woman to make a massive mistake where a man is concerned." *You're just not very good at hiding it.*

Jolene puts an arm around Catie and says, "I know this is hard."

"I'm fine."

"You're not fine, Catie. But you will be. Isn't it better to find out now instead of later, after you'd really fallen for him?"

The expression on Catie's face tells me she had already fallen pretty hard, but Jolene doesn't see it. A second later the look is gone, masked over with a half-hearted smile.

"You're right," she says. "I barely knew him. And we never went on a date. Not an official one, anyway."

I want her to stop being so resigned and share her heart with us. Clearly, she's hurting so why does she hide it? It's not like I expect her to play the heartbroken heroine of a Jane Austen story, throwing her hand across her face and weeping into her satin-draped sleeve. For goodness sake, though, can't she show some emotion? But Catie is far too practical for sentiment.

And I'm too sentimental to be practical. We're like the sisters in Jane's *Sense and Sensibility*. Me, the girl who wears her heart perched on her shoulder like a loud-mouthed cockatoo, and Catie, who hides her feelings behind a brick wall.

Still, not one of us likes this situation. We finally get a new, mid-forties GWP in our group and who does he want? The girl who claims she has no interest in ever getting married. The cute, young "white whale." Though I certainly hadn't fallen for Brian myself, this new reality hits me hard. Good men are hard to come by. Especially if they know they have a chance with someone who's out of their league. And Tess is definitely out of Brian's league. So is Catie for that matter. Not that it makes a pinch of difference now.

Still, I ask Tess, "Is it serious?"

"Well, it's too soon—"

"Has he kissed you yet?"

"Uli!" That comes from Jolene, who still turns to Tess as if hoping for an answer.

Tess blushes again. Which I interpret as yes, she's been kissed, and she's been kissed good.

Catie makes a sound like air coming out of a tire. "Tess, can you leave?"

Looking as deflated as said tire, Tess says, "Catie, if you'd just let me explain—"

"Please, Tess. I promise I'll meet with you at some point and we can talk it out and you can tell me everything. But this is not that time. I really need you to leave. Please."

Tess nods once more, grabs her purse and coat, and dashes out the door. As soon as she's gone, Catie crumples onto the couch. Jolene and I sit on either side of her.

Curiosity gets the best of me. "How bad is it? I mean, we knew you liked him but ..."

"I did like him. And I thought he liked me. How could I have been so stupid?" She still isn't crying, but her voice is hoarse, like she's getting over a cold.

"You weren't stupid," Jolene says. "You had every reason to hope."

Catie stands and starts gathering up plates and forks and napkins from dessert.

Oh yeah. It's my birthday.

"No, I didn't have any reason to hope." Clutching the trash like a lifeline, Catie stares at us. Actually, it's more like she stares *through* us. "All I had to do was look at my past, and I would have known it was all too good to be true. But I wanted to believe anyway."

I say, "There's nothing wrong with that," and plan to say more but she stops me with a look.

"There *is* something wrong with it, Uli. All of it. I need to let go of this ridiculous dream. It's just one heartbreak after another." She trudges into the kitchen and throws the remnants of my party away. Jolene and I follow. When Catie turns back to us, something in her eyes reminds me of a rabid dog. Maybe that's why Luna stayed in the living room.

"Do you know I have never *not* had a broken heart? It's been broken so many times it can't be much bigger than this by now." Catie holds up her thumb and index finger barely half an inch apart. "So what's the use? I'll just … I'll be happier once I accept the fact that God doesn't have marriage in mind for me. And I want to be happy. For once in my life, I want to be happy. And that kind of contentment can only come from God. Right?"

Well, that's what they say. But I can't tell her that, so I give her a half-nod and a quarter-smile. Pretty pathetic, I know. At least I'm trying.

Jolene, however, will not be so easily pacified. "Of course pure contentment can only come from God. We've always said that." She pauses and folds her arms under her chest, like she always does when she's about to make a point. "But that's not what's going on here, is it?"

"What do you mean?" Catie crosses her arms too. I feel like I'm in the middle of a Mexican standoff.

"This isn't about you choosing God. You're giving up on men and falling back on God as a last resort."

Catie stares her down for a second—a contest she should know she can't win. "I need coffee. Anyone else want some?"

Jolene and I both say no then watch as Catie pulls a canister of what looks like pretty expensive coffee out of the pantry. She measures and pours. We wait and watch. Once the brew starts percolating, Catie turns back to us, leans against the counter and—what else?—crosses her arms. The standoff continues.

"To be honest, I think I would be justified to not choose God at the moment. What has He done for me, anyway?"

My jaw drops. Good Christian Catie throwing blame

at God? Any minute now the earth will reverse its orbit, and Luna will start flying around the room. In a cape.

Jolene shakes her head. "Is that what it comes down to? Your faith in God depends on Him giving you what you want?"

"No! No, of course it doesn't depend on that." She covers her eyes with her hands then rakes them through her hair. "But would it be so bad? Am I asking for anything wrong? A job, a husband, a home. Security. These are good things, and you would think the God who professes to love me would say, 'Yeah, Catie, I'd be happy to fill your life with good things.' But instead He strips it all away, one deep, jagged cut at a time."

Well, she certainly has a point. I'm as anxious to hear Jolene's response as Catie. Maybe more.

"It's not wrong to want good things," Jolene says, "but it *is* wrong to make your happiness dependent on those good things. You need to be able to picture a great, happy life without a husband. But you're so caught up in this dream, I don't think you can."

Catie snags a mug from the cupboard, pours coffee to the brim, and takes a long drink. She doesn't even blow on it. If I did something like that I wouldn't be able to taste anything for two days. It doesn't seem to bother her, though, because she gulps down about half of it before saying, "You know what's frustrating?"

She stares at us as if expecting an answer. Okay, so apparently it wasn't a rhetorical question. I shrug. Jolene says, "No, what?"

"What's frustrating," Catie continues, "is that I wasn't like this ten, even five years ago. But I feel like the constant disappointment has eaten away at my hope until all that's left is, well, this." She swallows the rest of the coffee and pours another cup.

Catie then heads to the dining table and sits down. We join her.

"I read a quote on Facebook last week. Supposedly by Orson Welles. He said, 'If you want a happy ending, that depends, of course, on where you stop your story.'"

This time, Catie sips the brew more slowly as she stares at the cherry wood surface of the table. "If you had ended my story, say, fifteen years ago, when I was still in my thirties, loved my job, and had so much hope I believed I could be happy living single if that's what God wanted, everyone would have said, 'Wow, she has such a strong faith!' Or if God had brought a man into my life then, even I would have said He answered my prayer because I had learned to be content and, as they say, had stopped looking."

Jolene reaches over and covers Catie's hand with her own but doesn't speak. So Catie keeps talking.

"As we all know, that's not what happened. Instead I've had ten more years of disappointment and regret. I feel like I'm further from hope than I've ever been, and I don't know how to get back to it. I don't even know if God cares."

"Of course He cares!" Jolene insists, because she can't imagine the alternative.

But I have to force myself not to nod in agreement with Catie. If God cares, He has a funny way of showing it.

Chapter 17
Catie

My alarm jolts me awake at 6:30 a.m. on Tuesday, much as it has every morning since I started junior high. Even when I'm sick. Even when I'm unemployed. Even when I don't care. I roll over and punch it off, then sit up.

Of course, you could go back to sleep. The realization taps me on the shoulder. I could stay in bed. What do I have to get up for?

The weekend turned into an even greater failure than it started out. I skipped church only to spend my Sunday evening trolling through late night adult cable shows. After months of pursuing pure thoughts, I let myself fall. Again. I watched things I shouldn't watch and thought things I shouldn't think. When I finally clicked the TV off, I was too ashamed to cry, too heartbroken to pray. Then I stumbled into the guilt of regret. I begged God for forgiveness while never really believing He would. How could He, when I can't forgive myself?

I can tell myself it's not my fault I'm still a virgin at forty-eight. That I'm not made of stone. That I'm a flesh-and-blood woman with legitimate desires, and God is asking too much. I could point out that when you're almost fifty, virginity is no longer romantic. It's just sad. But no excuse can take away my shame and remorse.

The Bible is right of course. We hide our sin under the cover of darkness, thinking our secrets are invisible to everyone, including God. If I truly want to conquer this, I need to get it out in the open. Not the wide open but I need to tell someone. My accountability girls?

Not Uli. Certainly not Tess. Maybe Jolene?

God, make me brave enough to be vulnerable to a friend.

Please help me.

Because no one talks about this, except maybe, sitcoms. But at church? Perhaps they think if we don't mention it, then it doesn't exist. Like obesity. I actually went to a series of messages for singles about sex. The speaker—a married man who must have gotten his ideas about single sexuality from Grace Livingston Hill books—at one point recommended knitting as a substitute for sex. Like two knitting needles and a ball of yarn are all we need to fill that empty place inside us. But when I looked around the room, it seemed I was the only one who thought the idea was ludicrous. It wouldn't surprise me to learn most of them were sleeping around anyway.

What would that married man do if he went home and his wife said, "Not tonight, dear, I'm knitting"? I don't imagine he'd think it was such a great idea then. But I don't have to fix some random guy who doesn't have a clue what singles go through. I have to fix myself.

And I'm failing to a stupendous degree.

So, no, I'm not doing such a great job handling this Brian and Tess nightmare. If I'm not careful, I'll end up lying on the floor for weeks on end, listening to Sarah McLachlan CDs. *Motivation, Catie. It's what keeps you going.* I finally push myself out of bed and slide into pale-yellow slippers that are depressingly similar to the ones my Grandma—known to all her grandkids as Nanna—used to wear. Practical. Boring. Single.

Except Nanna wasn't single.

I shuffle to the kitchen. Start a pot of coffee. Feed Luna. Who noses her food onto the tile floor before eating it, and occasionally glances up at me with sad eyes. As I wait for the coffee to save me, I stare down at my feet and notice how "winter-y" my toes already look. Once, I told Jolene I didn't see the point in getting a pedicure during the colder months. I said,

"Who's going to see my feet when I'm wearing boots and close-toed shoes?"

Jolene shook her head at me like she was about to take me to school. "It's that kind of attitude that keeps you single."

Now, as I ponder my bare, dry toes peeking out from my decidedly unsexy slip-on slippers, I wonder if she was right. Can men tell when a woman has given up? I always try to look nice, but did Brian suspect I was holding back, afraid to show him how much I want a man in my life?

Maybe he just wasn't interested. Maybe he knew he could do better. *And maybe he did.*

The familiar voice drags at my heart like so many of my past disappointments. But this one's different. Brian was different. He made me feel young and funny and feminine. And desirable. He touched me, physically and emotionally, and I loved it. I even thought about what our life together might be like—something I never do. And all of it was nothing more than a figment of my sad, lonely imagination. *So are all of my feelings off? Can I ever trust my emotions again?* Even if I could, I don't think I will. I won't let myself go through this again.

It was all a dream. And, eventually, people wake up

from dreams.

I step outside and pick up the Colorado Springs Gazette from its spot on my front porch. Back inside, I toast an English muffin, spread it with apple butter, pour a mug of coffee, and sit down to read the Help Wanted section. Anything to get my mind off Brian.

Two hours, four cups of coffee, a half-dozen circled job leads, and several online applications later, the phone rings. Tess's name lights up the screen. Perfect.

"Tess, this isn't a good—"

She interrupts. "Catie, um. I'm calling with some sad news."

More sad than the past two weeks? "What's going on?"

"It's Ellen," she says, and straight-up grief cracks through her voice. "She ... passed away."

It takes me a moment. "Wait. Ellen who?" Silence, then it sinks in. "Not ... not Ellen Baker, from our group."

"Yes. Oh, Catie, it's so awful. They think she's been ... gone since Friday morning."

"What ... How could ... What happened?"

"They said she had a heart attack. Died in her sleep. Her co-workers got worried when she didn't show up for two days without calling and ..."

"And ..." It hits me like being slammed by an iceberg. "She was dead all weekend, and we didn't notice she wasn't around. Not even when she didn't come to Uli's birthday party."

Though Uli often dismissed her, Ellen doted on our blonde friend and had probably been looking forward to her birthday party for weeks. In fact, if we went through

Ellen's apartment, we'd probably find the cheerfully wrapped gift she'd picked out so carefully. I swallow back the tears.

What do I say to something like this? It makes the boo-hoo-iness of the last few days seem so minor. At least for the moment. But I don't have to talk because Tess says, "I'll send out a church e-mail with details about the visitation and funeral."

"Okay."

I hear her sniff again. "Well, I have to call some more people."

"All right. Thanks for letting me know, Tess."

Before I have a chance to click off the phone, a male voice says, "So, how did she—" and the call ends.

Brian.

He's there. With her. Right now. Holding her hand and comforting her. Grief hits me from all sides. For what seems like the millionth time since I got laid off, tears stumble down my cheeks. Tears for the job I no longer have and the man I thought I could.

And tears for Ellen. A lonely, kind woman just a few years older than me with hair that grayed too early and a life that ended too soon. A woman who didn't deserve to lie dead in her bed, alone and forgotten, for four days.

How long would it take for someone to realize I was missing? As of last month, I no longer have co-workers who'll hunt me down if I don't show up. My dad and my brother and his family live in another state, and we rarely talk. How many church services could I skip before someone noticed?

But I do have friends. Good friends. Surely Jolene

or Uli or even Tess would start to worry if they didn't hear from me for a day. Or two. Three?

Maybe I should get a roommate. Or at least teach Luna how to run for help. I glance down at my dog, sitting at my feet. She would care. At least I'm not completely alone.

Several decades of Sunday school lessons and long-winded sermons reminds me God is always with me, so I'm never *technically* on my own. Which, at the moment, feels like someone sticking a SpongeBob Squarepants bandage on a six-inch gash down my thigh. Ellen wasn't technically alone, and look what happened to her.

Wiping my face dry, I check the clock on my microwave. Wow. I've been brooding for over an hour. I should seriously consider getting something done, like job hunting or updating my résumé or at least fixing something for lunch.

Instead, I whistle to Luna, and we trudge into the living room and settle on the couch for a nice, long, late-morning nap. Sleep will give me a better perspective.

Somehow, despite extreme efforts to avoid it, I end up sitting two rows behind Brian and Tess at Ellen's memorial service on Friday. They are definitely a couple—he has his arm around her and, occasionally, she rests her head on his shoulder. How can I focus on what Pastor Owens says if all I can see is love blossoming in front of me?

I can't do it. With a silent apology to Ellen, I sneak out during the closing prayer. I made it through the service. So I miss the memorial luncheon. No one will notice if I'm not there. I just want to get in my car and drive somewhere. Anywhere. But I don't even make it to the front door before I'm ambushed by Jolene.

She stomps up to me in all-out intervention mode. "And where do you think you're going?"

"Home." I push through the door, shoving my arms into my dark-gray parka as a brisk November wind slams into me and vacuums my breath away.

"Okay, just wait a second." She grabs my arm. "I know this is hard, but it's not about you. We're here for Ellen."

"I realize that, and I can grieve for her at home just as well as I can here. Maybe even better because I won't be distracted."

"All right." Jolene lets go of my arm. Her pointed gaze tells me it's anything but all right. "I still think you should stay." She gestures toward the sanctuary. "The reality of Tess and Brian isn't going away. You might as well get used to the idea."

I bite my lip to keep from laughing. "Oh, come on. You don't really think they're going to last, do you?"

"Why not?"

"Well, first of all, we have Tess, who's always said she's not interested in marriage because she wants to serve on the mission field. And Brian? You don't honestly think she could fall in love with him."

"Didn't you?"

I stamp my feet. The chill slices through the parka and straight into my heart. "No, of course not. I liked him. But … I hardly knew him."

"And yet you're leaving Ellen's funeral because of

him."

How is she not cold? Must be the heat of being right all the time. I stare past the rows of cars in the parking lot toward Pikes Peak in the distance. Snow covers the top of the mountain and shimmers down the side, promising chilly weather ahead. Meteorologists say we can expect a bitterly cold winter.

They have no idea.

"What do I do, Jolene? Give up? Am I just meant to be alone? And if so, why can't I get over this?"

Jolene puts an arm around me and steers me into the relative warmth of the entryway near the church's fellowship hall. Then she puts one hand on each shoulder and looks me square in the face. "It's okay to be sad. You're grieving what you've lost. God understands that."

Her words steal my breath like another gust of wind. Is that what this is? Grief? Not just because of Ellen's death and my lost job but because of the husband and children I'll never have?

Recorded worship music bursts from the hall as Trevor pushes through the door. The expression on his face when he sees Jolene—and hers as she gazes back at him—tells me Jolene's time of mourning her singleness is past. As long as she doesn't do anything stupid. He steps up to us and asks if anything is wrong.

"A lot, actually," I say. "But nothing we can't work through."

I don't suppose he has a clue what that means because he simply nods.

Jolene glances toward the door he just walked through. "What are they doing in there?"

"Standing in line for chicken casseroles and orange fluff. And the family asked everyone to write down a favorite memory of Ellen in a notebook."

"Oh, that's a good idea." Jolene raises an eyebrow at me. "So, are you staying?"

"All right. But, can we sit … somewhere else?" Where I can't see Tess. At all.

Jolene says, "We'll follow you."

And they do. We find a spot on the far side of the room where I choose a chair with its back to Tess and Brian's location. For a little over an hour, I mourn a woman I never took the time to know and push all thoughts of my broken heart aside. Soon I'll be alone again and have plenty of time to coddle it.

But Jolene is right. This day isn't about me or Brian or Tess.

As I drive home it occurs to me this might be a good time to get away for a while. And though my relationship with my dad has been strained for years—and that's being generous—I feel a sudden urge to be near family.

I dial the number before I even get home. Dad doesn't know I lost my job, and this isn't the time to tell him. So all I say is I have some time off and wonder if I could come out early for Thanksgiving. I haven't celebrated a holiday with him in a decade, so he's surprised but says, "You know you're always welcome, Caitlyn girl," with what's left of the Irish lilt I love so much.

I spend the weekend shutting up my house and loading the SUV. Though it's a good twenty hours on the road from Colorado to Ohio, driving makes the most sense. I can stay as long as I want, pack as much as I want, and, most importantly, take Luna with me. She's a great travel dog and makes me feel safer.

Monday night, I meet my accountability girls—minus Tess—at Applebee's for the first time since the retreat. The reality of Ellen's death still hangs like a storm cloud over our evening. We each order a salad, and I tell them about my trip.

Jolene says, "When are you leaving?" at the same time Uli asks how long I'll be away.

"First thing tomorrow morning," I say, then shrug. "And I don't know when I'll get back. Probably not until after the holidays. Guess I'll see how things go."

So they tell me they'll miss me and wish me well. Then we spend some time in prayer. But I just want to be on the road already. I hug them good-bye and hurry home.

By seven the next morning, I'm on Highway 24, making my way toward Limon and Interstate 70. I blast Nichole Nordeman's song *Brave* through my iPod and concentrate on what I'm driving toward, not what I'm leaving behind. All I need is a little time.

Before I left the restaurant last night, I asked Jolene if she thought I was doing the right thing or if I was taking the coward's way out and running away. She said,

"There's nothing wrong with being open to new possibilities, Catie." The look in her eyes seemed almost jealous when she added, "We don't know what God has in store for you, but I hope you choose to believe you can have a different life."

A different life. Not necessarily a better one, but something new. Still, is *better* outside the realm of possibility? The words of Nichole's song weave determination through me. I like the idea of waving so long to what was as I courageously anticipate what's ahead. To even consider I might be traveling on the road God has intended for me all along gives me hope. If that's the case, then none of what's happened in my life has been the result of bad luck or because God just didn't care. If I keep moving forward, isn't it possible I will eventually know the purpose behind it all?

I really do want to be brave enough to believe I can have a happier life. One where I find so much joy in my relationship with Christ that everything else looks like dust in my rearview mirror. Where I can leave all the hurt and disappointment and unmet expectations behind me. I might not be there yet, but at least I believe there's potential. And that makes me want to be brave.

By mid-morning, I hit Kansas. The flat, over four-hundred-mile stretch of farmland reminds me what else I've left behind: my beloved mountains.

Just keep moving forward, Catie. Don't look back.

I only stop for gas, food, bathroom breaks, and to catch a few hours of sleep at a Super 8 about an hour west of St. Louis. The uneventfulness of the trip gives me plenty of time to think about choices, regrets, and hopes. I thought I had job security. I was wrong. I thought Brian was falling in love with me as I was with him. So wrong. On day two I cry almost all the way across Illinois.

Maybe it's time to stop thinking and start praying. It's worth a shot. I can't go on like I have. As I journey through Indiana, I embrace the opportunity to spend uninterrupted time with God. A voice keeps trying to interrupt, telling me I'm talking to myself, but I don't care. Things aren't always what they seem.

An hour after sunset on Wednesday, I make my way down the long driveway leading to the three-hundred-and-fifty-acre farm that's been in my family since Angus Delaney came to America during the Irish potato famine in the mid-1800s. Well, first he had to survive New York City, but through hard work and dedication, he saved enough to set up our homestead in Ohio.

"It's a legacy of which to be proud, macushla," Nanna used to say. She called all of her grandkids "macushla," an Irish term of endearment. Dad once told me it was easier for her than remembering our names.

My father, Collin, however, spent most of his childhood in Ireland, raised there by a part of the family clan that hadn't made the journey to America. But when Dad was thirteen, his uncle, Angus Delaney the third, died without an heir. So, my grandfather moved his wife, two sons, and three daughters to America to take over. And that's how acres of rolling farmland in the hills near Russells Point, Ohio, came to be part of my family heritage.

How I came to turn my back on that heritage is another story.

The six-bedroom, brick house at the crest of the hillside represents our family success better than just about anything, as does the substantial red barn nearby. My older brother, James, tore down the original farmhouse to build the five-thousand-square-foot home fifteen years ago. It's surrounded on three sides by corn and bean fields, and boasts a large stocked pond and a wooded area that three generations of children have spent hours upon hours exploring.

I pull up next to the three-car garage and let Luna out to roam the countryside. She's in her element when she can live outside, and I will probably not see her much while we're here. As I start to unload my bags, the garage door opens and my dad shuffles out. He's aged so much since the last time I saw him, I stumble a bit, tamping down my emotions with a smile.

"Hi, Dad."

He reaches out and pulls me into a hug that stretches way past what I consider comfortable. I still feel the wall between us, the wall I built after Mom died twenty-five years ago and Dad pushed me away. The one fortified by years of hurtful comments. Like when he said no man would ever want a girl as independent and stubborn as me. Or the first time I cut my hair short and he said I looked like one of Peter Pan's lost boys. It's true what they say—it's easier to remember the bad stuff.

Maybe now's the time to move past all that. I need to be close to my family. To not feel so isolated. I hug him back and manage to choke out, "I've missed you too."

Finally, he steps away. "How long are you planning to stay?"

"Well, I thought … maybe through New Year's. If that's okay."

"You stay as long as you want, Catie girl. We fixed up the blue room just for you." He turns toward the house. "James! Patrick! Come say hello to Catie and help her carry her things to her room."

And that's when the whole household descends on me. My older brother, James, and his son, Patrick, exit first. They're followed by my sister-in-law, Delia; their nineteen-year-old daughter, Angela; and Patrick's wife, Tawny, holding their toddler son, Will. Last but not least, Patrick's and Tawny's girls—Bella, five, and Bryn, four—skip down the steps.

"Wow," I say. "I wasn't expecting to see everyone."

Delia hugs me next. "Are you kidding? We love a good excuse to have the kids over for dinner."

I first met Delia when she and James started dating in high school. She would sit on the couch, gazing dreamily into my brother's eyes. If she even knew I existed back then, I'd be surprised. But, well, she was in love. And I was jealous to see my older brother in a serious relationship. Long story short, Delia and I never had a chance to get close.

Angela, whom we used to call Pookie, is like the little sister I never had. She sighs and wraps her arms around me. "It's about time you came for a visit, Aunt Catie. I was starting to think you didn't like me anymore."

I tickle her and say, "Don't be silly, Pookie. You're my favorite niece."

"No one calls me that anymore." She laughs. "But I guess you can."

"Gee, thanks."

"And I'm your only niece."

"Well, you'd still be my favorite if I had a hundred of them." I muss her thick, auburn hair, regretting the time we've missed. Sure, we've stayed connected through Facebook over the years, but that's a poor substitute for face-to-face interaction.

Everyone grabs a suitcase or bag, and we haul it all

inside. The door opens to the rich aroma of pot roast and fresh-baked bread. If anyone can put together a memorable meal, it's Delia. I'll definitely have to go for daily runs to keep the pounds off.

My family wraps around me, pulling me into their circle as if I'd never been gone. Could it really be this simple? We gather around the huge dining table my grandfather bought at a library auction in the 1960s. Delia passes steaming platters loaded with roast, potatoes, turnips, cabbage, and carrots. I'm almost overwhelmed by the noise of ten people sharing a meal. Add to that the racket coming from their three dogs—who've been joined by Luna—and the atmosphere couldn't be more different than my typical meals-for-one in front of the TV.

As I'm lifting a forkful of beef and potatoes to my mouth, Dad says, "So, Caitlyn, what aren't you telling us?"

I clear my throat. "What do you mean?"

"Don't think me daft, girl. Your job has kept you away from us for years because you couldn't possibly leave. Now you have all the free time in the world. So spill it, darlin'."

Everyone looks at me, except the kids, who are far more interested in finding ways *not* to eat their vegetables. "All right," I say. "I was laid off. There's not much more to it than that."

"Hmm." My dad is tough, rough around the edges, and as gentle as a down pillow. He worries about everything that's happening—or not happening—to his family. He once told me he took on all the worry of two parents after Mom died. So I say,

"I'll be fine, Dad. I'm sure I'll find another job in no time."

"Of course you will. But if you need anything—"

"I know."

"And you are always welcome to move back here."

I am? I don't say it but my face must have because he adds, "This will always be your home."

And a burden lifts off my shoulders.

After dinner, I help clean up our mess. Then I join Bella, Bryn, and Will at the table while they take crayons to pictures of Thanksgiving turkeys, which they plan to enter in a coloring contest in a local newspaper. The kids don't warm up to me right away but still seem happy to have me around. Their sweet faces tug at my heart, as does the warmth of the fire in the fireplace and the banter of the men as they watch a basketball game on TV.

I didn't expect this. Shouldn't I feel awkward and uncomfortable?

But I don't, which begs the question: Why did I stay away so long?

Chapter 18

Jolene

"We're ready."

Sara grins with satisfaction, hands on hips as she surveys what weeks of hard work have accomplished. I nod. She's right. I can't believe it, but we're good to go. Our first Grr-1 Stuff Saturday. The yard in front of Cocoon House looks like the best garage sale ever, and I couldn't be prouder of my girls. This is going to be a good day. Even the weather cooperated—not too cold for November and a cloudless sky so the sun could keep us warm.

If all goes the way I anticipate it will, we're going to make some serious money. In my head, I already have a list of things we've needed for I don't know how long. New bedding and curtains, dishes, pots and pans, maybe even a big-screen TV for movie nights.

I started advertising our funky furniture over three weeks ago, and the word is getting around. Several people have called, asking for more information. Someday soon, if we do this right, I predict people will line up early, anxious to get the first crack at great items.

Nothing wrong with dreaming big, right?

For the past month, Sara, Benita, and Jillie stripped wood, padded and upholstered chairs, and painted everything from old frames to broken-down crates. And now, to show for it, we have a yard full of unique items that I just know people will fight over. Which means it's only a matter of time until everyone in Colorado Springs will be showing off their Grr-l Stuff.

Hmm. That doesn't sound right. I pat Sara on the shoulder, and chuckle to myself as I stroll back inside to grab an armful of pillows and throws. Hopefully, the addition of homey, comfortable things will appeal to the buyers as they picture an item in their living room or bedroom or on their patio.

Sara has definitely taken charge. She's practically glowing, having found her element. It's been a long journey for the former prostitute, but she can finally see herself living a new life. A better one. And two months ago, when she gave her life to Christ, I cried for an hour.

That's why I do this.

I rejoin Sara on the sidewalk as we peruse our store. "I set things up according to the room they go in," she says. "And I tried to show how different pieces could go together."

"It all looks great." So great, in fact, that I'm tempted to buy a few things myself. But I won't, unless it's left over at the end of the day.

A horn beeps as Trevor drives up and parks across the street. He offered to help with sales and moving furniture, and I'm sure not going to say no to that. Maybe I should have. As he slides out of his car and walks toward me wearing a slick, Army-green muscle shirt, I bite my lip. Is it a mistake for me to bring such a fine-looking fella near my girls? Then he smiles. Trevor is a good man: strong, committed, godly. He's just the kind of guy these women need to be around.

And when they see how he cares for me, they'll see how they should expect a man to treat them. Since the girls are not allowed to date while at Cocoon House—at all—I don't want to flaunt my relationship. But I do want them to see what can be possible. I prepared Trevor last night by telling him what was okay with the residents and what wasn't. He'll be fine.

I believe in Trevor. And I trust him, which scares me almost as much as admitting I'm falling for him. Falling. That's all I can own up to for now. Not falling *in* anything. Just in the process of plunging. But certainly not in love. I haven't lost my mind. Yet.

Which means I can smile at Trevor like any other day as he says, "Good morning," and hands me a chai tea. The steaming liquid warms away the November chill.

He glances around our yard, clearly impressed. "Looks great. How can I help?"

"We have a few bigger items we still need to bring out. I could definitely use your muscle on that."

His eyes shine with warmth and just a little bit of heat. Memories of the particularly satisfying kiss we shared last night shiver through me. This is certainly not the time for that, so I push past him and try not to float into the house. *Boundaries, Jolene. There's plenty of time for daydreaming later.*

And then I remember I don't have to daydream because he's my boyfriend. My boyfriend. *My boyfriend.* The words echo in my head like music. It feels that good.

The sale officially starts at 8:00 a.m. At first, a few customers trickle in, and we sell some smaller items. As the day goes on, though, they just keep coming. Several arrive in pickups looking for specific pieces, which tells me people are talking about it. We make some good deals, too. Jillie shows a particular knack for negotiating.

The girls are enjoying themselves, wheeling and dealing and interacting with the community. Even the residents who chose not to participate seem to like watching the fun.

Uli shows up around noon wearing a cute purple skirt and flowery, lavender blouse. Definitely not work clothes. Not that I expected much anyway. She had offered to help—I'm still not sure why—and I'd asked her to come by early, before nine, if possible. Well, considering her late nights and tendency to sleep in, I suppose this is morning to her. She's just in time for lunch.

We set out three folding tables, paper plates, and napkins to enjoy the pizzas and cans of soda a nearby Little Caesars provided. Over the years, I've been able to develop relationships with several local businesses. It's an ongoing marketing job on top of everything else I do. In exchange for today's lunch, for instance, we've been handing out coupons to our customers for a one-day-only pizza special.

Grabbing a slice, Uli slides onto a seat at the same table as Trevor and me. She takes a bite of cheese and pepperoni and says, "How's the sale going?"

"Great. Better than I had hoped."

"Well, if you don't sell that frosty blue coffee table with the tray, let me know. I love that."

I laugh. "Yeah, it's one of my favorites too, so get in line."

She smiles back at me. "I suppose I can't afford it anyway."

"Probably not. Sara wants three-fifty for it."

"Three hundred and fifty dollars?" Uli glances

around at the rest of the crew. "Is that the kind of money you're making?"

"Well, everything's negotiable, but people love creative, one-of-a-kind pieces. Sara and the girls did an amazing job."

"I'm impressed. I wonder if I could do stuff like this."

Poor Uli. So full of optimism. So bad at following through.

Still, I say, "I don't see why not." I reach to take a second slice of pizza but a voice behind me asks, "Could someone tell me about this table?"

And it's back to work.

As I predicted, the venture is a success. We pull in over three-thousand dollars on our first day, selling nearly everything we set out. As we move the few leftover items back into the storage shed behind the house, my residents are as excited as I am. We get everything put away quickly, thanks to Trevor's strong arms. Even Uli pitches in before racing off to run errands. With the work almost done, all I have to do is make sure the girls are settled in for the evening with our weekend staff. Then I have a date. With my boyfriend and his strong arms.

Deep breath.

We walk back toward the front of the house, Sara describing her new ideas for some old furniture that had recently been donated. But as we round the front porch, a 1970s-era Lincoln tears down the street and rolls into our driveway. Benita gasps, and when I look her way, it seems as if all the blood has drained out of her.

"Girls, get inside." Whatever this is, it's not good,

and I'm glad Trevor has taken a stand next to me.

The women hurry up the porch steps and into the house as a short but stocky Hispanic man exits the car.

"Benita!" He strides toward the house, walking past me as if I'm invisible. "Benita, I know you're in there!"

I step in front of him and, as calmly as possible, say, "Can I help you?"

He stops, looking at me as if he wishes he had a gun in his hand and could use it. But if I let myself be afraid or intimidated by angry ex-boyfriends who are also ex-cons, I'd need to be in a different line of work.

"Who are you?" he asks, his voice raspy from years of smoking. Surprisingly, though, his face has a childlike quality—bright eyes and smooth skin that belie years of substance abuse and cruelty. He's like Dorian Gray, offering his soul in exchange for a youthful appearance. But I know what he really is.

"I'm Jolene Woods. I run this place."

"Oh yeah? Well, run inside and get Benita." He then spits out the derogatory term men like him use for just about every woman they meet. Spiteful, predictable, and dangerous. Someday, I will probably have to call the police on this one.

Lord, give me strength.

"No."

He growls. "Does Benita Jensen live here or doesn't she?"

"I'm not at liberty to give you information about any of the people living in this home."

"Is that right?"

"We'd like you to leave now."

Trevor takes a step closer and, in a voice that

doesn't sound even remotely civil, says, "Please."

The man—who I'm certain is Benita's former abuser, Diego—sizes Trevor up then shrugs. "Okay, I'll leave. But tell that—" and there's that word again—"I'll be back. She knows why."

And I realize there's more going on here than a jealous ex-boyfriend. I look toward the house and see Benita peering out the front window, her eyes wide with fear.

Apparently, we have more to talk about than I thought.

◊◊◊

I can't stop staring at Trevor. He's completely distracting me from the movie he plunked down over twenty bucks to see. The way he let me be in charge of the confrontation with Diego, yet made it clear he would protect me if he had to, has bathed him in a whole new light. He was fabulous before; now he's a superhero masquerading as my best friend and the man I'm dating. Clark Kent took off his glasses for a split second. I'm intrigued and infatuated and in so much trouble.

How long could this possibly last? How long before he realizes he can do better? Should I enjoy it while I can or run for the hills before losing him will hurt too much?

Like it wouldn't break my heart to lose him now.

I turn my attention back to the movie screen, having a devil of a time paying attention to the latest James Bond movie. Especially since the way Trevor's holding my hand doesn't allow me to think about much else. His fingers intertwine with mine but don't stop moving, like he wants to memorize every bit of that part of me. I'm glad I coated myself in hand lotion before I left Cocoon House. The dry Colorado air delights in drawing every bit of moisture out of my skin. It's a constant battle, but Trevor doesn't know that tonight.

The next time I glance at him, he turns to me, his eyes deepen to the color of dark, brown leather, letting me know he's not paying attention to the movie either. Well, it is James Bond. He'll fight the bad guys, drink martinis, and seduce women. And, in the end, he'll save the world from an evil mastermind. Are we really missing anything? The dark room surrounds us with privacy, even though it is full of people who actually do want to watch the film. As he leans toward me, I slide my arms around his neck, and our lips meet in a delicious kiss. I smile inside, glad we chose to sit in the back row.

It's been far too long since I made out in a movie theater.

The years fade away and, suddenly, I'm a teenager again. Trevor certainly has a knack for making me feel young. All of a sudden the final credits are rolling, and I realize I just spent the better part of an hour kissing my boyfriend. I can't get enough of him. The way his hands frame my face before plunging into my hair. His breath, sweet from the Twizzlers he ate before the movie, mingles with mine. Every move he makes is unexpected but so right.

We drive to my place in silence, sighing and smiling instead of talking. A Sade song slides off of the jazz station I tuned the radio to and massages the air around us like a caress. I keep telling myself not to get caught up in the moment, but I can't help it. If this doesn't last, at least I'll have a few fantastic memories to cling to in my old age.

When we're only a few minutes from my apartment, Trevor rests his hand on my knee. "I'm glad we did this."

I giggle, still channeling a sixteen-year-old me trying to get control of her hormones. "If we keep this up, we'll have to start double dating."

"Why's that?"

"Because we need to set boundaries." And, just like that, I'm forty-six again. Well, wanting to make sure Trevor and I keep a handle on our emotions—and previously mentioned hormones—doesn't mean I have to lapse into the stiff prudishness of spinsterhood. "I don't know what's going to happen with us, Trev, but we can't, you know, do anything we shouldn't."

"All right."

That's what he says. "All right." I'm trying to initiate an important Define the Relationship conversation, and he gives me an "all right." So I go on.

"Clearly, we have a lot of … chemistry. And years of friendship have drawn us close, so all this … kissing … has a certain … natural appeal."

"Sure does." He drives into my apartment complex parking lot, pulls into an open spot, and puts the Jeep in park. Then he turns and grins at me, raising his hand to trace a finger along the side of my face and down my neck.

Lord have mercy.

I steal my will against his appeal and push his hand away. "I just don't think it's wise to spend all of our time together making out."

"And what do you want to do instead?"

"Well, we used to have great conversations. Can't we just ... talk?"

He nods. And stares at my lips. *Good grief.*

"So," he says, "what do you want to talk about?"

Hmm. Perhaps I should have had a topic in mind. "Oh, well, Freddie wants to know if you can join us on Thanksgiving."

"I was hoping you'd ask." This wouldn't be the first time Trevor spent a holiday with us, seeing as his family lives in Cameroon, Africa. Still, it's never been something either of us takes for granted. Sometimes he celebrates with a friend, a co-worker, even, on occasion, a girlfriend. Every three years he saves enough money to spend two weeks in Africa with his family over Christmas.

He says, "You *will* make your French onion soup, right?"

"Of course." My family has a few unusual Thanksgiving traditions, like starting the meal with French onion soup and ending it with my mom's cherry cheesecake. And some not-so-unusual. We always eat way too much then spend the afternoon playing Capture the Flag. That's what the guys and kids do, anyway. The women clean up and make cookies. Then we eat the cookies while solving the world's problems.

Trevor picks up my hand, studying my fingers. "Does she know?" He looks up at me with warm, hopeful eyes. "Did you tell Freddie?"

"Are you kidding? She predicted it."

"Oh, really?"

"Yeah, about a month ago. She said I should choose you and stop making lists."

He chuckles. "What, I'm not on your list?"

I punch his arm. "It's a list of what I want in a man, doofus."

"Right. Let me guess. Tall, athletic, devilishly handsome?"

"Don't forget a good sense of humor." We both laugh.

The car has cooled off and I shiver. Trevor pulls me close, wrapping his arms around me. "So, what else is on this list?"

"Truth?"

"Please."

"I didn't know what I wanted." Then I smile and nuzzle into him. He should have the whole truth. Honesty strengthens a relationship. "But I didn't think I wanted you."

"I can see that."

With a shove, I push him away and glower up at him. "What's that supposed to mean?"

"You didn't exactly fall into my arms, Jolene."

"If I remember correctly, that's precisely what I did."

He grins. "Oh, right. We met. We became friends. And just twenty-some years later, you were all mine."

I sit back with a grunt. Well, if he's going to be that way about it.

He once again stares at my hand, as if memorizing every knuckle and nail. "After all this time, I still don't know where I stand with you."

"It's not like I'm trying to be all mysterious. Sure,

we've known each other forever. But this is still brand new." I put a hand on his face and kiss his cheek, breathing in his spicy aftershave and a hint of curry. "I just need time. I don't want to rush it. Any of it."

He nods and faces me square-on. "I hear what you're saying. But I don't agree." When he clears his throat, I take a deep breath. "Jolene, I've loved you almost as long as I've known you. For a while, I loved you as a friend. At some point it became more. I don't want to wait another twenty years to take the next step."

"Trevor, I—"

"I don't have a lot of patience when it comes to you." The raw desire in his eyes tears into me like scissors through tissue paper. Not too long ago, I would have given in to that desire. I didn't let things like biblical morality get in the way of fun during my younger years. But I didn't have a real relationship with Christ back then either. I just wanted to have a good time. Through it all, though, I was miserable without God and suffered so much pain because of the choices I made.

Trevor would definitely be a good time. The thought flits through my head like a movie trailer, tempting and teasing me. My past continues to haunt my present. But I can't let it dictate my future.

"Maybe I should go."

"Wait, Jolene. Don't freak out. I don't want sex." He clears his throat. "Okay, yes, of course that's what I want but when it's right. *After* we're married."

"M-m-married?"

"Oh yeah. Didn't I mention that?" He kisses me. Long and hard and I feel it from head to toe. This isn't helping. I push him away again.

"For heaven's sake, Trevor, unless you're going to marry me tonight, you can't kiss me like that."

He presses his forehead against mine, as breathless as I feel. "I just wanted to point out the main downfall of not rushing it."

"Point taken."

We stay that way, enjoying each other, for some time. I can't take it all in. To be on the brink of something I've wanted for so long; to have it here, in my hands, drops my stomach like I just crested the first hill on a rollercoaster. Something's bound to go wrong.

Doesn't it always?

Chapter 19

Catie

My first three weeks in Ohio zip by. I miss Colorado Springs—and my own bed—but I'm getting used to the rhythm of country life again. And Luna loves it here.

It hasn't taken long to draw close to Delia and Tawny. We have more in common than I would have imagined. Definite sister-like potential here. And that is why, one Sunday afternoon while we're cleaning up after a lasagna feast, I tell them about Brian.

"I really thought we had something. It seemed so ... meant to be." I set the tomato-sauce-and-cheese-crusted pan in the sink and fill it with water to soak. "I know how silly that sounds. But for a while there, it felt good to be the girl someone could fall in love with."

Delia passes me a stack of plates to rinse off. "Just because it wasn't Brian doesn't mean you're not that girl."

"You have so much going for you," Tawny adds. "I honestly don't know why someone hasn't snatched you up."

"That's what everyone says. And yet, here I am. More single than ever."

"Well, there must be something going on," Delia says. "Maybe you're not meeting the right men."

"At the moment, I'm not meeting any men."

Tawny looks genuinely bemused. "Well, there's got to be something."

"Oh, sure." I hold up my hand and count the somethings one finger at a time. "I don't know how to be myself. I'm too picky. I have low self-esteem. And, apparently, I put up walls. Would you believe a guy once told me I'm too independent? What does that even mean?"

Delia leans against the counter and shrugs. "Some men don't know how to handle a strong woman."

"I don't want to be *handled*."

"You know what I mean."

Tawny spoons the leftover Caesar salad into a storage bowl as she asks, "Is it possible you take what people say too much to heart?"

I grab a scouring pad and scrub the lasagna pan a little harder. Soaking takes too long. "I thought I'd make an apple crisp for dessert. And we have that French vanilla ice cream Dad bought yesterday."

They both stop what they're doing and share a look I'm completely left out of.

"Sounds yummy," Delia says. "And I thought it would be fun to watch a Muppet movie with the kids later if we can get the men to give up their Sunday night football game."

Tawny grins. "Good idea, Del. Maybe we could all work on a crossword puzzle together."

"While we're doing that, we can talk about the weather."

"And plan our menus for the next week."

I look back and forth between them. Well, aren't they funny? I finish scrubbing the pan, rinse it off, and put it on the drying rack. My "sisters" aren't done yet. Delia says,

"Don't you just love small talk? I could enjoy this all day."

"Oh, yes," says Tawny, speaking with such clipped precision she sounds like she's performing in an Oscar Wilde play. Years ago, I saw Tawny in a college production of *The Importance of Being Ernest*, so I guess the shoe fits. She should leave it on the stage. But she continues, "It is a delightful way to spend an afternoon."

I step between them. "Okay, okay, I get it. I do take things too much to heart, and I don't like confrontation. Are you happy?"

Delia snugs her arm around me. "No, we're not happy. I can see how much you're hurting. I wish you wouldn't place so much of your happiness on a man."

"Exactly," Tawny says as she wipes off the island counter. "I think you're giving marriage too much credit. Almost to the point of making it an idol."

To which Delia adds, "Marriage won't solve your problems. It will just give you new ones. I once heard someone say being married is a lot like being single, only with more laundry."

Spoken like someone who has a husband. But then I look in Delia's green eyes. She really believes what she's saying.

I take a deep breath. "Can I ask you something?"

"Of course."

"Do you think marriage is a good thing? That it's a gift from God?"

"Yes," Delia says, "but it's not the only thing. It needs to have the right place in your heart and life."

"I understand that. But you could say the same about any good thing God blesses you with: your job, your home, even your kids. All good but you shouldn't make an idol out any of them, right?"

Delia nods before I even finish. So I keep going.

"For some reason—maybe it's because of feminism, I don't know—it's become almost shameful for a woman to want to get married. Like it's okay to pursue a job or a home but not a husband. I don't see that idea coming from the Bible."

Tawny interrupts. "Well, Paul says as much in First Corinthians. He said it's good for the unmarried to remain single."

"What he says is, it's good for them to remain single *as I am*. It's his opinion." I sigh and search for the right words. "You can't read the Bible and see how God puts a blessing on marriage from Genesis 1 on then pull out a single section and say that proves you shouldn't want to get married. What about Ephesians, when Paul compares the relationship between a husband and wife to that of Christ and the church? Or the fact that marriage is the first human relationship God created?

"I mean, when God saw Adam's loneliness, He could have given a brother or a parent or even a friend so he wouldn't be alone anymore. But He gave him a wife."

Neither says anything for a moment. They're actually listening to me and considering the logic of my argument. Well, they should. I've thought about this for years. It would hurt if they dismissed my opinion because it doesn't fit the current talking points surrounding marriage and singleness. I gather the ingredients for apple crisp while they consider my words. It's not until I'm peeling the Granny Smith apples that Delia says,

"Okay, I agree there's nothing wrong with wanting to get married. But there's also something to be said about having the right perspective on it. I don't think God wants you to be miserable because you're single."

"God doesn't want us to be miserable about a lot of things. That doesn't mean we won't feel pain. You know that verse in Proverbs: 'Hope deferred makes the heart sick'?"

They both nod.

I put the paring knife down for a second. "Do you know the rest of the verse?"

"No," Tawny says. "I guess I always thought that was the whole verse."

"Actually, it's not. The whole verse is, 'Hope deferred makes the heart sick, but when the desire comes it is a tree of life.' Which tells me it's okay to believe that someday, this dream not only can, but will, come true. Maybe not in an actual husband, but in God meeting this need in my heart. Which would be okay. I think. It's just that—" I turn back to my apples, hiding my face, "believing is getting harder. I feel I'm moving further and further away from hope and becoming bitter and angry. Now I'm afraid someday my heart will harden to stone so I don't have to hurt anymore." I take a deep breath and push on. "What if I become one of those sour old maids who lives alone and doesn't love anyone?"

"Catie." When I look up, I see tears in Delia's eyes to match my own. "That won't happen to you. We won't let it."

She means it, and her love wraps around me like heat from a campfire. Maybe I am safe here. For the first time, Colorado Springs feels as cold and distant as it physically is.

What would my life be like if I moved back to Ohio permanently?

Am I brave enough to believe I can have a better life somewhere besides Colorado?

◊◊◊

Thanksgiving comes and goes, filled with enough turkey, laughs, and football to last at least until Christmas. On Black Friday, Tawny, Delia, and Angela somehow manage to convince me to go shopping with them while we leave the kids at home with the men. I have to spend carefully. My savings won't last forever, and I'd rather not dip into my retirement fund if I don't have to. But I won't let my situation stop me from buying a few Christmas presents.

We start the attack at a large department store, where I snag an old-fashioned popcorn popper for Dad, Barbie dolls for the girls, and a wooden stacking train to give to Will. Next, we set our sights on a favorite clothing store. There I find soft-as-silk cashmere sweaters and buy four—deep purple for Delia, red for Tawny, muted pink for Angela, and, because the price is so good, a royal-blue one for myself.

At the last store, I come across mugs with football team logos. We are a very diverse family when it comes to who we cheer for. I like the Broncos, Dad is a life-long Cincinnati Bengals fan, James loves the Steelers, and Patrick stays loyal to the Chicago Bears. It leads to a lot of in-house rivalry. So, just to stir things up a bit, I'll get the right mugs but hand them out wrong, then sit back and enjoy the resulting fireworks. Hee hee.

Just looking at the mugs makes me miss my Broncos. I've held season tickets to Denver games for almost a decade. I had several friends who would go with me, and we spent many cherished hours at what true fans will always call Mile High Stadium. Too bad I didn't get to enjoy many games this fall. I sold what was left of my tickets after I lost my job and, now that I'm in Ohio for the rest of the season, it's just as well.

Unemployment: the gift that just keeps giving.

We finish our retail attack by noon, drive through Arby's for a quick bite, and head for home. It's quite satisfying to look in the back of Delia's van and see it piled high with the day's loot.

I've just finished my roast beef sandwich when my phone rings. It's Jolene. I decide to take it since I'm sitting in the back, next to Angela. My niece has been serial-texting her boyfriend and giggling at his every response, so she won't mind. And Tawny and Delia can continue their chat without me.

"Jolene, hi!" Has it really been three weeks since I left the Springs?

"Hey, Cait. What are you up to?"

"Oh, heading home after spending money I don't have on Christmas presents no one actually needs. What about you?"

"Trevor's watching football, which, apparently, is on twenty-four-seven this weekend." She chuckles, then whispers, "I told him I would make brownies."

"Lucky guy. How are things going between you two?"

A moment passes as a heavy sigh trembles across the miles. "It's good. I think. Trevor is ... I don't deserve him. I guess it still feels a little weird, you know?"

Not really. "I'm sure it will work out. You two are great together."

"That's what Freddie keeps telling me. And that I need to stop running away from anything good. She thinks I have a tendency to freak out any time something gets serious."

"Do you?"

Another pause. "Maybe. But I sure didn't freak out at the great bargains we got this morning." Jolene has a gift for changing the subject. Just one more thing we have in common.

"Oh yeah? I got some pretty good deals too."

"Wait, that just sank in. You went shopping? On Black Friday? I thought you hated—and I quote— 'the commercializing of the holidays by exploiting consumer greed.'"

"Yes, I have said that. My sister-in-law made me see the folly of my ways."

"How'd she do that?"

Delia catches my eye in the rearview mirror and sticks out her tongue. I make a stink-face back at her. To Jolene, I say, "She can be very persuasive, especially when Thanksgiving turkey is on the line."

Jolene laughs. "She threatened you with poultry?"

"She threatened to *withhold* poultry."

"Well, that's downright diabolical."

I chuckle and cover the phone with my hand. "She said that's diabolical."

Delia throws back, "It worked, didn't it?"

We all get the laughter out of our system before I say to Jolene, "I did get some great deals and, truth be told, it was a lot of fun."

"Oh, so, you're in a good mood."

"Sure. Why?"

"Because ..." She pauses for so long I check to see if the phone disconnected. "I ... have news."

"Good news?"

"Well, not to you."

What could possibly have happened in Colorado that I wouldn't like? "Just spill it, Jolene."

"Brian and Tess—"

Oh crap.

"—are engaged."

Wow. "I didn't see that coming. Not this fast, anyway."

"I don't know if anyone did. Except Brian. Tess may have had some idea."

"But, engaged? Already? How could this happen? They hardly know each other." My voice catches, and I swallow my emotion. Plenty of time for the tears of broken dreams later. Great. I'm starting to think like a cross between Uli and *Anne of Green Gables.* I glance up and catch Delia's eyes in the rearview again. She looks sad. She's been listening. This day just keeps getting worse.

Jolene hesitates again. Then, "Do you really want to know?"

Do I? "Oh, go ahead."

Might as well pull the bandage all the way off.

"What Tess told me is she just knows it's meant to be."

"Oh, so their relationship is a Meg Ryan movie."

"In so many words, yes."

I changed my mind. I don't want to know. But Jolene keeps talking.

"She said they had a spark. It all just came together. The only downside being you." She takes a breath, and I can picture her biting a thumbnail. "She's miserable thinking you may have been hurt."

What do I say to something like this? "Of course I'm hurt. Brian made me think that I ... that we ... Does she even know everything that happened between us?"

"Catie, I don't even know everything that happened between you and Brian."

"Where do I begin?" Then I stop. Where *do* I begin? What exactly took place during all that time we spent together? Did anything happen beyond some flirting and phone calls? Didn't we have moments? Electricity? Or did I imagine it all?

I swallow. Hard. I've never been the daydreamer type, but maybe I let hope take over and convinced myself there was something there when there wasn't. Obviously, if he was falling in love with Tess the whole time.

In love. Something green with sharp teeth nibbles at my heart. It's not fair. But I won't say that out loud.

"Jolene? Could we talk more later? We're almost back to the farm, and I have all these bags to unload—"

"Sure. We can chat next week. Any time you want to talk, just call me."

"Thanks, I will. Happy Thanksgiving. And tell everyone I said hi."

"I sure will. Happy Thanksgiving, Catie."

After I hang up, I stare out the window as we pull into the driveway. By the time I hop from the van, I have control of the situation and my emotions. *I just won't think about it.*

I grab my bags and race into the house, as if the demons I've determined to ignore are hunting me down.

Chapter 20
Uli

The song about how many minutes are in a year will not stop running through my head. I've seen *Rent* twice, including once on Broadway, so I know the words. Actually, I remember just enough of it to be annoyed by it, like a two-year-old who keeps tapping his mom on the shoulder to ask the same question.

I woke up with random lines from "Seasons of Love" stuck in my brain, and I can't get them out. It must mean something. You don't flutter awake humming a particular song for no reason. Maybe my subconscious is trying to tell me something.

Or God is.

He would try to teach me a lesson through lyrics.

So, as the song says, you shouldn't measure a year in minutes but in moments. And what spectacular moments did this past year hold for me? Well, it started with a new boyfriend and ended with an old one. It did not include career success or a ring on my finger. I didn't even lose the thirty pounds I once again vowed to shed when I made my New Year's resolutions.

And Ellen died. I still cry about that every once in a while. Could I have been nice to her just once? We shared a room at the retreat just a week before she passed away, and I couldn't spare her one kind moment. Can I learn from this tragedy and stop being so selfish and treat all people with the love I long to feel myself? I don't know. I'm not sure I can express something I'm missing in my own heart.

Obviously, I'm not very good at this life thing. I haven't figured out how to make money doing what I love. Or even how to get and keep a job. I certainly don't know how to hang on to a man. Cole being the rare exception. I'm clinging to him like a cat to a string.

Keeping, now that I think about it, might be my biggest failing. I've never held a career position longer than four years and that was my first job out of college, working as a photographer for the newspaper in my hometown near Ames, Iowa. Then I decided I was ready for bigger and better things and moved to Colorado Springs. It seemed so providential at the time, like it was where God had been leading me all along.

That was fifteen years ago. Since then, work has been sporadic and men—up until Cole—were few, far between, and quickly gone.

Like I said, I can't seem to hang on to anything. Do I lose my keys? On a regular basis. Are my computer and e-mail passwords written on sticky notes taped to my laptop? Of course. Once, I took a shower and forgot to shampoo my hair. It might have been more than once. And that's just the kind of stuff that happens before I leave home.

Today I dart out of the apartment a little before eight, early for a Saturday, but I'm already late. I have ten minutes to make the fifteen-minute drive to the Presbyterian church on Weber. When I get to my car and see it coated with early morning ice, I add another five minutes to my arrival time. And I still manage to forget to grab a bite for breakfast or even the lunch I made last night so I'd have something to take with me.

All of which means I arrive at this year's Help-

Portrait event late, frazzled, and hungry. If I didn't keep diet Mountain Dews in the trunk of my car so I could pull out an ice-cold one all winter long, I'd be in a world of trouble.

Chuck Meissner, who heads the Colorado Springs event, greets me with a smile despite my tardiness and leads me to my station. He introduces me to Lisa Wissett, who has volunteered to help me and has, in fact, already organized the line of people waiting to get their picture taken. Though she seems quite nice, Lisa has a pinched and tired face, stringy, brown hair, and is so pale and thin I spend most of the day trying to find reasons to get her to sit and relax and eat something. Even if it's the candy canes I brought to use as props.

It's not long, though, before the passion for my work takes over, and I'm completely focused on the fun task at hand. We help the mothers fluff their hair and touch up their makeup and occasionally provide a festive scarf to add to their look, if requested. For the kids, I have a couple stuffed animals—including a fluffy-cuddly, white bear dressed in a blue sweater with white stars and a little girl puppet with golden pigtails—items I hope will get them to smile, maybe even laugh.

The morning flies past, and soon Chuck stops by to let us know we can take a one-hour lunch break. I make a quick run for fast food then meet Lisa in the gym where they've set up a few tables for Help-Portrait volunteers to eat. Several people are gathered there now, including a couple photographers I know, and I say "hi" to them before grabbing a chair across from Lisa.

"You've been a great help," I say, unwrapping my burger. "I wish I could hire you full time."

Lisa smiles. "I wish you could too."

I swallow the first bite of my sandwich before asking, "Where do you work?"

"Right now? Part-time at 7-11."

"Oh."

We chew in silence for a moment, then Lisa says, "Is photography what you do full-time, or is it more of a hobby?"

"No, this is how I make a living. Photography and some graphic design. I'm still waiting for my big break." I grin. And waiting. *And waiting.*

"What does your husband do?"

The question throws me. She might as well have asked if I own a luxury yacht, though that would be more likely. *Your husband.* If only. "I'm not married."

"You're on your own? No kids either?"

"Nope, just me. Mostly. I mean, I have a boyfriend. I guess." *Wow, Uli. Way to speak out with confidence.*

"Yeah? Me too."

Me too? Does that mean she has a boyfriend? Or she isn't sure?

"Cole's a great guy," I say. "We've been together a little over a year. He makes me smile and has a good job, and we have fun together and, well—"

I shut myself up by taking a long slurp of my chocolate shake, resulting in a brain freeze. *Just who are you trying to convince anyway, Uli?* I press the palm of my hand to my temple. And why didn't I mention I love him?

Lisa looks at me, then does a double-take, as if she just caught her reflection in a mirror. "Well," she says, "he sounds great. Kinda reminds me of my Torrey."

"Oh, is he your … boyfriend?"

"Sure." She says it like I just asked her if she wants chips with her sub. "I mean, we live together. It's, you know, comfortable."

Comfortable? Sounds like code for boring and predictable. "That's … nice."

This might be the most disingenuous thing I've ever said, but Lisa smiles at me and shrugs. "You get what you pay for, as they say."

I chew down some fries. She's talking about her own relationship, not mine, right? Besides, what I have with Cole is a completely different thing. First of all, I won't move in with him until the day he says, "I do." And second, we'll never be comfortable together. We fight too much.

Oh Uli, how you go on.

Just as I'm about to change the subject, Lisa says, "Well, at least my kids have a father."

I force a smile. "You have children?"

"Four." She laughs. "And they're a handful! But Torrey provides for us, and he helps out when he can."

"Well," I say, "you can't ask for much more than that."

Oh yes, I can.

◊◊◊

We finish our lunch and get back to work. The steady stream of people starts to slow down a little as the afternoon goes on. Though this gives Lisa and I more time to chat, we settle on mundane topics, like photography and shoes and who makes the best chocolate chip cookies. As soon as I discover Lisa has some experience with a professional camera and a passion for taking pictures, I let her try her hand at a few shots, talking her through lighting issues and various shutter speeds and getting the focus just right.

The day finally comes to an end, and we pack up my seamless white backdrop and the stand I hooked it to, as well as a few Christmas-y props like the aforementioned candy canes and festive red-and-green pillows. As we're rolling up the backdrop, I say,

"I think you might have a good eye for this, Lisa. You should think about taking some classes."

She grins. "You really think so?"

"I do. In fact …" I stop mid-packing. Should I? It's a bit of a sacrifice, but why not? "I think my mom is getting me a new camera for Christmas. If she does, would you be interested in my old one?"

"Only if you let me pay you for it."

I laugh. "Of course! I can't go around giving stuff away. How about … fifty dollars?"

Lisa shakes her head. "Oh, no. I happen to know it's worth a lot more than that."

"Fine. If you're going to push, I'll make it forty. But that's as high as I go. And this is on the condition you let me teach you how to use it."

"You drive a hard bargain, Uli." She sticks out her hand and shakes mine. "But you got yourself a deal."

And that's how, for the second year in a row, I make a new friend at Help-Portrait.

◊◊◊

Though the photos have been taken, my work for the charity event isn't over yet. I still have to edit the pictures and get them back to the church by the end of the week.

Before I get to all that, though, I have a date with Cole. Not really a date since we're going to his work Christmas party, but after that we might go to a movie. Or something. That's my boyfriend's go-to date-night plan. More likely, he'll want to go back to his place, which sounds less appealing every day.

I refresh myself in a long, warm shower before slipping into a twirly, red dress with a handkerchief hem. After sliding on a pair of knee-high black boots, I spin around in front of the mirror. At least I look good. Let Cole's co-workers point and smirk. I'll get through this just fine.

The requisite pep talk taken care of, I throw on my black, wool coat and a thick, blue scarf, and grab my purse and the requisite White Elephant gift. Feeling a need for a bit of cold night air, I step outside to wait for Cole on the porch steps. The snow that started earlier this afternoon has thickened to heavy, white flakes, covering the ground with a deep, wet sludge. It's cold enough to snow, if not cold enough to be considered a substantial winter storm. My guess? The sun will melt it all away not long after it makes its appearance tomorrow morning.

Cole announces his arrival with a quick beep, and I hurry to his truck, ready to get out of the cold. As I hop in, he says, "You look nice."

"So do you." For his work party, Cole went all out: a good pair of jeans and a white, short-sleeved dress shirt that's so tight he didn't have to iron it. No tie, of course—let's not go crazy. But this he'll do for his job buddies. For just me, I'm lucky if he brushes his teeth.

We arrive at the party only twenty minutes late. To clarify, it's not so much a holiday celebration as it is a kegger and pizza in the back room at Old Chicago's. The night also includes the requisite White Elephant gift exchange, which merely gives a bunch of soused construction workers a chance to laugh at neatly wrapped, half-eaten McDonald's hamburgers and a cup of earwax-coated Q-tips someone collected over the past year. Yes, that's the one I got. At least all the other women are as disgusted as I am. My made-in-China glass snowman collectible ends up being the nicest gift available, and I take some satisfaction in watching everyone fight over it.

Okay, the women fight over it. The men are much more interested in a six-pack of Bud Light, which Cole somehow manages to win. Yay.

The festivities start winding down around ten— *thank You, God.* We're about to make our escape when one of Cole's drunk chums throws an arm around him and bellows, "Dude!" I've learned that, in man language, "Dude" can mean just about anything. This one sounds a bit like, "I didn't know you were here!"

Then, to my horror, he puts his other arm around me. He squeezes me so tight it's a miracle my head doesn't pop off.

Dude pushes my boyfriend away and weaves his finger in front of Cole's face for several seconds, then somehow gets his digit to hold still and says, "When-a you gonna marry this girl?"

He says "marry this girl" slowly, like each word is its own sentence. The finger turns to me as I hold back a smile. *You tell him, buddy.* Then he ruins it by adding, "You gotta make an honesh women outta her, or I gonna steal 'er away. Unless you knock 'er up."

His eyes finally focus on a spot somewhere near my left temple. I don't know his name. But, it would seem, he's single. Or not. He grins and sighs a beer-and-garlic-laden breath in my direction. "You," he says, his chubby face softening into a look of pure adoration, "have the eyes of an angel."

And with that, he plops down onto the closest chair and plants his face into what's left of a bowl of spinach-artichoke dip. Cole cracks up laughing and grabs my hand. "Come on, angel eyes. Let's get out of here."

Pulling me quickly through the room, Cole waves good-bye to his pals. I manage a few farewells myself before we're out the door. That's when we discover the snow has turned to an icy sleet. I slow down just in time, glad I'm wearing boots with decent traction instead of the three-inch heels I briefly considered earlier. Sometimes I'm just not in the mood for sore feet.

But I still slide and slip all the way across the parking lot while Cole strides easily toward his truck like he's walking on Berber carpet. I cling to his leather jacket-clad arm for the sake of my stockings, my dress, my modesty, and because I don't want to end up bruised and shivering on the asphalt.

We finally make it. Cole opens the door and practically lifts me up onto the seat. I pull the scarf, now slick and soaked with shards of ice, off my head. The cold slices through my coat, and I'm glad when Cole jumps in, starts the truck, and cranks the heat. Slowly, warmth starts to seep through the vents, but I can't stop trembling.

"So," he says, "you still want to go to my place?"

That was the original plan. "I d-don't think so. N-not with this weather. And, of course, I have church to-mo-morrow."

"Right."

Then, as I have nearly every Saturday for the last year, I ask, "Would you like to g-go with me?"

He doesn't always just say no. Sometimes he has an excuse, legitimate or not. Like tonight. "Probably not. I need a day off."

A day off? From what? Me?

I'm happier not knowing.

So we head off toward my apartment. Slide off, I should say. In good weather, it takes thirty minutes to get from the Old Chicago on Academy to my apartment on the west side of town, near what everyone calls The Scar—a mining area along the side of the mountain. But tonight Cole has to take it easy and watch out for other cars skating along the ice. Silence fills the cab as he concentrates on driving. One couldn't be safer with him at the wheel—even with the three or four beers he drank—yet my hand clasps the seat so tight my fingers start to ache.

As we crest the top of the Austin Bluffs hill, I'm struck by the sight of the city shimmering white and gold below, like the inside of a snow globe. The road curves around before sloping downhill, right toward a busy four-way intersection. If we can just make it through that stoplight, the rest of the trip shouldn't be so bad. Still precarious but more doable.

The timing couldn't be more perfect. We come up to the light not long after it turns green, giving us an easy crossing. My grip on the seat lets up, and I take a deep breath. Several lights and turns later, we are only a few blocks from my apartment. It's a more-wooded area of the Springs, sitting close to the base of the mountain. It should be smooth sailing now. Which, of course, is when a small animal—a coyote?—darts in front of us.

This must have caught Cole off-guard because he slams the brake, sending us into a spin. The car whips around like a Tilt-A-Whirl. I shriek and grab my seatbelt. Cole fights the ice, trying to steer against the spin. If there hadn't been a van parked on the side of the road, we probably would have made it. But there is, and the front passenger side of the truck slams into the back of the van. My door takes the brunt of the crash, pressing in and trapping my leg under the dashboard.

In only a few seconds, it's all over. The engine shudders one last gasp and dies. We sit in silence, surrounded by a night illuminated only with Christmas lights blinking from a few nearby homes. Our anxious breaths mingle with the sound of sleet spattering against the truck.

Cole turns to me, putting his hand on my arm. "Are you okay?"

I try to shift free, then grimace. "My leg. I can't move it."

He scoots closer and leans down. After feeling around a little, he slides back to his side of the cab and gets out. Seconds later, he's at my door. I'm not sure what he's thinking. It's far too smashed in to open the usual way.

They'll have a hard time pulling me out. Ooh. Maybe that means they'll have to rescue me using the Jaws of Life. That could be—

Pain shoots up my leg, reminding me it might be a little too early to start working on my near-death experience story. Time to call the pros. So I get out my phone and dial 9-1-1.

I finish giving the emergency operator our information as Cole gets back in the truck on his side. He slicks his hands through his icy hair and wipes the moisture on his pants, then takes his jacket off and puts it around me. He's still not cold. Unbelievable.

"I'm sorry I can't get you out."

"That's okay." The warmth from his coat drapes me in safety. He takes my hand. Blood rushes through me, and it's not only the cold making me tremble. "I'm sorry about your truck."

"Eh." He shrugs. "That's why I have insurance."

We smile at each other for a moment. Glancing out the window, I see the sleet has turned back to snow. It swirls around the truck in the gentleness of a memory through tinted glass. Now we're *in* the snow globe. Cole's hand brushes my cheek, and he turns my face to his, then kisses me, soft and sweet. This is why I fell in love with Cole. The way he used to make me feel like a treasure, something to cherish, something beautiful. His rough, construction-worker hands caress me as gently as a Caribbean breeze. His mouth slides from my lips to my neck, then up along the side of my face as his hands cradle the back of my head. I melt into it.

Best of all, it's just kissing. With my leg still

wedged under the dashboard and EMTs about to arrive at any moment, it can't go any further. I can enjoy not doing anything I'll feel guilty about later. All I'm aware of is his strength. Not the pain in my leg or the fear in my heart.

We finally pull apart. Cole says, "I really do love you, Uli."

"I love you too." *Oh God, please let this work out.*

"You've been so patient with me this past year. I know it's been tough." Then he chuckles. "I'm not the easiest guy to get along with."

Before I can take another breath, he reaches into his shirt pocket and pulls out a tiny, sparkly diamond ring. "Uli, this is what I want." He clears his throat. "So let's get married."

This is it. Exactly what I've been waiting for. And, for all I know, no one will ever ask me again. I've already given him my body. Doesn't that make us one in God's eyes anyway?

So I say yes. Of course I say yes. Cole smiles and hands me the ring, which I slide onto my finger. And that's that. It's not fancy or pretty or extravagant but it's done. I'm engaged before Christmas. A giant weight lifts from my shoulders.

Only to be replaced by a brand new—and much heavier—one. The kind of burden that hits when you make a major life decision and don't ask God about it first.

Chapter 21

Catie

I *have to win.*

Over the years, my family has continued many of the Irish Christmas traditions my dad enjoyed in his youth, with our own personal modifications. Traditions I've missed while spending so many holidays in Colorado. Like the ugly sweater exchange with the coveted prize for the winner.

Despite all my time away, I fell quickly back into the pace of a Delaney family Christmas. The Saturday after Thanksgiving, we took the children into the back woods and cut down the perfect scotch pine tree, which we set up in the family room and decorated with white lights, red beads, and silver ornaments. Then, a few days before the holiday, we made popcorn garlands to hang around the main room. We don't skimp on the lights, either. Folks can see our house from a hillside three miles away.

The fun or work—depending on one's perspective—escalates on Christmas Eve. First, we make our Holly ring to hang on the front door and string mistletoe over the entryway. After that, we bake Irish soda bread stock-full of raisins and caraway seeds. This all leads up to the ugly sweater exchange.

On the night before Christmas, the Delaney adults, which adds up to a pretty impressive number, assemble in our large living room, eager to see the array of red and green hideousness, while what seems like a hundred children run wild through the house. After eating too much stew, boiled cabbage, and potato bread, we pass around the two dozen or so pillow-like packages.

And I have to win. I have to prove I didn't lose my ability to recognize a truly ugly sweater. I'd forfeit my Delaney clan card. Besides, there's a tin of biscuits from Barker's Bakery for the winner, which includes coconut creams. Yum.

One by one, everyone opens their package until, finally, it's Dad's turn. And, wouldn't you know it, he picks mine. The fashion nightmare is supposed to look like a reindeer wearing an elf suit, complete with a hood with antlers for the head. I'm a shoo-in for the prize.

Slowly, Dad pulls out the monstrosity to the gasps of everyone watching. It looks like a bear emerging from Santa Claus wrapping paper. Dad throws it over his shoulders, pops the hood up with a growl, and starts chasing kids around the room.

Minutes later, I relax into my chair and munch on my well-deserved coconut creams while I enjoy being surrounded by my family. But even as the children laugh and everyone tries on their sweaters, eats cookies, and drinks hot cider, I'm not in the middle of it. I'm an observer. The littlest ones giggle and run to their parents for protection from my dad. The couples take their turn kissing under the mistletoe. And, to my relief, my aunts don't ask me why I'm single. It seems I'm not the only one who's given up on the chance I'll ever marry.

It's better this way.

But just when I think I'm off the hook, sweet Aunt Honoria turns to me and says, "How's your work going, Caitlyn?"

Any other year it would have been a fine question.

But now, it's a whole different can of worms. One I'd rather keep closed. Since that's no longer an option, I say,

"I'm … not really working at the moment."

"What?" she asks, loud enough to quiet the whole room. "What are you saying, dear?"

"I'm, well, unemployed."

She leans in closer. "You need to speak a little louder for your old aunt, honey."

Really? So I clear my throat and try again. "I said I'm unemployed."

"Oh dear." Aunt Honoria turns to her brother. My father. "Collin, what's this about our Caitlyn being unemployed?"

And he says, "They dumped her."

"Dad!"

Why does being with family always make you act like you're in high school again?

Everyone looks at me. Maybe I'd rather be an observer after all. "I … was laid off. In October." I suppose it had to come up sooner or later. But I would prefer much later, say, after I was back in Colorado.

All three aunts say, "Aw, honey," in unison and surround me in a hug. Dad's sisters, Alma, Doreen, and Honoria, all followed remarkably different paths—Alma married young, birthed half a dozen kids, and now dotes on her fifteen grandchildren; Doreen and her husband, Bernie, spent thirty years serving as missionaries to Argentina and raised a daughter with Down's Syndrome; Honoria is a tenured engineering professor who never married. But though they're unique in their situations, they could be triplets in looks and personalities.

Now they join forces to console me, and each one has something to say. I hear, "What are you going to do now?" "Have you started looking for a new job yet?" and "Maybe you should let your hair grow out" all at the same time.

Oh, and they have ADD. That last comment probably came from Alma, but it's so hard to be sure.

"I've already applied for about two dozen jobs and have a list of a dozen more. I'm sure I'll find something soon."

Doreen says, "Of course, you will, honey," then yells, "Who wants some pie?" all in one breath.

Minutes later, every person has a plate of pecan or pumpkin pie, Honoria has challenged Dad to a game of chess, and Alma has returned to her favorite pastime: scolding her grandkids for staring at their iPhone/iPod/iWhatever during quality family time. By the end of the night, she's confiscated seven electronic devices, and we're all standing around the piano singing Christmas carols.

Not much has changed. Except, maybe, me.

It's good to be home.

◊◊◊

Christmas morning dawns with a fresh dusting of snow, just as it should. The sun streams through the window, waking me without an alarm. I dress in my new, green-plaid pajamas, which were way too nice to sleep in, and matching, not-like-Nanna's slippers, let Luna out, then shuffle to the kitchen. I promised Bella and Bryn I would make cinnamon rolls. It will be a smaller group today, without the aunts and first cousins and second cousins and all their offspring. Delia is already at the sink, rubbing a freshly washed turkey with butter, salt, and pepper. Before I do anything else, though, I start the coffee.

We work in silence, our attention captured by the beauty of the day bouncing through the big bay window. Since the kitchen connects to the dining area and opens to the living room, we can enjoy the snowy vista from two sides. The piney perfume of our ten-foot Christmas tree overwhelms the space, waiting to be replaced in a few hours by the scent of turkey and apple pie. It's so idyllic, I swear I hear jingle bells.

Tawny joins us as I'm rolling biscuit dough into a cake pan. She clicks on the TV and flips it to a holiday music station. After putting the turkey in the oven we have in a second kitchen in the finished basement, Delia turns her attention to making homemade dinner rolls. Tawny gets to work on homemade cranberry sauce. The sense of camaraderie and Christmas washes over me like a sunrise as a piano version of "Silent Night" fills the room.

All is calm, until Delia clears her throat.

"Catie, there's something I've been wanting to say, and I guess now's as good a time as any."

What? Now? Since my cinnamon buns are now baking away, I won't have another project until closer to meal time. So, I lean against the counter and enjoy the morning's first cup of coffee. Loud thumps, eager voices, and running water tell me the rest of the house is stirring, so the chances of this being a drawn-out conversation seem slim. Thankfully.

Delia shapes her dough into a large ball, kneading and pounding it as she talks. "I've been thinking about what you said last month, about wanting to get married and how you feel you're losing hope that it can still happen for you."

"I'm sorry about all that and how grumpy I was. I blame PMS." That's not what it was, though. My cycle has been sporadic at best for several months now. It's one of those things I prefer not to think about.

"No, I'm the one who's sorry." Delia does, indeed, appear heartbroken. "It was so hard for me to understand what you're going through. But the more I think about it, the more I get it."

"Really?" I ask. "What do you get?"

After putting the dough in a large bowl, Delia covers it with a towel, then rinses off her hands. Tawny puts her cranberries in the fridge at the same time and pours her own mug of coffee. Their work done, they turn their complete attention to me. Delia says,

"You're grieving."

The idea knifes through me. That's the word Jolene used at Ellen's funeral. I still have a hard time with it. "I won't deny my situation hurts, but 'grief' is a little too strong."

"Is it?" This comes from Tawny. She and Delia must have talked about it earlier. Does that make this some kind of weird, spinster intervention?

Tawny continues, "It just seems like a lot of what you're feeling is similar to what someone goes through when they're grieving a loss."

"And isn't that what you're dealing with?" Delia says. "A loss?"

"Well, yes, I suppose." It's not a completely strange concept, but it is an unpleasant one. After all, this is the life God has given me. And, as such, I should be content, even happy, in knowing I'm in His will.

But the sister-thought to this is that I'm *not* in His will. That, because of my hard-headed stubbornness or fear or high expectations or all three, I somehow managed to miss my chance at love. What if God brought him into my life, and I pushed him away? Can I still grieve if my situation is all my fault?

It's something I'll have to think about later, because three kids and four more adults join us in the kitchen en masse, and the rest of the day disappears in the joy of Christmas.

A joy that sits under the cloud of realizing Delia is right.

I'm grieving. And I don't know how to stop.

◊◊◊

My phone rings the next morning while I'm playing a game of Disney Princess Monopoly with my nieces, one of the presents I gave them yesterday. I check the number on caller ID—it's from Colorado Springs, but I don't recognize it. So I tell the girls I'll be right back, then head to the small den next to the kitchen for a quiet place to talk.

A woman's voice says, "Is this Caitlyn Delaney?"

"Yes, it is."

"My name is Rhonda Messenger. I'm the HR manager for the sales department at Tasker Pharmaceuticals here in Colorado Springs. I've been looking over your resume, and I must say I'm quite impressed. I think you have great potential as a pharmaceutical sales rep. Are you still looking for a new position?"

I clear my throat. "Yes, actually, I am."

"Wonderful! Well, we would like to meet with you." She pauses—to check her calendar, I imagine. "Would you be able to come in for an interview tomorrow?"

"Oh, unfortunately, no. I'm in Ohio for the holidays. The earliest I could get back would be Friday afternoon."

"Of course. We do have an opening at three on Friday. Would that work?"

I would have to leave right away. The excitement of a job interview spars with my disappointment over having to pack up and hit the road before lunch. But I say, "Yes, that sounds great."

"Very good." After she gives me a few more details, I hang up, still in shock.

Now I have to tell my family I'm heading home as soon as I can load up my car.

◊◊◊

"Luna!" I stand at the door, calling my dog for the fourth time in the past half hour. She still won't come. I know she likes it here, but we need to leave.

James walks behind me on his way to the living room. "Still no luck?"

"No, and I don't know where she could be. I really need to get going if I want to get as far as Kansas today."

My family's three dogs are in the front yard, rolling around in the snow. Luna's not with them, which worries me. "I'd better go look for her."

"We'll all go," James says. Then he yells, "Everyone, get your coats! We need to help Catie find Luna."

In less than five minutes, the whole family heads off in different directions. Delia, Tawny, and the children explore closer to the house while James, Patrick, Dad, Angela, and I split up into the family's two ATVs and one golf cart to explore farther in the fields. Fortunately, we only have a thin layer of snow and it's too cold for the dirt trails to be muddy. I make my way to a wooded area, worry eating at me with each turn. I'll cancel my interview if I have to.

I hope I don't have to.

Please God, let my dog be all right.

The quiet of the woods turns the gray day even gloomier. Branches creak in the wind, black and stark against the snowy hillside. Cold air nips through me. It's like someone opened the caskets in a musty old cemetery and let all the ghouls go free.

Well, let them grab at my jacket and howl in my car. I'm not leaving without my dog.

I get to a denser, wooded area and leave the ATV behind so I can investigate on foot. Weaving around dead trees and sharp brambles, I keep my ears open for any sound out of the norm while continuing to call for Luna. Once through the first stand of trees, I cross a barren cornfield to a check-mark-shaped bit of woods near the back of the property. I've now been out looking for almost half an hour. The long cross-country drive I have ahead of me quickens my step. When I stop to pull some thorns out of my coat, I hear what sounds like a faint whimper. I freeze, not daring to breathe.

Yes, there it is again.

"Luna!"

The cry comes from a tangled mess of trees and brush and broken branches. As I draw closer, the tortured breaths of an injured animal grow louder. Certain it's my dog, I start clearing a path until, finally, I see her. She must have gotten herself snarled in the brambles, and the more she struggled to get free, the more entangled she became. Now she's bloody and breathing heavy. I can't get her out on my own, so I take out my phone and call James.

While I wait, I break off branches and pull at the thorny vines blocking my way. Soon I realize it's not just thorns. Luna somehow got herself caught in a rusty, old, barbed-wire fence. No wonder she's so badly wounded. And, I fear, in danger of contracting tetanus.

At last, the men and Angela show up with the truck and several large pruning shears. Even working together, it still takes us almost twenty minutes to cut her free. Once Luna's out, I wrap her in an old blanket. When I pick her up, she licks my face. My brother takes her while I jump in the back of the truck, then James hands the dog to me. As we head for home, I hold her close. She's so badly hurt she barely moves. Tears scratch at my eyes, and I brush them away.

Dad called the family veterinarian, Dr. Walker, as soon as he found out Luna was injured. Fortunately, the vet agrees to meet us at his clinic, just a mile away. While we all wait for him to examine her, I pace the reception area, rubbing my arms.

Angela asks, "So, what are you going to do?"

"Honestly, I don't know."

"I think you should go back to the Springs," Dad says. "You don't want to miss your chance at a job interview."

"You did say this sounded like a great opportunity for you." Angela sits on the edge of an orange, plastic chair, plucking burs out of her jacket. Then she looks up at me. "Maybe you could postpone the interview?"

"Well, I could, but it wouldn't make for a good first impression. And since Monday is New Year's Eve, the earliest we could reschedule would be Wednesday. What if they want to make a decision by then?"

James nods. "I agree with Dad. You need to follow through with the interview." He comes over and puts an arm around me. "We'll take good care of Luna for you."

I know they will but … when will I get her back? And what will I do without her? I don't even want to think about shuffling around my big, empty house without Luna trotting along beside me.

None of this matters, though, because they're right. After talking over treatment with Dr. Walker and making sure Luna will be okay, I say good-bye to my dog and my family. When I finally get to I-70, I'm more than two hours behind my original plan.

The road stretches ahead of me. I'm not ready for a long drive or a long night or a job interview in two days. I make good time but night still falls far too soon. As I race through Missouri, I crank the volume on an eighties XM station, hoping music from my younger days will help me stay awake and alert. I'm determined to get past Kansas City, maybe even to Topeka, tonight, but it won't be easy. I call Jolene and Uli but neither answers.

Guess I'm on my own. Again.

Somehow, I make it to Kansas around 1:00 a.m. and start looking for a place to crash for a few hours. But I have a second wind, so I pass several exits without stopping. I can definitely make it to Topeka.

I fly by yet another exit boasting several hotels. *Just a little farther.* And then, just like that, I've left Topeka behind, and I'm on a straight-away with nothing ahead but dark cornfields and, well, not much else.

Brilliant, Catie. You know you're too tired to keep going. But I have to. I yawn and force my eyes to stay open. Not working. So I power down the window, hoping the cold air will help.

This is not good.

And that's when the voice starts to whisper.

You're all alone. No one cares that you're out here, not a soul in sight, facing a choice of falling asleep at the wheel or pulling off the road and placing yourself in a different kind of danger.

No one cares. Not even God.

Is that true? Do You really not care? Or are You here, in this car, watching over me? And, if you are, why do I still feel alone? I'm tired of being on my own. I'm tired of the struggle and the frustration and the regret. I'm so tired.

You could, the voice suggests, *drive off the side of the road. Speed up. Hit a tree. Just hard enough. You wouldn't be shirking any responsibilities. Luna has a home. And all this could be over.*

Just like that.

Just like that I could give up. Let God know He pushed me too far. He abandoned me too long.

Funny, isn't it, how quickly one can go from hope to despair?

A large oak looms ahead, calling to me. So easy. I push down a little harder on the accelerator. Tears trickle down, stinging my eyes. I don't need to see anything anyway.

Then my phone rings.

I glance at the screen and see it's Jolene calling me back.

Don't answer.

The same voice.

Speed up. Don't get distracted.

Another trill from the phone, followed by a different voice. *Catie, answer the phone.*

It doesn't matter.

It does. This is Me, not abandoning you. Answer the phone.

Finally.

I accept the call. "Jolene?"

"Hey, girlfriend," she says, chipper as a blue jay. "I saw you called. Sorry I missed it."

"I'm not." The words catch on a cry.

"Oh really?" She must have heard it in my voice. "What's up?"

So I tell her. I tell her everything. My struggles. My sin. My lack of faith and attempts to do things on my own. The overwhelming grief I can't seem to shake. And just how close I came to ramming my car into a tree not a minute before she called.

She listens without comment. Then, as I'm pulling into the parking space at a Holiday Express near Junction City, Kansas, she offers to pray for me.

Now I can close my eyes.

◊◊◊

The interview with Tasker Pharmaceutical went better than I expected. Everyone I talked with seemed easy-going yet professional. I have a good chance.

With that weight lifted, I can enjoy the rest of the weekend, reconnecting with friends and enjoying Sunday services at my church for the first time in two months. To my relief, Brian and Tess aren't there. Uli tells me they're visiting her family in Texas but plan to be back in time for our annual New Year's Eve party. That gives me a little over twenty-four hours to prepare.

After a lunch of chicken quesadillas with the gang at Margaritas, I go home and change then drive over to Cheyenne Canyon to hike Mount Cutler. It's an easy climb with great views—a perfect re-introduction to the Colorado altitude. And the first time I've gone hiking without Luna since I adopted her four years ago.

I bundle up in my warmest quilted parka, plus a hat, scarf, and gloves, hoping to ward off temps in the low twenties. At least there's no wind, but it's still frigid-cold. I move quickly. It's the best way to warm up.

Once I reach the top, I simply stand there, taking a moment to catch my breath and admire the view. This would be a good time to pray. I'm alone up here. I have so much to say, I'm not even sure where to start.

A low layer of clouds block out the sun as flecks of snow drift around me. I probably should head back down soon. Instead, I hike a little farther across the summit. Trip over a tree root. Stumble. And twist my ankle.

Again.

Only this time I don't have someone to carry me down the mountain.

"Really, God?" I say, out loud. And that lets loose the torrent. I can't stop yelling. About everything. I'm glad I'm alone and no one can see me, screeching to the heavens, tears streaking down my face and mingling with the snow.

But I'm angry. At God. And guilt joins hands with the anger. I shouldn't be mad at God for this situation, especially since so much of it is of my own making. Yet if anyone could do something about it, that would be God and, still, all I feel is His silence. Years of silence.

Over a decade ago, I spent a month in a prayer-filled semi-fast, specifically seeking God's direction about my perpetual singleness. Instead of eating breakfast and lunch, I set aside those meal times for concentrated Bible study and to journal my thoughts, wanting to know if He had a husband for me.

At the end of it, I believed He told me, "Yes, I have someone. Soon."

I was wrong. Either I heard wrong or I let myself hear what I wanted. I've been wrong so many times, I doubt I've ever heard God's voice. Or ever will. Even the words that stopped me from driving my car into a tree just a few nights ago seem unreal in the light of day. Another illusion of hope and my desperate imagination.

The memory of that time of fasting and the disappointment since stirs my anger like a cement mixer.

"Has any of it ever been real?" Then I scream, "Where are You? What do You want from me?"

You, Catie. I just want you. But can you just want

Me?

I do just want You.

No, you don't. You want what I can get for you.

The words hit me like a Mack truck. Is it true? I stumble to my knees, my heart breaking more than it ever has.

He's right. All the time I've wasted longing for something instead of God. I can tell myself over and over how what I've wanted was a good thing based on a desire He gave me but, in the end, I placed marriage as my ultimate prize and God as the horse I would ride to win it.

And now, I've been whacked in the face with what I've lost—the time I could have spent basking in Him, enjoying His love and presence rather than moping and whining and asking God why He hated me so much. Was it hate that yearned to know me without anyone else getting in the way? Was it hate that gave me so many years to come to know Him intimately?

"God, You are the prize, the goal," I whisper into the cold snow whipping around my head. "You didn't let a husband get in the way of that. But I did. Even though I didn't have one, I let him come between us. A fantasy of my own making."

Then, because it has to be said, I add, "Please forgive me. And please take me back."

A silly thing to say, of course, considering *I* left Him.

When I stand up, my ankle feels surprisingly better. I'm able to hike back to my car without any trouble, knowing I'm not alone.

◊◊◊

"Cute dress!"

The light in Uli's eyes tells me she means it, and Uli doesn't throw compliments around. I bought the sleek and shiny green dress a few years ago on a whim but never had a legitimate chance to wear it. Instead, I kept it wrapped in plastic, hanging in the back of my closet. But tonight, an extra ounce of courage seemed in order.

"This old thing?" I spin in a circle to show off the widely flaring skirt. This might be the first time I've ever twirled. "I've had it for years."

Our annual New Year's Eve Party—offered to all the Christian singles in Colorado Springs—isn't typically a fancy affair. Still, a frilly dress and kitten heels aren't unheard of. This year, the committee secured a ballroom at the Broadmoor, so I had license to go a little overboard. The five-star hotel is far from cheap, but it's worth every penny. And though I'm content to focus on my renewed relationship with God, I'd be blind not to notice a roomful of GWPs.

Uli, on the other hand, is doing all she can *not* to notice. She spends the night focusing everyone's attention on her engagement ring and fiancé, in that order. Jolene e-mailed me Uli's news weeks ago, after she made the official announcement. It's hard to be happy for her, though. She could do so much better than Cole. Mafia Dave, Star Trek Sean, even Scott would be better than her cold-as-granite, black-eyed fiancé. Oh, wait. Sean and Amy stand near the refreshment table, holding hands and grinning at each other like they're the only ones in the room, so apparently, he's not available.

But still. There are others.

Of course, Jolene only has eyes for Trevor, their arms clasped around each other like they've been glued together.

For a singles party, there sure are a lot of couples.

I wander around the room, chatting with close friends as well as people I haven't seen since last year's New Year's Eve bash. All the while, I make sure I'm where Brian and Tess aren't. One sparkly engagement ring seems like enough for the night, no matter what revelation I've recently had.

With my mind focused on keeping the happy couple at a distance, I run right into a man. A tall man with blue eyes and a military buzz cut. I've never seen him before.

"Sorry," I say. "Guess I need to watch where I'm going."

"That's all right. It's pretty crowded in here."

Then he smiles at someone behind me and walks away.

God, just so you know, this is still really hard. The intense emotion that overtook me on Mount Cutler and led to a much-needed epiphany didn't last long. I still believe everything I realized yesterday. But the process of taking that knowledge from my head to my heart will take time. Good thing God is more patient than I am.

Will it ever be easier? Will I ever have answers? Maybe. Maybe not. My future happiness, though, can't depend on getting what I want but on giving what I have.

Across the room, Brian and Tess laugh at something Uli just said. Brian has his arm around his fiancée's waist and she's leaning against him. A twinge of jealousy tweaks through me, and I slap it down. He's not mine. Never was. Brian leans over and whispers something to Tess. She blushes. There's something right about the two of them together.

I take a deep breath, then start toward them. Tess sees me. She looks nervous. Brian looks oblivious. When I reach them, I grin, take Tess's hand and say, "I'm so happy for you both."

And, it turns out, I really am.

Study Questions

1. The story begins with a glance Catie's romantic history—or lack of one. What are the highlights of your life where love and romance are concerned? What are your regrets?

2. "I am more single today than I have ever been." Is this how you feel? Or have you ever felt this way? If so, why?

3. Who are your closest friends? Do they understand or, better yet, can they empathize with your feelings about your singleness? How do you and your single friends support each other? Are you a part of an accountability group? If yes, how does it encourage you as a single, Christian woman?

4. Jolene runs a transition home for women just out of prison. What kind of ministries have you been involved with? How has that involvement affected your life? Has it had an impact on you as a single woman? If so, how?

5. Have you tried online dating? What did you like about it? What didn't you like?

6. Each of these women have made mistakes in their relationships. Who did you most relate to and why?

7. How did you feel when Catie lost her job? Has that happened to you? If so, how did you handle being unemployed and single?

8. While at the retreat, Uli's emotions get the best of her and she lashes out at her friends. Then she tries to salvage the situation, but fails. Have you ever felt out-of-control, emotionally, while in public? Did you hide your feelings or let them loose? What happened? How did

you deal with the situation, then or later?

9. When Catie learns Brian is dating Tess, she is, of course, devastated. Not only that he's not interested in her but—as Uli points out—that he ended up with someone so much younger than him. Is this something you've dealt with—watching GWPs date younger women? How does this affect your hope for finding someone?

10. What kind of relationship do you have with your parents? Are you close? Estranged? Somewhere in-between? Is it something you'd like to change? Has that relationship been shaped by or had an effect on your singleness? How?

11. Do you think Jolene is right to be concerned that dating Trevor could ruin their friendship? Why or why not? Have you ever dated a best friend? What happened?

12. When Cole finally proposed to Uli, were you happy for her? Do you think she made the right decision?

13. Have you ever considered suicide? What stopped you? Did you seek counseling afterward?

If you are currently struggling with thoughts of suicide, I encourage you to contact a supportive friend or loved one and openly and honestly share your heart. Don't keep it inside! And if you don't have someone who fits that description, you are more than welcome to contact me. Even if you simply want someone to pray with you.

Consider finding a licensed counselor as well. The American Association of Christian

Counselors offers you access to approximately 50,000 state licensed, certified, and/or properly credentialed Christian counselors. Their website is www.aacc.net.

In addition, Focus on the Family has on-staff counselors you can call free-of-charge at 1-855-771-HELP (4357) Monday through Friday between 6:00 a.m. and 8:00 p.m. Mountain time. Also, Focus's website provides a form you can fill out to find a counselor in your area.

14. In the final chapter, Catie realizes she has spent years longing for something instead of God. She states, "I can tell myself over and over how what I've wanted was a good thing based on a desire He gave me but, in the end, I placed marriage as my ultimate prize and God as the horse I would ride to win it." How did you react to this? Have you made God your number one prize and goal?

15. Do you feel hope when it comes to your singleness or are you grieving? Or do you feel a mixture of both? If hope, is it that you will get married one day or that God has a plan for your life even if you remain unmarried? What can you do today to encourage hope in your heart?

My Recipe for Chili—Just Like Mom Used to Make

It's been over 30 years since I lost my mom to breast cancer, but I've managed to hold on to a few of her recipes. Well, at least close to how I remember her making them. It's one small way of keeping her memory alive.

One of those recipes I've kept is for chili. It really hits the spot on those cold winter days! So, here's how I put it together (adjust according to how much soup you want to end up with):

Brown about half a pound of hamburger with onions and half a green pepper, chopped into small pieces. Since I'm not too fond of onions, I substitute a few teaspoons of onion flakes—it's easier and not so oniony. But that's entirely up to you. Make sure you give the meat a few dashes of salt and pepper too.

While that's cooking, stir together a can of diced tomatoes, a can of stewed tomatoes and a can or two of kidney beans in a large pot. I like the dark red kind but choose your favorite. If you rinse the beans off in a colander until the foam is gone, you'll be less likely to cut loose any evidence of chili later, and potentially avoid the problem Uli experienced at Cole's house.

Now, here's my mom's twist: she added 32 ounces of V-8 Juice. This gives it a unique veggie flavor. Try it! Then stir in the meat, a dash or two of garlic powder, and some chili powder to taste, and let it simmer until you're ready to eat.

Though most people eat chili with crackers, I prefer some good crusty bread with butter. All that's left now is to settle in with a favorite movie while you eat.